SCIENCE PROJECT

BAD BOYS OF REDWOOD ACADEMY

EMILIA ROSE

CONTENT WARNING

Explicit sexual assault by an immediate family member, thoughts of suicide, mention of suicide, death, degradation (and not the fun kind).

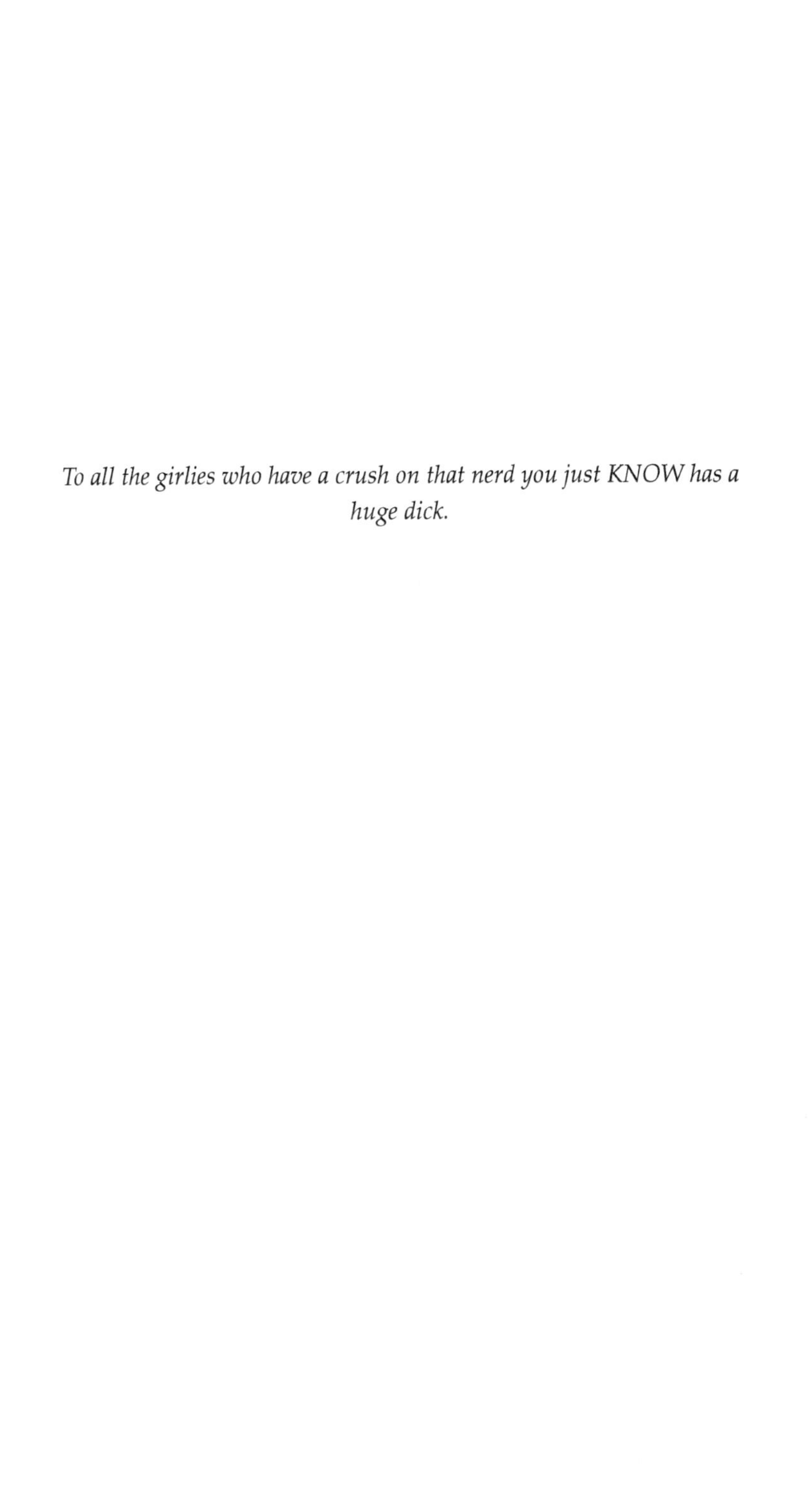

To all the girlies who have a crush on that nerd you just KNOW has a huge dick.

NICOLE

"FUCK, YOU FEEL SO GOOD," Dad grunted into my ear, one hand on my hip and the other groping one of my bouncing tits. He pounded ruthlessly into me from behind, fingers digging into my sensitive skin. "You like that, you dirty slut?"

I bit back a whimper and nodded.

After seizing a fistful of my hair, he yanked back on it harder than he ever had and forced me to stare up into the vicious eyes of my own father. Tears stung my eyes. I dug my manicured fingernails into our leather sofa—the same place Dad had watched his work buddies fuck me after he lost a game of poker this weekend.

"You're a worthless whore." He spit on my lips. "Say it."

"I'm a worthless whore," I said, my voice cracking.

He tightened his grip on my hair. "Say it like you fucking mean it."

"I'm a worthless whore!" I cried. "I'm a worthless whore! I'm a worthless whore!"

And I believed it, too, because that bastard forced me to say it to his face every morning.

Just like this.

A moment later, he released the grip on my head and slammed hard into me from behind. I stared down at the couch and bit back another sob because worthless whores didn't shed any tears. Or else they received a punishment.

"You got your shot this month, didn't you?" he asked after he already came inside me.

As he pulled out of me, I nodded. If I said anything, I feared that my voice would crack and Dad would see how many tears threatened to stream down my cheeks. And I didn't want to be punished before school. He'd make me do something embarrassing again.

Force me to seduce happily married men and ruin their marriage.

Dump all our trash out and make me crawl through it.

Chain me up to a pole in our backyard, naked and in the cold.

I squeezed my eyes closed and swallowed hard. That couldn't happen. Not again. I wouldn't survive another punishment like that. Last time, I'd almost lost my fingers from the freezing temperature.

Once Dad rolled over onto the couch next to me, I slipped off it, grabbed my sweater off the floor, and draped it over my shoulders to cover myself from him. I glanced over at Dad's phone lighting up on the side table—6:45 a.m.

Only fifteen more minutes with him. At most.

He leaped off the couch and stalked over to me. "We need to talk."

"About what?"

He ripped open my sweater. "These."

When he looked down at my tits, I held my arms over my chest and averted my gaze. He had seen them, touched them, *fucked* them hundreds of times and had let his buddies do the same, but this time, there was disgust on his lips.

"I've scheduled an appointment for you with Dr. Aldridge. She's a plastic surgeon."

"Why-why do I need a plastic surgeon?"

He fondled one of my breasts. "Because these aren't doing it anymore. You can only go so far with tits like this, Nicole. My business partners are losing interest." He gently slid his thumb across my chin. "Can't have that now, can we?"

"I'm getting a breast enhancement?" I whispered, a lump in my throat.

"Yes. F cup or larger."

Tears burned my eyes, and my chin quivered. But I didn't want to get any enhancement. If anything, I needed a reduction. I always mentioned to him how much my back fucking hurt me every day because he … because he hadn't gotten me a brace for my scoliosis when I was growing. It wasn't *that* bad, but some days … it killed me.

"I don't think they're becoming uninterested," I said in an attempt for him to reconsider.

"*I'm* becoming uninterested in them." He turned around, headed into his bedroom, and grabbed his uniform for work at the police station, then walked back out. "And if I'm becoming uninterested in them, then everyone else will surely follow. Besides, Pope's daughter has bigger ones than you."

I turned away so he couldn't see my tears and bit back a sob. "Please, I don't want it."

"I'm not asking you, Nicole. I've already made the appointment for the first consultation."

My fists tightened so hard that my nails split through the skin on my palms. I inhaled deeply in an attempt to calm my racing heart. But I … I didn't want to do this. I didn't want to do any of this anymore. I never did.

"Yui's son," Dad said, buttoning up his shirt. "You know him?"

Yui, as in the leader of the Redwood mob?

"What's his name?" I asked quietly.

"Akio. You have Anatomy and Physiology with him."

"I don't know him."

It wasn't my fault that I didn't know anyone else in my class besides the people Dad wanted me to know. Between cheer and … following all his orders, I didn't have time for much else, never mind make friends.

"Well, get to know him," Dad said. "I want information on Yui. I don't trust her."

"But you're work—"

Before I could finish my sentence, Dad's hand collided with my cheek. I stumbled back and grasped my burning flesh, immediately dropping my gaze and pressing my lips together so he wouldn't hit me again.

"Don't fucking talk back to me," he growled, spinning around and heading through his bedroom door while he buckled his belt and pulled up his zipper. "Do your job, like the good little bitch you've always been."

My eyes stung with tears, but I hurried toward my vanity in my bedroom to cover the light swelling and redness so nobody would suspect a thing. But it wasn't even like anyone would care. Everyone at Redwood hated me anyway. Nobody would believe me if I told them what really happened behind closed doors, what my father actually did to me, and what my fate would end up being.

Dumped into the Atlantic Ocean. Pimped out, used up, and dead.

Just like he had done with Hannah.

Or maybe I'd end up killing myself like Mom had because she couldn't handle the thought of what Dad did to his own daughters. Maybe I'd take the easy way out and end it all myself. Because the thought of this being the rest of my life …

I dabbed the corner of my eyes with a tissue so my mascara wouldn't run. Couldn't have that happen and ruin Dad's perfect image with Yui, the rest of the police force, or the town. To him, we were the flawless family who had tragically lost two of their loved ones.

The only thing that I was holding out for was Jace or Carter, two of Redwood's football players, or *someone* to see my pain, ask what was wrong, and rescue me from this living hell. But that'd never happen because nobody at Redwood cared about anyone but themselves.

Maybe it'd be better if I was dead.

CHAPTER
TWO

AKIO

"WHERE THE FUCK IS IT, AKIO?" João—the leader of Poison, Redwood's most feared student-led gang—asked after he, Landon Caddell, and Kai Koh had cornered me in an empty hallway before school started Tuesday morning.

"I don't have it."

Landon—the brawn of Poison—grabbed ahold of my jacket and hurled me against the lockers. Then, his fist followed, slamming square against my jaw. "Where's the fucking shit?" he asked through gritted teeth. "We gave you a fucking job."

With blood spraying out of my nose, I threw my fist back at him in a weak attempt to protect myself. My fist barely landed on Landon's lower lip. They could kill me and make it look like an accident, but I had something that they needed, so they wouldn't murder me.

At least not here.

Before I could pull it back, Landon smashed me into the lockers so hard that the red metal dented behind me. I grunted, my gaze darkening for a moment as footsteps approached from my left.

"Stop it!" someone shouted, pushing Landon away from me.

I slowly blinked my eyes open to see Imani Abara—the girl that Dad kept trying to convince me to date. She stood in front of me as if we were friends, but most importantly like she didn't fear Poison at all, her stance strong and stoic.

Characteristics that I only hoped to have one day.

"You lucked the fuck out today," Landon spit at me and nodded down the hallway in the opposite direction from where Imani had come from. "Get the fuck out of here and don't come back without the damn shit."

I scrambled past Imani, hurried down the hallway, and rounded the corner. Screw João for always needing that medication. Just because I worked at the pharmacy didn't mean I could steal pills for him whenever he felt like it.

Blood continued to spray from my nose. I pinched it shut and tilted my head back, hurrying down the corridor toward the restroom because, apparently, I now had to sit in class with toilet paper stuffed up my nostrils.

As I rounded another corner and slammed into someone, I tripped over my own two feet and landed on top of them. Blood continued to pour from my nose, stars dancing in my vision for a moment until the woman underneath me screamed.

"Ew!" Nicole screeched.

She shoved me off her, shuffled to her feet as her heels scratched against the floor, and stared down at her white jacket, stained with my blood. When she unbuttoned it and pulled it off, my eyes fell to her low-cut top.

Fuck.

"You ruined my jacket, *jerk!*"

Her jacket, Akio. Focus on her jacket. Not on her—

"Are you even listening to me?" she exclaimed in a huff.

"I'm sorry!" I scrambled to my feet and pinched my nose closed again because if I didn't, I would seemingly bleed to death through two small holes in my face. "I'm so sorry, Nicole. I didn't know you were—"

"Forget it." She twirled around, her blonde hair drifting through the air, and headed toward the women's restroom, then murmured, "My dad is going to kill me if he finds out," underneath her breath.

"I'm sorry," I shouted before she slipped into the restroom.

After sighing—because I'd definitely ruined all chances that I might have had with her—I walked into the men's restroom and slipped into a stall to grab some toilet paper. I stuffed it up my nose and walked out to the sink to wipe the blood off my face.

Carter, Redwood's quarterback, sauntered into the restroom with one of his friends, laughing with each other. I splashed my face with water and rubbed the blood off my chin, glancing over at them.

"Heard Jace found you with his girl in the locker room."

"With Nicole?" Carter chuckled. "Harbor was pissed."

"Pussy good?"

"Best in Redwood."

The friend nodded in the mirror at me. "The fuck you looking at?"

"Sorry," I mumbled under my breath.

My gaze dropped to the red blood mixed with water in the sink. Nicole was a prize that every guy at Redwood wanted to claim, and I would never have a chance. Especially when I had to compete with Carter and Jace. Hell, she didn't even know my name.

Besides, it was probably better this way.

Mom wanted me to get closer to her so she could use Nicole against her father. And I wasn't about to be a part of her illegal games. Never had been, and I had vowed never to be. I hated living with her.

I glanced up to catch Carter not even washing his hands as he and his friend exited the restroom. I finished up and walked out of the restroom to my locker, making sure to avoid Poison at all costs.

Once I grabbed my books from my locker, I spotted Nicole

walking with her friends on the cheer squad down the hallway to their first period. I wanted to apologize again, but I kept my mouth shut as they passed me and inhaled her apple cider perfume.

Didn't even recognize me as the fuckup who had bumped into her this morning.

When she disappeared around a corner, I sighed through my nose and dragged my feet to the main doors to head across the quad to Calculus with the infamous Mrs. Dawson. Mrs. Dawson flirted with all the popular guys at Redwood, and it was the only time I didn't wish I were one of them.

But if I were popular, maybe Nicole would notice me. I had had a crush on her since elementary school, but she never looked my way. Not once. Not even today! She never went for guys like me, and she never would.

I was last on that list.

Though I still wished that I weren't. I wished that she would notice me—or for that matter, that *anyone* would notice me—because I hated being so alone. I hated Mom and Dad for forcing me to live a life of dealing drugs and guns. But most of all, I hated being a useless nobody in Redwood.

CHAPTER
THREE

NICOLE

"WHY DON'T we just skip our last class today and have some fun?" I asked Carter, twirling a finger around the end of his thick dirty-blond hair, my other arm draped over his shoulders at his locker.

Dad had given me *multiple* people to get friendly with this semester.

And unfortunately, Carter was one of them. He was even stupider than Jace Harbor, but I only had a couple of months until football season ended, and then Carter wouldn't be as important to Dad. I had been counting the days.

I dropped my arms around his abdomen and slipped my hands underneath his shirt to rub his muscles the way that I knew he loved. I had done it yesterday to seduce him in the locker room before Jace walked in on us.

Carter shrugged. "If I miss another class, Coach will sit me out for the next game."

After standing on my tiptoes, I placed a lingering kiss just below his earlobe—right where he liked it—and slid my hand underneath his jean buckle. Then, I wrapped my fingers around his hard dick. "Are you sure about that?"

While he eyed my tits, he blew out a low breath and pulled my hand out of his pants. "You know I'd love to eat that wet pussy again, but it's important that I kick Harbor's ass on the field every day until he quits football."

"Whatever," I huffed, turning away from him to walk toward Anatomy and Physiology.

I stared down at my heels and blew out a breath. I honestly didn't care what kind of rivalry he had with Jace or about actually sleeping with him in the back of his smelly car.

Before walking into science, I popped off the top button of my shirt. Mr. Woodward sat at his desk while scanning our textbook, wiry gray hair brushed back atop his head and thick glasses magnifying his eyes.

"Mr. Woodward." I placed my hands on his desk and leaned forward.

Since I was twelve, Dad had told me that my tits were my best assets and that I should use it to get what I wanted. And now, he thought otherwise, but I would prove him wrong.

"Yes, Nicole?"

"Last class, you said that we'd be paired for a project." I moved toward Mr. Woodward and curled my fingers around his tie, gently pulling him closer. "Do you think you could pair Akio and me together for this one?"

Cheeks red, rounding, and blotchy, Mr. Woodward giggled like a schoolboy, his gaze dropping to my chest, and nodded. My stomach twisted as another wave of guilt and disgust rushed through me at the thought of what I was doing.

As the class began to pile into the room, I straightened myself out and scanned the room to see if I could even *recognize* an Akio. But I didn't know most of the students in my class, never mind in the entire Redwood body.

My gaze met Willie, who smirked at me like he always did whenever I caught his gaze. I stiffened as a shiver ran down my spine. Out of a class of twenty-five, he was the only guy I recognized. I could never get those piercing demon eyes out of my head.

Not since he'd watched his uncle rape me last year.

I reached up to tug on Hannah's gold necklace that she had given me the night before she was murdered, then turned toward my seat. A nerdy kid up front peered at me for a moment, and then he turned back to his open textbook with flushed cheeks.

After I slid into my seat, the bell rang, and Mr. Woodward stood up on shaky legs with the help of his desk.

"We'll be working on a project that's due by the end of the semester. I've chosen partners for you."

Willie leaned back in his chair and placed his forearm on my table, flashing me a disgusting smirk. "Hope we'll be partners, babe."

Deciding to ignore him—which came off as me being a bitch to most people—I stared ahead at Mr. Woodward and hoped that he'd actually follow through with his promise to me.

"Sarah and Willie. Harry and Winslow. Nicole and Akio ..."

I released Hannah's chain and straightened my back. *See, Dad, I'm not useless yet.*

"I'll be up front if you have any questions," Mr. Woodward said, sitting.

With big, goofy glasses nearly falling off his face, skinny arms holding a stack of textbooks, and a *Dragon Ball Z* T-shirt that had blood all over it, the same nerdy kid from earlier slipped onto the stool next to me, avoiding eye contact.

"H-hi, Nicole."

"You're Akio?" I asked, staring at the assignment on my desk with my stomach in knots.

Akio might've been Yui's son, but considering she was Redwood's mob leader, I'd expected someone a bit more ... bad boyish. Akio was one of the geekiest guys I had ever laid my eyes upon with out-of-style glasses and pimples scattered across his forehead, which he tried to hide with his hair.

How was I supposed to get any information out of a good guy

like him? I didn't want to corrupt this poor guy. He didn't deserve it, and while I didn't feel bad about trying to get information out of anyone else because of their history in Redwood, I did with him.

"Sorry about this morning."

I furrowed my brow. "This morning?"

"When I got blood all over your jacket."

My eyes widened slightly. "That was you?"

Well, that would explain the blood all over his shirt.

He stared down at his open textbook. "I couldn't see where I was going."

"What happened?"

"Poison."

"Poison?" I asked, raising my brow. Maybe he was a bit more bad boyish than I'd thought.

"They kinda beat me up."

Scratch that.

"Well, your *Dragon Ball Z* shirt is ruined. Use distilled white vinegar to get out the blood."

He snapped his gaze up at me. "You know what that is?"

Fuck! Why'd I say that?! What normal kid knows how to get blood out of a shirt? Maybe Poison, but someone like me *shouldn't.*

"What?" I giggled softly, twirling my finger around my hair.

"You know what *Dragon Ball Z* is?"

Oh, he is talking about how I know what anime is and not about the blood …

After shifting uncomfortably in my seat, I cleared my throat. "Sorta."

Nobody knew that it used to be Hannah's and my thing.

"Anyway," I said quickly before he could ask any more questions, "let's get started."

"Right …" Akio adjusted his glasses and opened his spiral notebook that held all his notes from this entire semester. "Mr. Woodward is letting us do the project on anything that we learned this semester. What do you want to do?"

Dad's promise flickered into my mind. He had already made an appointment with a plastic surgeon for me, but if I proved to him that I could get information out of Akio and anyone else he told me to, then maybe he would reconsider.

Maybe he wouldn't make me get any surgery.

So, I leaned closer to Akio and placed my hand on his knee underneath the table.

He tensed. "We-we can do the musculoskeletal system or endocrine or …"

I moved my hand up his thigh. "Or maybe the reproductive system?"

CHAPTER
FOUR

AKIO

"GET OUT, AKIO," Mom growled at me from outside of the car. She stood next to Dad with her arms crossed over her chest and her silky black dress blowing slightly in the fall breeze. "We don't have all day."

After grumbling to myself, I stepped out of the backseat and followed them into the restaurant. We were meeting Imani Abara and her family for dinner because Dad loved to try to set me up with a smart, rich girl.

"Yui," the hostess said to Mom with a tense smile. "Right this way."

She led us through the busy, upscale restaurant in the heart of Redwood and gestured to a table large enough to sit six people. Dad peeled off his coat as the hostess leaned into Mom to whisper something.

Instead of sitting down with Dad, Mom snapped her sharp claws around my upper arm and continued to push me toward the back. We stumbled through the kitchen, and the cooks scrambled out of the way to let her through.

"Where are we going?" I asked.

"You're going to do something for me."

I dug my heels into the ground. "No."

She pushed me out the door and shoved me onto the gravel. "You don't get a choice."

Before I could land on my hands and knees, I caught myself and took a few more strides forward to regain my balance. My gaze landed on a man who looked vaguely familiar, kneeling on the ground with his hands tied behind his back.

Mom held out a gun for me. "You're going to kill him."

"No."

"Akio."

"I'm not going to kill anyone," I said again. "You already know this."

Eye twitching—which meant that she was pissed the fuck off —Mom cleared her throat and nodded to the guards she used in the Redwood mob. "Release him."

I didn't know why the hell she continued to try to make me part of these games that I didn't want to play. Every time that Dad tried to help, she was way too controlling to let him do anything for her. Or maybe she just wanted to protect him.

This bitch must've wanted me to die, didn't she?

Once the man was untied, she tossed the gun at his feet.

"Kill my son, and I'll set you free," Yui said.

What the—

With the gun at his knees, the guy stared between Mom and me for a few moments, as if he didn't know what kind of game Mom was playing. But I did. She was doing this to get what she wanted from me.

"Kill my son, and I'll set you—"

Before she could finish the promise, the man picked up the gun. I roundhouse-kicked him across the face so hard that one of his teeth flew out of his mouth and underneath the green dumpster. A bullet whizzed through the air, but hit the garbage bin instead of me.

Growling to myself, I kicked him straight on this time, my foot colliding with his chin and sending him flying back. When he hit the ground, unconscious, the gun slipped out of his hand. I took it and dropped all the bullets out of it and onto the ground at Mom's feet. Then, I shoved the gun into her hands.

"You're not finished."

"He's unconscious," I snarled. "You finish it."

After storming back into the restaurant, I readjusted my tie and nervously picked at the scab on my finger from when Mom had dragged me to the shooting range with her. Because if I was her son, the least I could do was learn how to shoot a gun.

That was all she wanted me for, apparently.

Once I slid into my seat, Imani and her parents followed the hostess to our table. After the overzealous greetings, Imani sat across from me and sank into the plush chair. She looked like she hated being here almost as much as I did.

Or maybe she hated how much my dad and her mom tried to pair us together.

I glanced toward the kitchen, waiting for Mom to waltz out and sit with us, but she never did. Hell, I wouldn't put it past her to put seven bullets straight through that man's head and throw him into the dumpster to get rid of him.

My hands balled into fists underneath the table. Mom was the reason why I couldn't involve myself with Nicole—even though I loved working with her during class because she was so pretty and smelled so good and, hell, she even knew what anime was. Mom already wanted information from Nicole about her father. If she found out we were working together on a science project …

Dick twitching in my pants, I pressed my hand against my thigh and wished that it'd disappear. But I hadn't been able to stop thinking about her since Anatomy class. She had placed her hand on my thigh, and I had gotten so hard almost instantly that she had to have seen it. She even suggested we do our project on the reproductive system.

Had she been flirting with me?

I shook my head and pushed the thought away because,

surely, Nicole wouldn't flirt with anyone like me. She didn't even know my name. Besides, she was tied up with Carter and Jace Harbor drama.

Still, that hadn't stopped me from jerking off to the thought of her in the restroom after science and this afternoon … and probably when I finally get out of this stupid dinner too.

Dad laughed obnoxiously beside me, snapping me out of my fantasies. I cleared my throat and looked up at Imani, who stared down at her lap while sipping her water. She gazed up at me through big brown eyes.

"How'd it go with Poison?" I whispered.

She sucked in her cheek and stared through me.

Story of my life.

"Uh, Imani …"

She blinked a few times, then shrugged. "Good, I guess. I slapped Landon in the face for you. You're welcome." She glanced at Mrs. Abara and leaned across the table. "Why are they after you? What did you do?"

I tensed and sat back, then stuck my fork into a piece of bread and plopped the entire thing into my mouth. Dad scowled at me for eating so poorly, then turned back to Imani's mom. While Imani was a nice girl, I didn't want to tell her what Poison wanted from me.

Mainly because I didn't want her to see me like everyone saw Mom.

"Akio has an internship at the pharmacy," Dad boasted to Mrs. Abara, wrapping his arm around my shoulders and pulling me close—something he only did when he wanted to brag about me. "I'm so proud of this boy."

Sure he is …

Imani arched a brow at me. "The pharmacy? Do they give you access to all the drugs?"

Mrs. Abara smacked Imani's shoulder. "Oh, honey. Stop it. I'm sure he's working in the front room."

"Actually, right alongside the pharmacists," Dad said.

He can't shut the hell up, can he?

I sank lower in my seat as Imani murmured, "Interesting ..."

And while I had wanted to keep it a secret from Redwood, Imani wasn't stupid. She was one of the brightest people I knew, and she had surely put it all together now. Over the course of the past few months, I had become the supplier for the most feared gang in town.

CHAPTER
FIVE

NICOLE

MOUTH SALTY with cum from a man I hardly knew, I walked out of his home and down the front yard in the dark toward Dad's car parked on the side of the Redwood slums. His car hummed lightly over the fall wind.

"Go good?" he asked through the open window.

"Yes," I whispered.

"Did you get what I needed?"

After blowing out an unsteady breath, I reached into my bra—trying hard not to wince at the bruises on my chest from the man's harsh grip on me—and pulled out a small note. I handed Dad the piece of paper and shrugged my shoulders forward. "Here."

"Good girl."

I shivered in disgust at the nickname that most girls found sexy. But I couldn't.

At least not from him.

Across the street, João from Poison sat on his porch steps and watched us. I shielded my face with my bangs and hoped that he didn't say anything because I feared that I'd burst into tears in front of Dad. And I couldn't do that.

"Get in, Nikki. You have another appointment."

"Dad," I whispered from outside of the car, "please. I need to study."

Not that I could care about school … I wanted to, but I didn't have the energy or time.

"We're going to see Dr. Aldridge, then going home."

"Okay," I whispered, peering over at João again, who was now smoking with Landon.

Once I slipped into the car, Dad placed a hand on my knee. I stared out my passenger window and watched the houses fly by as he drove down the road, manicured fingers digging into my palms. I glided my tongue across my teeth, wanting the salty taste out of my mouth.

"Any news on Yui?"

"I'm partners with Akio on a science project," I said.

"Oh, yeah?" he murmured. "How's that going?"

"Fine," I whispered.

When he stopped at a light, he peered over at me. "It'd best be going better than fine."

"I don't have any information yet," I said quietly. "It's only been a day."

He dug his fingers into my thigh and continued driving. "It used to take you a couple of hours to get what I needed."

"I'm sorry."

"I want something by the end of the week."

"Okay."

"I'm being serious, Nicole. No more second chances."

"Or what?" I said before I could stop myself. I immediately smacked my lips together. "Sorry."

Dad slammed on the brakes in the middle of the road and seized me by the throat. "Or what?" he repeated. "Or fucking what? You know what will happen to you if you don't do exactly as I ask, Nicole."

"I-I'm sorry," I whispered, attempting to peel his fingers off me so I could breathe. "I'm sorry."

He ripped Hannah's gold necklace off my neck. "Don't forget about your sister."

After dragging his hand away, he shoved the gold necklace into his pocket. My lips trembled as I stared through the windshield ahead of me, finally having—what I considered—proof that he'd had something to do with her death.

"I'll have something for you by the end of the week," I whispered, tugging out my phone.

As we pulled into the doctor's office parking lot, I scrolled to Akio's contact. Still in shock.

Me: Wanna work on the project tomorrow night after cheer?
Me: Your house?

"Get out," Dad ordered.

I followed him out of the car and into the office. "Can I have my necklace back?"

"No."

So, I snapped my mouth shut and glanced down at my messages with Akio. He typed and typed and typed and didn't send anything. We walked into a large office and sat across from what looked like a sweet woman with big brown eyes.

"What can I do for you today?" Dr. Aldridge asked.

Dad began diving into everything that he wanted me to get done without my consent while I prayed that Akio would send me a message so I'd have an excuse not to listen to the horrible things that Dad desired.

Akio: Okay.
Me: We don't have to …
Akio: No, no. I want you to come over.
Akio: My parents won't be home, if you're okay with being alone.
Me: That's totally fine. :) I'd prefer that anyway.

"We can schedule that to be done in a couple of weeks. Sound good?" Dr. Aldridge said.

"The sooner, the better," Dad said, flashing her a smirk.

"All right, is there anything else you'd like done?" she asked Dad.

Of course she wouldn't ask the woman who would actually be having the procedure. I didn't have any say in my body, my life, or even my future. Why would I? All I was, was Dad's toy that he could do whatever the hell he wanted with.

"Leave, Nicole."

With tears in my eyes, I grabbed my purse and shuffled out of the doctor's office before he could force me to stay, before they could ask me more questions, before they could decide my entire life for me.

Once I slipped into the passenger seat of Dad's car, I burst out into tears. My mascara ran down my cheeks, but I couldn't care anymore. Dad didn't have any more work for me to do tonight, and it was too dark for anyone to truly see.

It had always been too dark for people to see my pain.

To see how much I fucking hurt.

I slammed my fist into the dashboard repeatedly and screamed, "Someone, help me!"

CHAPTER
SIX

AKIO

AT SEVEN THIRTY—AFTER Mom thankfully left for *business* down at the Overlook—Nicole pulled into my driveway and knocked on the front door. I had turned off all the security cameras so Mom wouldn't see Nicole and hopefully bribed the guards with enough of Mom's money to keep their mouths shut.

I took a deep breath and swung open the door. "H-hi, Nicole. How was practice?"

She tucked some blonde hair behind her ear and stepped into the house. "Good." After peering into the living room—where I had paused Raid of Durnbone, the video game—she cleared her throat. "Would you mind if I borrowed one of your shirts? I just want to get out of these sweaty clothes before we start."

My eyes widened slightly, and my dick stiffened at the mere thought of seeing Nicole in one of my shirts with nothing underneath it, her nipples pressing against the thin fabric. I twirled on my heel before she could see how excited it made me and headed for the stairs.

"Follow me." Once we reached my room, I opened a dresser in my closet. "What kind of—"

"Anything is fine."

When I turned back around to give her an Attack on Titan tee, Nicole had stripped off her shirt and was kicking off her shorts.

"Oh fuck," I whispered, cock throbbing inside my sweatpants.

Nicole reached around her body, unclipped her bra, and let the straps fall down her shoulders. With one arm draped across her chest to cover her nipples, she took the shirt from me and smiled. "Thanks, Akio."

Fuck.

Cheeks boiling hot, I twisted around and fast-walked to the door. "I-I'll meet you downstairs." As soon as I closed the door, I pressed my back against it and placed a hand on the front of my pants against my aching dick.

Before I had the chance to run downstairs, the door opened behind me, and Nicole stepped out of the room with my T-shirt on her body, hanging down to her mid-thigh, her nipples pressed against the front of the shirt.

With a small, seductive smile on her face, she stared up at me through thick lashes and curled her hand around my forearm. "You know, we could just skip the project and do something else instead," she whispered into my ear, trailing her manicured fingers up my chest.

"I-I, um … if you don't want t-to work on the project"—my gaze fell down to her breasts, my dick throbbing hard and aching for her to touch it because, God, I had been dreaming about this for so long—"I-I can do it myself."

She followed my gaze, then dropped it even lower to the bulge in my pants and pulled me back into the bedroom. "Do you think I'm that stupid that I can't even help you with a simple project?"

"N-n-no, not at all. I just—"

When her legs hit my bed, she lay back on it and spread her thighs so I could see her pretty, bare pussy, all on display for me. My lips parted slightly, heart pounding hard in my chest, and I placed a hand over my dick.

"Come here," she purred. "I know you need a break."

"Y-you do?"

"You've been hard since Anatomy." She pushed two fingers against her clit and teased herself as my shirt rode further up her stomach.

God, my dick throbbed so badly as that pussy drooled all over my bed.

"Do I turn you on, Akio?"

"Yes," I whispered, gripping my dick now.

She curled around on the bed, so she sat on her hands and knees with her bare ass against my bulge and began slowly bucking her hips against me as she stared back through her curtain bangs. "Tell me how long you've wanted to fuck me."

I gently grasped her hips. "So long."

After sitting up so her back was against my chest, she placed her hands over mine and drew them up her curves and over her breasts. I couldn't hold back the grunt that escaped my lips and could just barely contain the orgasm that wanted to rip through me right now.

When she drew my hands across her nipples, my eyes rolled back into my head, and I came right there in my pants as she continued to grind her ass against it. I groped her full breasts as hard as I could and pressed my bulge against her round ass, plea-sure rolling through me at full force.

"Oh f-f-fuck …"

"Did you make a mess?" she murmured. "Why don't you let me clean you up?"

Before I could even realize what was happening, Nicole crawled off the bed and dropped to her knees in front of me. She moved her hand across my bulge over and over while pulling my sweats down my hips.

My cock, drooling with cum, sprang out of it, and Nicole had my head on her tongue almost instantly. I pushed my glasses up my nose and glanced around the room, wondering if this was actually happening. This … we …

She glided her tongue across it, then suddenly sucked every

inch into her mouth until I was buried down her throat and her lips were pressed against my hips. I stared down at her, watching her eyes fill with tears as she forced herself down further despite her gagging.

"Fuck," I murmured again.

She looked up at me through her lashes, then bobbed her head up and down on my length, licking up all my cum. Spit and drool rolled down her chin.

"I bet you've dreamed of having my lips wrapped around your cock, huh?" she asked, sucking my balls into her mouth.

I nodded in a daze, getting harder again. If she kept this up, I'd come twice in—

"What about having my tits bounce in your face as you fucked my tight pussy?"

I didn't even have time to say anything coherent before she shoved me down onto the bed and crawled on top of me, her big tits swaying in my face. Again, she set my hands on her breasts, letting me squeeze them.

"Go on," she whispered. "Suck on them."

My dick throbbed against her cunt, and I sucked one of her nipples into my mouth, unable to believe that this was happening. Soon, I'd wake up from this dream, covered in a shitload of my own cum. I was sure of it.

"God," she moaned, throwing her head back. "That feels so good."

Heart racing, I sucked harder on her breast and pressed them together to easily move my mouth from one to the other. Nicole was perfect—so fucking perfect. And I loved every single second of this. Even if it was a dream.

After reaching between us, she grabbed my hard cock in her small hand and positioned it at her entrance. She slowly lowered herself down onto me, her pussy squeezing my dick harder than I ever could with my hand.

"Shit, shit, shit, you're so tight," I grunted against her breasts.

I sucked on her tits as they bounced against my face, her pussy sliding up and down on my cock. And when I couldn't handle it any longer, I raised my hips to meet hers with every thrust, which only made her wilder.

"Faster," she moaned.

I pounded my hips up against hers as fast as I could, feeling the pressure build up inside me twice as quickly as it had before. She crashed down onto me, her breasts against my chest and her mouth against my own.

"I'm going to come," she cried against me. "And I want you to come inside me."

"C-come i-inside you?"

"Please, Akio," she begged. "I need you to come in—"

She didn't have to repeat herself before I slammed my hips up and stilled deep into her pussy. She screamed out in pleasure, her entire body trembling on top of me.

"G-God, I have a feeling you're going to be my new favorite partner."

CHAPTER
SEVEN

NICOLE

AFTER THE PLEASURE WORE OFF, I rested back against
the bed. Akio backed up a few feet and leaned against the nearest
wall, one arm on his abdomen, which was skinnier than Carter's
or Jace's or even any of the creeps at the police department.

"That's it?" I whispered, tears pricking at the corner of my
eyes.

Akio's face dropped, and he turned away from me and shoved
himself back into his pants. "I-I'm sorry. I didn't think I would … I
would come so quickly. I really didn't want … I know that I don't
live up to Carter or Jace or—"

Tears suddenly sprang from my eyes and rolled down my
cheeks. That was all? There wasn't any yelling or calling me
names or staring smugly at me like he had taken advantage of a
young piece of meat?

"A-are you crying?" Akio asked. "I'm sorry if I did something
wrong. I tried to be gentle …"

"Gentle," I repeated in a whisper.

Usually, Dad's friends threw me around, pulled my hair,
smacked me anywhere they wanted. I'd expected Akio to do the

same, but nobody had been so gentle and caring with me before, and it almost seemed fake.

Another sob escaped my throat, my shoulders pulling forward.

And I had taken advantage of him.

I'd fucking taken advantage of the nerdy kid, all for my father. For the bastard I hated.

"I'm sorry, Nicole," he said, readjusting his glasses. "I …"

"I need to leave," I whispered. I ran to the door. My throat was closing, my heart pounding, and my thoughts were racing so fast that I couldn't even hear them. But all I knew was that I needed to get out of here. Now.

"Wait," Akio said, grabbing my wrist as my back was still turned toward him. "I-I'm sorry if I—" Again, he paused for a long time. His grip on me loosened, and then he gently twisted my arm around. "D-did I do that to you?"

I glanced over my shoulder to see Akio staring wide-eyed at the bruises that Dad had given me the other morning. I usually covered them up with makeup, but I must've sweated it off during cheer practice.

"Nicole, I—"

Before another word could come out of his mouth, before he could ask about where I had gotten them or if he had given them to me, I ripped my arm away from him, sprinted out of the bedroom door, and slammed it behind me.

What had I even been thinking, coming here and using Akio? I didn't want to hurt him or drag him into whatever drama my father had planned. He didn't even seem like his parents were part of the mob. He was so … so sweet.

Tears wavered in my eyes.

Too sweet that it couldn't be real.

There was no way.

I hadn't met anyone in Redwood that selfless. Nobody that really cared. Not about me.

"Nicole," he said from the other side of the door. "I didn't mean to hurt you. Can I—"

"No," I shouted after biting back a sob. "I'm leaving, Akio."

I didn't want him to touch me, to make me feel better, because I didn't deserve it. I deserved to be treated the way that Dad and his buddies treated me. I was mean and rude and deserved all the bad things that came my way.

And I sure as hell wasn't worth all of Akio's kindness.

So, I hurried off to my car, slipped into the driver's seat, and drove to the Overlook—the rocky mound before the Atlantic Ocean. Waves crashed against the rocks. The salty breeze permeated through my car from the windows. And I barely turned the engine off before I burst out into uncontrollable sobs.

I didn't know why I was crying. Akio had just been so gentle with me. And *usually*, I kept my emotions together. But I … but I … I didn't know what to think. I had no problem using any of those stupid jocks at Redwood or Dad's friends for information.

Akio though …

It was so cruel.

A car pulled ahead of me in the dark and parked. I stared at it through stinging eyes, my vision blurred from the tears, and then I watched a couple of students from Redwood leap out of the car and stare out at the ocean, his arms wrapped around her shoulders from behind, his head tilted and his cheek on the top of her head.

My lips quivered, and my chest tightened at the sight of something that I would never have.

Young love. Maybe not even love at all if my father thought I wasn't worth it anymore. If he decided to bring me here one day —not to use me, but to dump me off like a whore that nobody cared about. Like Hannah.

I reached up for my necklace—*her necklace*—but it was gone. He still had it.

Leaning forward, I rested my head on the steering wheel and cried. And I cried and I cried and I cried and I cried until my body began shaking uncontrollably. I must've leaned too far forward because the horn suddenly blasted.

The couple jumped in surprise and hurried back to their car, driving off into the night. With tears stinging my eyes, I stumbled out of my car, slammed my door shut, and wobbled toward the rocks.

Waves smashed against the rocks a little ways down, and part of me hoped that I slipped and fell into the ocean, washed away, just like Hannah had. It wasn't like anyone would care if I suddenly disappeared. Hell, it'd probably make everyone's lives easier.

So, I jumped down onto a lower rock, one closer to the ocean.

Then another.

Then another, until a couple of inches of water soaked through my shoes.

One more step. That was all it'd take for the waves to crash against my legs, for the pull of the water to whisk me away into its depths, to take me under and swallow me whole. Just one more small step.

My phone buzzed in my pocket, jolting me out of my thoughts. I ignored it, and then it stopped buzzing, but a moment later, it started up again. I leaned back against one of the rocks and pulled the phone out of my pocket.

Two missed calls from Akio and one text.

Akio: You left your clothes.

I clutched the phone in both of my shaky hands and stared down at his contact, then back up at the crashing waves. If he had called me a few minutes later, I wouldn't have noticed. I would have been swept up, and I …

Truly, I didn't want that.

Akio had saved me, and he didn't even know it.

AKIO

I SAT across from Imani in her parents' dining room the next weekend. Dad and her mother were in a heated conversation *again* about who would be at the top of the senior class once we graduated, but they obviously didn't know that Sakura Sato had already claimed valedictorian. Her GPA was too high for even me to reach now.

Imani played with her peas with a fork, rolling them around, stabbing them, and crushing them between the tines. I stared emptily at the table in front of me, barely having touched my food.

God, I was so bad that Nicole had *cried* the other night.

The first and only time I'd ever had a chance to be with Nicole, and I'd had to completely fuck it up by making her cry. I wasn't even sure what I had done wrong. She'd seemed to enjoy it, but maybe I said something or touched her wrong. And had I given her those bruises?

Had she even come?

I hoped that she had. It had been my first time ever being with someone, and I didn't know if I had done it right. Maybe I would be the laughingstock of Redwood when she returned to school, whenever that was. She had practically missed the past week.

Imani kicked me hard in the shin under the table. When I glanced up at her, she nodded to the other room and excused herself from brunch.

Her mother gave her a dirty look, but Imani hummed, "We're going to talk in the other room."

My dad and her mom were always trying to get us together. So, they were overjoyed to let us spend some time together.

After stuffing my hands into my pockets, I walked into the other room and sighed. "Thanks for that."

"Don't worry about it," Imani said. "I couldn't last another second in there."

"Me neither."

She scratched the back of her head. "About last night ... I'm sorry about Kai."

Oh yeah. Last night, when I had gone to the football game— *why did I think that'd be a good idea?!*—to warn Imani about Poison, Kai, the quiet hacker from Poison, had put a gun to my stomach and warned me to stay away from her.

"It's fine," I grumbled, staring out the window at the orange and brown leaves.

She paused. "I also ... kinda wanted to ask you about the pharmacy."

I arched a brow. The pharmacy?

The only reason that Poison ever wanted to talk to me was because I worked at the pharmacy. They wanted drugs, not to sell, but for more personal reasons. And Imani had been hanging out with them a lot lately. It was almost as if they all had become a couple or a throuple or whatever their relationship was.

"Is this about João?" I asked.

She chewed on the inside of her cheek. "Maybe ..."

"You want information about why he needs that medication from me?"

"No," she said quickly. "I know why he needs it. I just want to know who else gets it too."

Who else was prescribed medication specifically for HIV?

I tensed. "You know I can't give you that kind of information, Imani."

"Please, Akio," she begged, grabbing my hand. "It's important to me."

After pulling my hand out of hers, I looked toward the doors to make sure our parents weren't listening in on our conversation, then lowered my voice. "I'll tell you, if you promise to hang out with me this week, maybe study for Barnes's class with me."

"Why do you want me to hang out with you?" she asked.

Well, I really couldn't tell her that I had been desperately trying to get my mind off last week with Nicole. Because she hated Nicole. But also because I didn't want all the questions about what had happened or the drama leaking out to anyone else.

Especially Mom.

So, I glanced down at my feet, jaw twitching. "Because, Imani, nobody else understands what it's like to have parents like ours. The other rich kids become like their parents, and the kids who live in the slums hate us. I don't …" I swallowed hard and shook my head. "I don't have anyone else to talk to about this shit."

Great semi-lie, Akio.

Though … it was partly true. I didn't have any friends who understood the struggle of having parents who were fucking psychotic sometimes. Imani's parents weren't as bad as Mom was in terms of … hurting and killing people, but I saw the expectations they had for Imani.

Imani nodded. "In exchange for names, I'll hang out with you. We can go get ice cream with Allie or something."

I pushed my glasses up my nose. "Really?"

"Yes, really."

After I nodded as a thank-you, we returned to the other room just as Dad pushed in his chair. I blew out a breath, said goodbye to Imani and her mother, thanked myself for thinking ahead and bringing my own car here today.

When the front door shut behind us, Dad cleared his throat. "Your mother—"

"I have something to do," I said, hurrying down the walkway to my car.

Nicole hadn't been in school for days now—thankfully, our project wasn't due until the end of the semester—but her being absent meant that I hadn't been able to return her clothes. And I wanted to make sure she was okay.

"Akio!" Dad called.

But I had already slipped into the driver's seat of my car. "I'll be home later."

A few hours later, after I had found her address, I pulled onto the curb in front of Nicole's house. I grabbed her fresh clothes from the backseat, walked to the front door, and knocked a few times. When nobody answered—although I knew she was home by her car in the driveway—I knocked again.

Someone shouted from inside the house.

I pushed my glasses up my nose and waited a few more moments, thinking they were shouting that they'd be down to open the door for me soon. But when nobody came and the shouting continued, I peered into the window next to the door.

The foyer looked empty, but I could see two figures in the next room.

In order to try to get a better view, I walked around the house and peered into the side window. My eyes widened when I spotted Nicole bent over her family's couch with a man much, much older inside her.

Chest tight, I stared at the way he used her in terror. His large hands were around her throat, his fingers digging so deep into her skin that they turned white. Nicole stared down at the couch cushions, emotionless.

I clenched my jaw and pulled my gaze away.

Just because she fucked you doesn't mean she likes you, Akio.

How stupid was I to believe that she'd liked me like that at all? She'd probably only come over to sleep with me so I'd do the entire science project myself.

By the looks of it, I wasn't even her type. She wanted someone to be rough with her, someone much older and bigger than my scrawny ass was.

Because I couldn't help myself, I glanced into the window again to see her staring at me in horror through wide eyes. The man—who looked familiar, but I couldn't put my finger on how I knew him—had pulled out of her and collapsed onto another couch. But she hadn't moved from her bent-over position.

Suddenly, she shot up, matted down her skirt, and ran over to the window to close the curtains. After cursing under my breath, I walked toward the front of the house, where I had come, only to hear the back door open and footsteps approaching. Quickly.

So, I picked up my pace and walked to the car.

It was wrong for me to be here. I shouldn't have come.

And I didn't want Nicole to think that I was stalking her ... or that I liked her.

"Akio!" Nicole whisper-yelled from behind me.

But I slipped into the driver's seat of my car before she could say another word.

CHAPTER
NINE

"WHAT ARE YOU DOING HERE?!" I exclaimed, sliding into Akio's passenger seat before he could drive off.

He had been knocking at my door for so long while Joe Santos was inside me and then peeped through my windows.

Thank God that I had turned off the security cameras and alarm system before Joe came over. I didn't want Dad to know I didn't have the damn cold-blooded heart to mess with Akio, so I'd invited over someone else in his mother's mob family to get information.

The car was slowly inching forward, and then Akio pressed on the brakes. "What are you—"

"I saw you peeping into my house—that's what I'm doing here! Now, drive!"

I didn't want Dad to return home and see Akio sitting at the curb.

Akio pressed on the gas and drove down the road, heading toward the beach.

"Now," I said, crossing my arms, "tell me why you were at my house."

When we stopped at a traffic light, Akio reached into the backseat and then set clothes in my lap. "You left these at my house the other night, and I wanted to return them to you. I washed them all."

One by one, I picked up the neatly folded clothes on my lap. Shirt. Shorts. Bra.

No underwear.

While I had no business getting all warm in places that I shouldn't be around him, I couldn't stop myself from pressing my legs together and thinking about Akio purposefully leaving my underwear at his house … *for reasons.*

Like closing one of his textbooks before he was finished studying. Turning on some hentai—because Akio didn't seem like one to watch *regular* porn. And stroking his huge cock with my thong while thinking of me.

At least, that was what I had done last night in the shirt he had given me. Touched myself until I came, thinking about nobody else but him, how innocent he truly was, how easily he had come *twice* for me, how turned on I'd made him, just as I was with no need to look any different.

Fuck.

I blew out a breath and tried to shake the thoughts from my mind. *Focus, Nicole.*

He had just waltzed into my house and put himself in danger! I couldn't let that happen ever again. And I needed to make sure that he knew it too. No more randomly coming over, just to hand me some clothes. He could do that at school.

"Don't get any ideas about anything happening between us just because we hooked up once," I said, crossing my arms and glaring at the side of his cute face. "You shouldn't have come to my house."

"I-I know," he said, his lips curling into the smallest frown. "I'm not your type."

When those words came out of his mouth, I wanted to take it all back.

But I needed to keep the facade up around him. I didn't want to drag him into this mess.

"No, you're not." But he was.

"Okay," he whispered. "I'm sorry for coming to see you."

Tears wavered in my eyes, and I wanted to hug him. So badly. He didn't deserve to be treated this way, but I couldn't stop now. I couldn't let him know that I … that shit happened to me behind closed doors. For all I knew, he might try to get in the way and get hurt in the process. Hell, he had come all the way to my house, uninvited, in the middle of the night!

"You should be," I forced myself to say, my chest so tight that I could barely breathe.

A long silence plagued the ride down to the beach. I leaned my head against the cold window and stared at the desolate road where the buildings had been closed for the quickly approaching winter months.

We reached the very end of the road, and Akio glanced toward the street that led to the Overlook. But instead of heading that way, he turned left and headed toward town to drop me back off at home.

While I had made my intentions clear with him, I had secretly hoped that he'd turn right. I yearned for a chance to be that couple that I had seen the other night, perched at the Overlook, his arms around my shoulders, kissing my neck, happy.

At least with someone.

When we reached Route 1—which had about three Dunkin' Donuts, a Walmart, and a dozen other restaurants, pharmacies, and gas stations—I cleared my throat. "You didn't see anything."

Akio glanced over at me. "What?"

"You didn't see anything at my house. Got it?"

Again, he stayed quiet until we reached my neighborhood. Akio paused at a Stop sign a few streets down from my house and parked the car, staring ahead through the windshield with an expression that I had never seen on his face prior to tonight.

"Who was he?"

"Who was who?" I asked, though I knew exactly who he was talking about.

"Who was the guy with you at your house?"

"It's none of your business, Akio."

"Yes, it is," he snapped so suddenly.

My eyes widened at how loud his voice had become, and then I cleared my throat. "It's no—"

"He works for my parents, doesn't he?" Akio asked.

"If you knew who he was, then why'd you ask?" I said, not wanting to talk about him anymore tonight. I had done what Dad had asked me to do, and now, it was my time to decompress, and I really didn't want to do that by talking about that bastard Joe. Or the reasons I'd asked him to come over tonight ... because I didn't want to use the boy sitting in the driver's seat.

"Did he hurt you?"

"They all do," I murmured to myself, glaring out my passenger window.

"What?"

"Nothing."

Akio clenched, then unclenched his fist a few moments later. Then, as if all that ... *anger*—if that was what it was—disappeared, he put the car into drive and headed back to my house. Too quietly.

He parked at the curb and offered me a small smile. "I'll see you at school."

I narrowed my eyes at his sudden change of emotions, then gathered my belongings and exited the car. "I'll see you later, Akio." Before I shut the door, I leaned down and looked into his car. "Remember what I told you?"

His smile didn't falter. "Don't worry."

"Okay ..." I said suspiciously, shutting the door and heading up the walkway.

Before I slipped into the house, I glanced back at him. The car lurched forward erratically. As if Akio wasn't planning on an easy ride back to his house. And by the looks of it, he wasn't heading that way either.

CHAPTER
TEN

AKIO

I REPEATEDLY FLASHED my high beams at Joe Santos from behind him in the darkness.

Joe Santos had been driving around Redwood for two hours, talking on his phone, probably to his buddies about fucking a barely legal academy student and the police chief's daughter. And I had been following him for that long at a distance, waiting for him to pull over.

But I was fucking done trying to be subtle.

The longer I stared at this scumbag through my windshield, the more I fucking loathed him, the harder I dug my fingers into the steering wheel, and the heavier my foot pressed on the accelerator.

After glancing in the rearview mirror and spotting my car behind him, he turned onto a more discreet road that led to the Overlook. I followed behind him, turning on my high beams for good and hoping that it blinded that asshole.

A few moments later, he parked on the side of the Overlook. I slammed on my brakes behind him, threw the car into park, and stormed out of it just as he was opening his car door. My hands shook with rage, and I … I … I couldn't help myself.

"Akio, if I had known that it was you—"

Before he could say another word, I ripped him out of the driver's seat and hurled him toward the rocks so hard that he fell backward down the first few of them, knocking his head on his way down and landing on one near the water.

There was nothing between Nicole and me. Absolutely nothing.

She had made it clear that I wasn't her type, that she didn't like me, and that she wanted absolutely nothing to do with me. But I didn't care. Because when she'd slipped into my car, it wasn't anger etched into her face.

It was fear.

Fear of something I couldn't quite decipher then, but I could now.

After Nicole had whispered that they all hurt her, that *he* hurt her, it was clear that she hadn't really wanted it. Or maybe she did, but he had taken it too far. And I wasn't going to let any of Mom's scummy men hurt the one girl I had liked since elementary school.

"Akio, what are you—"

I slammed my foot into his side.

He reached for his gun, but I pulled out the one that Mom forced me to carry around with me and shot off his hand before the gun could make it out of his waistband.

Screaming out in pain, he grasped his wound with his empty hand. "What the fuck are you doing?!"

"You hurt her."

"Yui is fine!" he shouted. "I didn't touch—"

"Not my mother." I smashed my foot into the side of his head. "Nicole."

"Who?"

A low growl escaped my throat, and I dropped to my knees in front of him and hurled my fist at his face. Rage seized hold of me, the way I had seen it take hold of my mother since I had been a kid. And yet, I still couldn't control myself.

Nor did I want to.

Not after I saw him inside Nicole.

Not after she admitted that he hurt her.

Desperate to shove me off him, he reached for the gun again, this time with his unwounded hand. I kicked it with my boot so the waves washed it away, and I climbed onto him to keep him still.

I had never been a physically strong guy like Mom wanted me to be, but she had taught me how to fight. And I was going to use that to kill one of her men because he fucking deserved it for everything he had done.

Once I grabbed his collar, I slammed his skull into the rocks repeatedly.

Not stopping until blood gushed out of an open wound on his head.

Screaming and shouting and shrieking, he attempted to push me away, to hit me back, to stab me with whatever type of sharp rock the waves had washed up into his grimy hands. But there was no stopping me.

Crimson gore stained my hands. My knuckles had split open. Salty water soaked the bottoms of my pants. But seeing this man struggle underneath me, tasting his blood spraying back up at me from his worthless body, feeling the life leave his corpse …

Made it all worth it.

When he didn't even twitch after one last punch, I released his collar and stood over him on the rocks. Then, I spit on him like I believed he had probably done to Nicole. He'd just seemed like that kind of asshole.

My chest rose and fell harshly at the sudden burst of energy and adrenaline. And I could barely see straight. But I wasn't worried about what I had just done. I would do it over and over again if I had to.

So, after slipping his phone into my pocket, I used the heel of my shoe to shove him into the Atlantic Ocean. With waves this rough, his body would be shredded by morning. And if anyone did find him, nobody would care. He was just another pawn in my mother's game, just someone expendable. Like anyone else would be if they hurt my girl.

CHAPTER
ELEVEN

NICOLE

ME: **Wanna meet up tonight?**

I leaned against my locker the next day, impatiently tapped my foot, and stared down at the message I'd sent Joe Santos three hours ago. Should I text him again? Why wasn't he returning my messages? Men like him usually did within minutes.

After tearing off some skin on my inner cheek with my teeth, I double-texted.

Which I had never done to someone like him.

But, damn, I was desperate as fuck not to use Akio for my father's dirty work. I didn't want to get him involved at all and would much rather suck it up and let the mob's grimy hit men use me so I could get information.

Me: Maybe a quickie after I get out of school. xx

Still nothing.

But the Delivered message turned to Read.

I tightened my hands into fists and then I shoved the phone into my purse because he obviously wasn't interested, and if I couldn't get any information from anyone, then maybe Dad was right.

My body just wasn't cutting it anymore.

The bell rang through the hallway, and I strolled down the corridor to Akio's locker. When I turned the corner, I spotted Akio dressed in an oversize black anime shirt, pulling books out of the metal compartment, his hair all over the place, as if he'd had a long night.

"Akio!" João shouted down the hallway, storming toward him.

Eyes widening, Akio slammed his locker closed and hurried in the opposite direction of João while juggling a stack of textbooks that he hadn't gotten to put away. João stormed after him, seething.

"You'd better have it tonight," João growled, catching up to him. "Don't be late for work."

"I can't keep giving you drugs!" he whisper-yelled at him.

João seized him by the collar and slammed him up against the lockers. "You'd better—"

With my heels clacking against the tiled floor, I ran across the hallway, grabbed João by his shoulder, and pulled him away from Akio, whose glasses now sat crooked on his nose. "Leave him alone."

"This is none of your bratty bitch business," João growled.

"Leave. Him. Alone."

After looking between us, he snickered. "What, are you guys fucking now?"

I expected Akio to say no, but when neither of us said a word, João smirked and ripped himself away from me. "For the first time in my life, I actually have some respect for you, Akio." He headed down the hall. "But you'd still better have the shit tonight."

Once he disappeared, I turned to Akio, who readjusted his glasses.

"So," I said with a small giggle, "you're a drug dealer."

"Don't listen to João. I don't—"

I gently pushed him. "It's just a joke."

But what had João said about Akio having the drugs for him

tonight after school? Maybe he actually was working for his mother, selling drugs to the drug dealers themselves. But then why would they have the confidence to bully Akio? It should've been the other way around if Akio really was the dealer's dealer.

"Are you okay?" I asked.

"I'm fine. I have to get to class."

"Wait." I grabbed his wrist. "I want to talk to you."

The second bell rang through the hallways, signaling that we were already late for our next class, which was, as luck would have it, science. Some of the good girls hurried to class, and the troublesome kids lingered in the hallways, waiting for restorative officers to discipline them.

Akio glanced over his shoulder at the troublemakers, who threw glances our way. "What're you doing, talking to me here? We can talk about the project in science. You don't have to go out of your way to—"

"This isn't about the project."

"Then, what is it about?"

I paused, my stomach twisting at the thought of what had happened last night. What he had seen. How I'd reacted. And what I'd said to the poor, innocent kid who seemed to have had a crush on me for a long, long time now.

"I wanted to apologize"—I tugged him to a quieter section of the hallway—"for yesterday."

"What about it?" he asked, fiddling with the bottom of his *One Piece* graphic tee.

"About what I said in the car," I whispered.

Akio paused for a long time, then swallowed and looked away. "Which part?"

How could I say the *you're not my type* part without saying the *you're not my type* part?

He shouldn't have come to my house, but all the other things that I'd said, I hadn't really meant them. I had been trying to protect him from my father and from what any of those guys would do to him if they caught him.

I shrugged and tilted my face away so he couldn't see my blush. "About all of it."

After a long and tense pause, he gazed down at the tiled floor and shuffled his shoes, again pulling his already-oversized shirt away from his abdomen—the way Mom used to do after Dad would bully her for the belly fat she could never lose from childbirth.

But Akio didn't have an ounce of belly fat.

"You don't have to try to make me feel better," he said, turning toward our science class.

"I'm not trying to make you feel better."

"That's what it seems like."

"Why can't I apologize to you because I'm remorseful?"

"Because."

After shaking my head because I still didn't understand, I said, "Because why?"

Grasping the handle of the classroom door, he paused. "Because I don't blame you."

"What does that mean?"

Again, another pause. "You don't have to worry about it, Nicole."

"Worry about what?"

He slipped through the door. "Any of it."

CHAPTER
TWELVE

AKIO

"AKIO, YOU'RE LATE," Mr. Woodward said from the board.

Keeping my head down, I scurried into the classroom and muttered an apology. My usual seat was taken by a girl named Piper, so I quickly walked to the back and sat in one of two open seats next to each other.

My pants began buzzing from the phones shoved into each of my pockets. I discreetly pulled them out and stared down at Joe Santos's phone, which had been lighting up all morning with messages from Mom's business partners.

But this message was different. It was directly from my scumbag mother.

Yui: Where are you?

Yui: I need you back at the Sandbox now.

The Sandbox … meaning the beach, one of the places she did business.

Then, *my* phone buzzed in my other hand.

Mom: We need to talk. After school.

After grimacing at the message, I turned off my phone and shoved it back into my pocket. I didn't want to know what she wanted to talk about, and I honestly didn't care. Besides, I had work at the pharmacy after school, and I didn't have time for her.

A few moments later, Nicole walked into the room with her head held high, not apologizing to Mr. Woodward once and her hips swaying side to side with ease, the way they always did. After marching right up to me, she slid into the seat beside me and leaned closer.

"You told me that I shouldn't worry," she whispered. "But you should."

"What?"

"You should be the one to worry," she said even more clearly in my ear, her voice velvety smooth, "about how you're going to survive three more classes after you make a mess in your pants again."

My entire body stiffened, and my pants tightened. *Fuck.*

Last week, she had seduced me so I would do our project. I was completely aware that she would never really want someone like me, but still … I couldn't stop thinking about her all morning. Even after I saw those messages she'd sent to Joe Santos.

"What are you talking about, Nicole?" I asked, my throat dry but my dick twitching.

She leaned back on her stool, and my gaze dropped down to her hard nipples pressing against *my* shirt. I hadn't even realized it earlier when she stopped me in the hall. But that was my anime shirt on her body, the one I had given her.

Without any shame, she reached up and grabbed one of her nipples, then tugged on the bud. I gritted my teeth and looked away, my balls heavy. She placed her manicured fingers on my thigh underneath the table. My cock stiffened inside my jeans even harder, and I sucked in a breath, glancing around nervously to make sure nobody else looked over at us.

What is she thinking?! We are in class!

"Relax," she murmured, drawing her nails higher and higher up my thigh.

Relax?! How can I relax with her—

She placed her hand on top of my bulge. "So hard for me already."

"Nicole," I warned underneath my breath.

"Are you going to come?" She giggled softly. "Right in the middle of class?"

When she undid my jeans button and slipped her hand inside my pants, grasping my hard cock, I clenched my jaw and stared down intensely at my notebook. I was supposed to be listening to Mr. Woodward, but I couldn't focus.

Not with her hand moving up and down my cock like that.

"Nicole …"

"I couldn't stop thinking about you all night," she whispered.

Fuck!

I balled my hand into a tight fist underneath the table and prayed that I didn't come. Not in class and definitely not in my pants. Again. I needed her to stop, but, God, it felt too damn good. Better than anything—except being with her.

Her pussy tightening around my cock had felt amazing.

So amazing.

"Want to know what I did in first and second period?"

"Someone is going to see," I whispered.

Yet she didn't seem to mind as she grabbed my hand and slipped it underneath her skirt to her wet cunt. Another small giggle exited her throat, and she shoved two of my fingers into her pussy. "Touched my little pussy and thought about you."

It had to be a lie, but I couldn't seem to care anymore.

My balls were heavy, aching, and full of cum that I wanted inside her. I wanted her to crawl right up into my lap like she had last week and bounce on my cock over and over, her tight pussy gripping my dick harder than my hand ever had.

"Your body's so stiff," she murmured. "Were you thinking about me too?"

"Yes," I breathed, succumbing to the pleasure. I squeezed my eyes closed. "All night."

She slipped her hand deeper into my pants, taking a better

grip on my dick, and pulled my head out of my jeans. She leaned over and let a wad of spit dribble from her lips and onto my cock, and then she swiped her thumb across it, mixing it with my pre-cum.

"I'm going to make you come," she murmured. "So hard."

She moved her hand faster, harder, the soft sounds drifting through the quiet room. I stared up at Mr. Woodward, my cock twitching. My balls felt heavy and warm as she pushed me closer and closer to the edge.

Nicole leaned closer to me. "Maybe tonight, I'll let you fuck me ag—"

My hips jerked slightly, the pleasure shooting through my body. I bit my lip and dropped my gaze to her hand around my cock as my cum drooled all over it. She smirked and continued to stroke until every last bit came out.

"Good boy," she praised. "That's my good boy."

CHAPTER
THIRTEEN

AKIO

FUCK.

I pulled into my driveway behind Rick Santos's car and tightened my hand around the steering wheel. What the hell was he—and the rest of the mob—doing here tonight? They never came to the house. Mom usually didn't let them.

After debating whether I should stay out later, I finally grabbed my book bag and headed for the door. I didn't want to deal with a hundred and one questions, especially after I ignored all of Mom's texts today. But I had to study.

Once I slipped through the side door, I tiptoed toward the stairs near the front.

"Akio!" Mom shouted. "I know you're home. Come here."

Growling underneath my breath, I shuffled to the living room, where Mom, Dad, Rick Santos, and a handful of other mobsters stared tensely at each other. Rick looked especially pissed off with his teeth gritted and eyes glossy.

"What did you get on Nicole?" she asked me.

I stiffened and tightened my grip on my bag. "What do you mean?"

Her gaze hardened. "I asked you to get information on her."

"Why?"

She grabbed me by the collar and yanked me closer. "Don't fucking talk back to me. Joe Santos is missing, and my sources say that the last person to be seen with Joe was Nicole. So, start fucking talking."

"Who's Joe?" I asked.

But Joe and I had gotten to know each other very well.

"He's my fucking brother," Rick Santos growled. "Don't play stupid."

"What was a sixty-year-old doing with a senior at my school?"

Mom only let small pieces of her business through to me, but I had collected enough of them to draw my own conclusions, to start the puzzle that she had presented me. And by the way Nicole had been acting …

Mom clenched her jaw. "We tracked his phone and found it at your school."

I pulled out Joe's phone and tossed it to her. "Oh, you mean this phone?"

The chattering suddenly stopped, and everyone gazed at the phone.

Then, Rick lunged at me, seized me by the collar, and shoved me against the nearest wall. He could bully me all he wanted, but he wouldn't kill me. At least not in front of my mother.

"Where is he? Where the fuck is my brother?!"

I stared blankly at him. "I'm not sure."

"Don't fucking lie to me."

"The ocean is vast. He could be a hundred miles off shore—"

Rick slammed his fist into the side of my face and sent me flying to the ground. My glasses fell right off my face, and Rick stomped on them, the sound of glass shattering and of metal snapping echoing through the room.

Pain radiated from my face and down my neck, and my vision was cloudy.

"He deserved it," I gritted out.

Loud footsteps approached me from the left.

"Rick," Mom warned.

The toe of Rick's boot collided with my left cheekbone. I flew backward and landed on the hardwood floor again, the iron taste of blood filling my mouth. After rolling over onto my knees, one hand posted on the ground and the other clutching my face, I spit up the blood.

"Your brother deserved everything that fucking happened to him," I gritted out.

Rick slammed his heel into my ribs with even more force. My hands slipped, and I face-planted into the hardwood, hitting the left side of my face a third time. I grunted and attempted to lift myself back up, but my arms were too weak.

I hated Rick. Almost as much as I hated his asshole brother.

"If Joe hit as hard as you do, he wouldn't be dead," I sputtered.

After releasing his anger in the form of a shout, Rick tightened his fists.

"Rick," Mom warned again, "stop it."

"He fucking killed my brother!" Rick shouted, readying to lunge at me again.

This time, before Rick could make contact with me, Mom lifted her gun and pressed it against the back of his head. "If you touch my son one more time, I'll put a bullet through your head and kill you too. Calm the fuck down and let the boy explain."

Balling my hands into fists on the floor, I wanted to so desperately pound them into Rick too. He had bullied me for so long, always put me down in front of my parents, and was far more of a nuisance in my life than Poison ever had been.

"Why'd you kill Joe?" Mom asked me.

"He hurt me."

She didn't need more of an explanation than that. Joe fucking Santos had hurt Nicole, in turn hurting me too. Of course I'd had to kill him, just like I would with anyone else who even touched her in a way that she didn't want.

"How?" Mom urged.

After spitting up some more blood, I lifted my head and met her stare. "He. Hurt. Me."

"He's fucking lying," Rick growled, lunging at me.

Another one of Mom's men grabbed him by the collar and shoved him toward the front door.

Rick shouted and hollered, screaming at my mother to punish me because, "Joe didn't deserve to die," but he didn't know what Joe had done to Nicole.

Or maybe he did know and just didn't care.

Mom crouched down to my level and grabbed me by the chin, fingers digging hard into my cheeks. "If I find out that Nicole killed him and you're covering for her, there will be consequences. Do you understand me?"

"You're not going to find out shit," I said through my teeth, raising my hands to show her the scabs on my knuckles from pounding my fists into Joe Santos's face in a wild rage last night. "You see where my knuckles are split open?"

"That doesn't mean anything, Akio."

"It will when you find his face bashed in," I said.

Nicole couldn't have done that.

Mom held my glare for a few moments, then released me. "Joe was one of my men."

"And I'm your son," I growled, knowing that I was digging a deeper hole for myself, setting bigger expectations. "Your son who you should be proud of. After years of trying to get me to do it, after years of training me, you got your fucking wish. I killed a man."

After standing, Mom headed for the front door, followed by Dad and the rest of her men. "But why, Akio? Why now? Why him?" She paused at the door, not looking back at me. "I don't know yet, but I will find out."

CHAPTER
FOURTEEN

NICOLE

AT EIGHT P.M., I parked in Akio's driveway and turned off the car. I really didn't want to be here just so I could get information out of him for my father, but Joe Santos wasn't calling me back, and we did have a project to finish.

I peeked into the rearview mirror and dabbed some extra concealer over my bruises. Last time, he had literally sucked the concealer off my chest and thankfully hadn't noticed the marks on me. But I wasn't taking any chances.

Because … I couldn't answer the questions he'd ask about them.

After finishing with concealer, I fished around in my purse for mascara, but came up empty-handed. I turned on the overhead light, tossing out the contents of my purse and cursing because I must've left it at school.

My lips curled into a frown, and I hoped that I didn't look too bad. My eyes felt so bare without mascara, eye shadow, or eye liner. Stupid me had washed my makeup off after cheer practice, completely forgetting that I had to see Akio tonight.

Deciding that I couldn't go back now, I exited the car and

walked up the walkway to the front door, feeling so self-conscious. I didn't even knock twice before Akio opened the door with a small smile on his face.

"I didn't think you were coming."

Besides the flash of the television screen in the next room lighting up the right half of his face, the other side was shaded by the darkness. Thank God Akio couldn't see how terrible I looked tonight because there would be no way that I could seduce him or even get any information out of him like this.

After smiling at him, I kept my head down and walked into the other room, where *To Your Eternity* was playing on the TV. Akio went for the remote to turn off the anime, but I plopped myself down on the couch and grabbed the remote before he could.

"Leave it on," I said. "It's one of my favorites."

But I would also rather use the light from the screen to work than him turning on the light.

"You've watched this one?" Akio asked with wide eyes.

"Looks like you have some catching up to do," I teased. "You're only on episode one."

"What episode are you on?"

"I've finished it." My lips curled into a smile. Memories flooded my mind—of when Hannah and I would watch anime every day, how she'd always turn it up loud while Mom and Dad fought so I didn't have to listen to them, when she was still here to protect me, to take a punishment for me. God, I had been so selfish to let her go through all that alone. "I used to watch anime with my sister every morning." Tears built in my eyes. "Before she died."

Akio peered over at me. "What happened to her?"

I couldn't look him in the eye. "Someone killed her," I whispered.

But I would never let him know that it wasn't just anyone. That it was my own father.

Not wanting to continue the conversation, I cleared my throat and looked back at the television. "Can you even see the screen without your glasses? Where are they anyway?"

Akio scratched the back of his head. "Oh, just trying out a new look. What do you think?"

"I like you with your glasses better," I murmured, butterflies fluttering in my stomach at how adorable he looked with them on, always readjusting them when he was nervous around me. "They're cute on you."

Akio tilted his head away from me and bit back a smile. "Really?"

A small giggle escaped my throat, and I glanced away because I hadn't meant for that to come out of my mouth. I hadn't meant to admit that I thought he was one of the sweetest guys at Redwood Academy. "Maybe ..."

When I looked back at him, he had his head angled toward me, and the screen was illuminating the left side of his face. His left eye almost looked ...

I gently grasped his chin and tilted his face toward me, spotting a huge bump and purple bruise that he had been attempting to hide from me. My eyes widened. "Wh-what happened to you? Who did this?"

He stiffened and turned back toward the screen. "I fell. Don't worry about it."

"What do you mean, don't worry about it?!" I exclaimed, taking his hand and leading him toward the kitchen.

After searching the freezer for an ice pack, I wrapped it in a washcloth so the ice wouldn't be in direct contact with his skin and walked over to him.

"What really happened?" I asked.

"I fell."

"Why are you lying?"

No response.

"Was it João?"

"No."

"Because if you need me to kick his ass for you, I will," I said.

"It wasn't João," he said, his voice sharp this time.

I pressed my lips together and gently tapped the ice against his cheek so he'd get used to the cold feeling. Every time I had to use an ice pack, the chill was always so biting, and I hated it so much.

"If you want people to believe your lie, you have to believe it yourself," I said, not wanting to get into it because he didn't seem to want to either, but I was also worried. "Or at least look the other person in the eye when you speak."

When he didn't say anything for a few moments, I glanced up at him. In the middle of the brightly lit kitchen, Akio stared down at me with his lips set in a line, gaze drifting around my face. And I tensed.

Because I wasn't wearing any mascara or eyeliner and I probably looked dead to him.

Nobody saw me without eye makeup ever. Usually not even without lipstick.

I dropped my gaze again, chest tightening at the thought of him judging me. Dad had convinced Mom to start swiping lipstick across my lips when I was four. I had accepted the fact that I would never be naturally attractive without makeup.

Suddenly, he tucked some hair behind my ear. "God, you're so pretty."

Warmth exploded through me, and I snapped my gaze up to his innocent one. "What?"

But I ... I had to have heard that wrong. I was so ugly right now.

"You're so pretty."

A giggle bubbled up inside me. Nobody had ever called me pretty before. Sexy? Sure. Hot? All the time. But pretty? My lips curled into a small smile, and I had to bite back my laugh so Akio didn't think I was some weirdo.

Akio scratched the back of his head. "Sorry, I—"

"Do you really think so?"

Akio pressed his lips together and dropped his embarrassed

gaze to the space between us. Then, he shuffled his shoes across the floor, cheeks growing even redder. "I know it doesn't mean anything, coming from a guy like me, but—"

Before he could finish his sentence, I stood up on my toes and kissed him.

CHAPTER
FIFTEEN

AKIO

NICOLE'S soft lips were pressed against mine, and I was frozen to the spot.

I had never been kissed.

Not by a girl that I liked and definitely not by one as pretty as Nicole.

She curled her fingers around the back of my neck, and she pulled me down toward her. Her mouth tasted like mint, and her hair smelled of strawberries. Butterflies fluttered through my chest. And I tried to force myself to grab her by the waist, the way I had seen so many guys do to her.

To seize her hips. To pull her closer. To kiss her more passionately than anyone else.

But I was scared that I'd do something wrong.

A few moments later, she pulled away.

Come on, Akio! What was that?! You didn't even kiss her back!

"Sorry," she whispered, tucking some hair behind her ear. "I'm not sure why I did that."

I stared down at her, wide-eyed, and opened my mouth to say something—anything—but not even a word would come out.

Did Nicole …

Did that really happen?

Sure, I hadn't kissed her back, but I was so shocked that it had even happened.

"We should get back to work," she whispered, wiping the spit off her lips.

She disappeared into the living room, and I followed her.

What is wrong with me?!

After sitting in silence for fifteen minutes, both staring at our textbooks without speaking a word or flipping a page, Nicole's phone screen lit up the dark room, and she picked it up from the coffee table.

While I didn't want to make it obvious, I glanced over her shoulder at the phone, maybe a little jealous, a little possessive that someone was taking her away from her spending time with me. We weren't an item, and we wouldn't ever be, but still …

Dad: Karmeen Kaiser.

She sighed through her nose, glanced over at me, and definitely saw me staring at her phone. I looked away and shifted on the couch. After standing, Nicole walked to her purse on the table and stuffed the phone into it. "I have to go."

"Right now?" I asked.

"Yes."

"Okay." I followed after her as she rushed to the front door. "Is everything all right?"

Before she left, I wanted to apologize to her for not kissing her back. But I was so nervous. Nervous that she'd say it was a mistake. That this *all* was a mistake. That I was a bad kisser and would never get anyone, especially her, to like me.

"Everything is fine," she said without looking me in the eye.

After she ran out the front door and slipped into her car, I grabbed my keys from the side table in the foyer and watched her pull out of the driveway. When her car disappeared down the road, I ran to my car, determined to follow her.

While I stayed a ways away from her car so she wouldn't see

me, I caught up with her at a traffic light. She turned down a side road and then another, heading toward a slummy neighborhood on the opposite side of town.

She parked in front of Karmeen Kaiser's house and headed to the front door.

I parked a few houses down.

Karmeen Kaiser didn't work for Mom, but they often did business together. Kaiser also worked for the Redwood Police Department, not as an official police officer, but from what I knew, Nicole's father and Kaiser knew each other. Well.

My hands balled into fists on the steering wheel, and I waited.

And waited and waited and waited.

Whatever I'd felt tonight wasn't real.

Nicole had been using me, and while, in the beginning, I had been okay with that, I couldn't shake the feeling of how I'd felt tonight. I so desperately wanted it to be real for her too. I hadn't ever found a girl like her at Redwood—one who was not only pretty, but enjoyed watching anime with me and liked my glasses.

Why had I been so stupid tonight? She had given me a chance to kiss her back, a chance to prove to her that I could be more than just someone she thought she had to use to get a good grade. And I'd ruined it.

Blowing out a breath, I leaned back in the driver's seat and ran my hands over my face.

Get it together, Akio. She'll never like you like that.

But to me, it didn't matter.

All that mattered was that I had her attention. At least until the end of the semester.

Suddenly, the front door opened. After running her hand through her messy blonde hair, Nicole walked to her car, slipped into it, and grasped the steering wheel without driving off. She opened her mouth as if she were screaming and then rested her head against the wheel.

A few moments later, she lifted her head, started the car, and drove off. When her brake lights disappeared down the road, I slipped out of my car and headed straight toward Karmeen Kaiser's back door.

CHAPTER
SIXTEEN

NICOLE

"DAD," I whispered, staring out my windshield, "someone will see."

With his hand fondling my breast, Dad leaned back in my passenger seat and stared out the windshield with me. "People will turn blind with enough money, Nikki. Don't worry about this. I'll protect you as long as you do everything I say."

I pressed my quivering lips together and sank down in my car. We were in the student parking lot, an hour before school actually started, and while there weren't many students here yet, João had parked in the corner of the lot about five minutes ago.

"Have you gotten me any information about Yui yet?" he asked, seizing my nipple.

When he squeezed, my body jerked from the sudden pressure, and he placed his hand over the growing bulge in his pants. I shoved back the tears and hoped that he'd stop, get back into his police car parked beside me, and drive far, far away.

Drive into the Atlantic Ocean. Drown.

"A bit from Joe Santos," I whispered.

While I'd received the information last week, I hadn't told him yet because I wanted to drag this out for as long as possible. I didn't want him pushing me to get closer to Akio for more and more information.

"Joe Santos?" Dad repeated, pinching my nipple even harder. "He's dead."

"What?" I asked in a breath.

Then, he used his fingernails to dig into my nipple, like he usually did as punishment.

"You're lying to me," he growled. "Where'd you get the information?"

"I-I am not lying," I whispered.

"He washed up onshore last night. Dead."

My eyes widened. "S-someone killed him? But I was with him just the other day …"

Dad's hand snapped around my throat, and he squeezed hard, his other hand dropping between my legs. He shoved his hand up my skirt and thrust two fingers into my dry pussy. "Why didn't you tell me sooner?"

With stinging eyes, I shook my head. "I-I don't know. I'm sorry."

After tightening his grip around my throat until I could barely breathe, he pounded his fingers deep into my pussy. I bit down on my lip hard enough that I could taste the blood pooling in the bottom of my mouth.

Tears streamed down my face. "P-please, stop."

"Why did I think a bitch like you could do anything right?" he growled, spitting on my cheek. "You should've fucking told me the second you found out. Makes me think you're hiding other shit from me."

"I'm not," I cried. "I p-p-promise."

"Bullshit, Nicole. I know when you're lying."

"Please." When I couldn't take it anymore, I grabbed his wrist. "Y-you're hurting me."

Instead of stopping, he added a third finger and stretched me out even more. I stared at him in desperation, stars clouding my vision and my head lolling slightly to the side. It was … getting harder to breathe.

"Dad," I said, my voice dry, "please."

He squeezed my neck even harder for another moment, then released me. But instead of storming out of my car, driving away, and getting into a car accident, like I had wished would happen for years, he dropped his now free hand to my tits again, fondling and squeezing them.

Just how he liked.

"Your sister took punishment better than you do," he sneered. "No crying from her."

Lips quivering, I sniffled and attempted to stop the tears. But they kept pouring down my face as he ripped open my button-up shirt and slapped one of my tits. I dug my fingernails into my thighs, enough to cut through the skin, all to keep quiet.

To be good.

So he wouldn't hurt me more.

"What information do you have for me?" he snarled.

"I-it's in the glove compartment."

After another moment of him slamming his fingers into me, he pulled them out and opened the glove compartment. Inside it was a single yellow envelope that I had taken off Joe.

Dad grabbed it, exited the car, and slammed the door. I sank down in my seat and watched him drive off through the tears in my eyes. Once he was gone, I wiped my cheeks, reapplied some makeup, and buttoned up my shirt.

Pussy stinging, I stepped out of my car and smoothed out my skirt. Since it was still almost an hour until school started, I marched over to João, both to confront him about Akio and wanting to hurt someone because I hurt.

Being mean never made me feel better in the long run, but it gave me a sense of control for a few moments. And a moment of control in a life that I didn't control made me feel powerful. Even if it didn't last forever.

My heels clacked against the pavement, but João didn't even look up.

"Have a good conversation with Daddy?"

I seethed at João. "What'd you do to him?"

Leaning against his car with windows tinted darker than what was legal, he scrolled through his phone. "To who?" he asked. "Carter, Jace, or your little boyfriend that you're trying to keep a secret from Red—"

With my teeth gritted together, I smacked the phone out of his hand and kicked him straight in the balls. Who did he fucking think he was? João knew exactly who I was talking about because Poison had beaten him up just last week.

Grunting, he fell to his knees.

"What the fuck?!" he growled, clutching his *precious* jewels. "You bitch."

"I might be a bitch, but I asked you a question. What did you do to Akio?"

"I didn't do shit to Akio," he said through his teeth. Using his grip on his car, he slowly stood back up, his hand over his crotch and a low grunt leaving his mouth. "Why do you have to be a fucking bitch to everyone?"

"If you didn't do anything, why does he have a black eye?"

If I couldn't protect myself, the least I could do was protect someone I cared about.

Like Hannah had done for me.

"Crazy fucking thought, you bitch," he growled, "but maybe ask him?"

I crossed my arms. "I don't appreciate your attitude."

"I don't fucking appreciate that you just kicked me in my fucking balls."

Fuming with anger that either João was lying or Akio was being beaten up by someone he refused to tell me about, I twirled on my heel and stormed toward the building. "Hurt him again, and I'll kick them so hard that they come out through your throat."

"Fuck you," João spit.

After throwing up my middle finger at him, I crossed the teachers' lot and hopped onto the sidewalk that led to my first class. If João hadn't hurt Akio, then who had? Barely anyone knew who he was at Redwood.

Which meant that … it had to have been someone he knew. Well.

CHAPTER
SEVENTEEN

AKIO

AFTER SCHOOL, I sat across from Imani at Beestra, a fast-food restaurant where all the Redwood students hung out on the weekends. I picked at a fry on my plate and stared down at my Biology textbook.

My phone buzzed beside my book, Mom's name lighting up the screen.

Mom: Since you're a big boy now, I need your help in an hour.

Lips curling in disgust, I glared at the phone. I hated her.

Mom: Be home by six.

Once I flipped the phone over, I returned to the textbook. If she thought that just because I'd killed Joe and maybe Karmeen Kaiser, I'd start doing her dirty work for her, then she had another thing coming. I wasn't going home until eight tonight.

Maybe later.

"I don't know why Barnes decides to give us tests every other week," Imani said.

"Because he has nothing better to do."

I tapped my finger on the table and tried to focus on the material, but all that had been running through my head today was not kissing Nicole back last night. Why had I just stayed frozen to the spot? Nicole liked guys who took control, not geeky, nervous kids like me.

"We don't even cover this much material in class," Imani grumbled, angrily biting a fry and staring at the chapters. "Does he expect us to teach ourselves, understand the material, *and* ace the test?"

"We do, don't we?" I asked.

She snarled, "Yeah, but still, he's annoying."

A couple of the football players strolled in to grab a milkshake after practice, Jace Harbor being one of them. The other guys stopped to flirt with girls from Redwood while Jace seemed highly unamused and uninterested. He typed aimlessly on his phone and barely looked up at the woman who was flirting with him at the counter.

Of course, he was probably texting Nicole. Making plans to hook up later.

Because I couldn't even kiss her back.

Once Jace grabbed his milkshake, he turned around and made eye contact with Imani. He nodded at her, as if to say, *What's up?* and followed the others out of Beestra.

Jealousy pooling inside me, I glared at the textbook.

Snap out of it, Akio. Nicole doesn't like you like that.

Imani slammed my book closed. "All right, enough studying. Let's talk."

I readjusted my glasses. "About what?"

"Are your parents as annoying as mine are?" she asked me, dipping another fry in ketchup and kicking her legs back and forth under the table so hard that she accidentally kicked me.

But it didn't hurt as badly as Karmeen Kaiser's punch had last night when he was trying to defend himself from me.

The ketchup on Imani's fry was almost as dark as his blood that I'd washed off in the sea.

She rolled her eyes and popped the food into her mouth, coily dark hair bouncing on her shoulders whenever she moved her head. "My mom literally scolds me if I don't do the smallest things right. I just … ugh …"

If Imani thought being scolded was bad, she should try having a mom who wanted her to be a killer.

I ran a hand across my face. "My dad isn't *that* annoying, but he pushes me to get together with you. He wants me to be with you so badly, and it's so annoying," I said. "All he does is talk about you when I'm at home. How I have to be just like you, how we'd work well together. It's nonstop, Imani."

"Well"—she smiled—"I'm off the market."

She accidentally kicked me again, so I kicked her back.

"Well, I don't like you anyway."

"Who do you like?" Imani asked, leaning forward and suddenly interested.

I shrugged and looked away, chewing a fry. "Nobody."

How could I tell her that I liked Nicole?! She hated her.

"Who?"

"Nobody."

"Oh, come on! You wanted to hang out and be friends. This is what friends do. They tell each other who they like, so their friend can go out, stalk their crush, and secretly make it happen!"

Brow arched, I stared at her like she was crazy because was that what friends really did?! That sounded horrible and traumatic if it didn't work out.

I blinked a few times and shook my head. "Exactly why I can't tell you."

"So, you're going to live the rest of your life alone?" she asked.

"God, you're so dramatic."

Tossing some curls over her shoulder, she smirked. "Thank you. I try."

After rolling my eyes, I glanced behind her at a group of cheerleaders who had walked into Beestra. Nicole walked a few feet behind them, dressed in the tightest pair of leggings that formed perfectly to her ass and a white crop top.

"Ugh, she's so—" Imani started, but then stopped. As if it all clicked. "You like her?!"

Cheeks growing hot, I snapped my gaze back to Imani. "Can you not scream that?"

She lowered her voice and leaned further across the table. "Nicole?" she whisper-yelled at me. "The head bitch of the cheer team and the police chief's daughter?" She fake-gagged. "Gross. She sleeps with, like, the entire school."

Ouch, that hurt.

"And you sleep with the three most dangerous guys in Redwood," I said.

"All right, you got me," she said with a smile and raised her glass of water. "Cheers to being a slut … but she's the rudest damn person that I've met, and she has the unhealthiest obsession with Jace, Allie's … stepbrother."

"So? I think she's hot," I said, trying to brush off my jealousy as if it were nothing. "It doesn't matter. She would never like me anyway. And if, miraculously, she did, my father would never approve of her. He'd take one look at her and judge her, the way that he judges everyone."

But really, it was mostly the former reason.

Because Jace Harbor had a billion dollars he could give Nicole. He had the Redwood fame and prestige and a future in the National Football League that was almost certain. They'd be perfect together.

Unlike her and me.

"Every decision you make doesn't have to be for him," she said, offering another smile. "Sometimes, the best ones are the decisions you make for yourself because being the perfect son in his eyes will never be achievable. I've tried, so don't worry about what he thinks. You do you."

After mumbling a thanks that I wasn't even sure she heard, I sank down in my seat and picked at another fry. Imani's advice would be great, if my mother didn't kill people for a living and my father wasn't the dog who sat by her side, both expecting the best and worst life for me.

When the girls moved closer, I stared down at my textbook and wished that I could disappear. Nicole had skipped Anatomy and Physiology today, and it was probably because of how awkward I had been with her last night.

I ignored the girls until they began their stampede to the exit. Then, I dared to look over to see Nicole one last time. But instead of talking with the others, she clutched a brown paper bag in one hand, a milkshake in the other.

And she was staring back at me, her eyes wide and a frown on her face.

After her gaze drifted to Imani, she gritted her teeth and walked out of Beestra.

Not looking back again.

CHAPTER
EIGHTEEN

NICOLE

THREE HOURS after seeing Akio out on a date with Imani Abara, I sat parked in front of his house. I had been driving around Redwood for God knew how long, trying to wrap my head around what I had seen at Beestra tonight.

I had just wanted to get some dinner, and I had gotten a whole eyeful of something else.

Of Akio out with someone better than me, of course.

Why was he out with Imani?!

The question played in my head over and over, but I already knew the answer.

Imani was smart, pretty, and had everything going for her. Me, on the other hand? I might've had some decent looks, but I wasn't as pretty as I used to be, and I definitely wasn't intelligent and didn't have *anything* going for me.

Except a father who wanted to make me pretty again.

I looked through the windshield with tears in my eyes. The longer I stared at Akio's front door, trying to get the balls to march up to the door, step inside, and show him what he was missing out on, the more my chest tightened.

I wasn't good enough for anyone anymore. Not even the guy I'd thought liked me.

Hell, he hadn't even kissed me back last night!

Clenching the steering wheel, I bit back a whimper. *What is wrong with me?*

I had vowed *not* to fall for Akio because I didn't want my father to hurt him, and now, I was in front of his house, crying.

Akio's garage door opened, and a car backed out. I sank down in my seat so whoever it was wouldn't see me basically stalking his house now and watched the woman, who I assumed was Akio's mother, turn right to head down the road.

A moment after his mother disappeared, the car parked behind me turned on its lights. I squinted my eyes and looked into the rearview mirror, watching the car drive into the road and then up Akio's driveway.

What the hell?

Once the car stopped near the garage, Akio hopped out. I furrowed my brow at the shape of his skinny, lengthy body in the darkness, the moonlight hitting his graphic hoodie.

Was he waiting for her to leave?

Deciding that I didn't have time for questions that I would never get the answers to, I jumped out of my car and ran up the driveway in hopes to catch Akio before he slipped into his house and slammed the door in my face for awkwardly staring at him earlier at Beestra.

As he fumbled with his keys, I grabbed his elbow. "Aki—"

Suddenly, he twirled around, keys dropping from his grasp and hand snapping around my throat, shoving me up against the front porch post. My eyes widened, and I tugged on his hand in an attempt to breathe.

His eyes widened. "Nicole."

Almost immediately, he dropped his hand from around my throat. I leaned forward, coughing and trying to catch my breath. I had been choked before by I didn't know how many guys, but I hadn't expected it from Akio.

Damn, his grip was stronger than my father's this morning.

"Nicole," Akio said, crouching down in front of me, "I'm so sorry. I didn't know it was you."

I shook my head. "It's my fault for not saying something."

After fumbling around with his keys once more, he opened the door and led me into the house. "Let me get you some water or ice or something. I'm sorry. I didn't mean it." He headed straight toward the kitchen.

Before he could get far, I grabbed his elbow. "It's okay. I'm fine."

And I was used to it.

Akio tilted my chin up to look at my neck. "There are bruises."

My entire body stiffened, and I pushed him away. "They're not from you."

"What do you mean, they're not from me?" he asked. "Who are they from?"

With my lips pursed, I stared at him and wanted to crawl into a hole and fucking die. Why had I even left my car? Had I actually thought this would be a good idea? What had I even been planning to ask him again?

"Nicole," he said, his voice softer, "who did this to you?"

"Do you like Imani?" I blurted.

"What?"

I crossed my arms. "Do you like Imani? I saw you on a date with her."

"We weren't on a date," Akio said.

But I had seen them laughing and smiling together. And I could never make anyone laugh and smile like that. So, he had to be lying. He had been out on a date with her and had a great time because they had so much in common.

So much that I would never be able to relate to, never be able to understand.

"You don't have to lie," I snapped, jealousy pooling within me. "We were studying."

"Studying, huh?" I asked, more so to myself. "Like we do?"

A confused expression crossed his face, which was quickly replaced with bewilderment. "No. Not like we do. My parents know hers, and ..." He rubbed his elbow. "I don't really have any friends, so—"

I didn't know what came over me, but I seized his face in my hands for a second night in a row and kissed him. There was so much that I wanted to say to him, but I didn't know how to communicate like a normal human being.

Dad paid off all my teachers to give me a passing grade so I wouldn't fail when I didn't do the homework because I was busy with his work.

And now, all I knew was how to seduce men.

Akio froze to the spot and didn't kiss me back.

My chest tightened, and tears were heavy in my eyes as I pulled away.

"Fuck," I whispered, wiping the string of spit off my lip and looking away. "Sorry."

Again, Nicole?! What is wrong with you?!

He hadn't kissed me back last time. Why had I thought tonight would be any different?

Before he could throw me out, I twirled on my heel and ran toward the front door. I needed to get out of here. Dad was right, like he always had been. I didn't have it anymore, and now, I was falling for some guy who would never like me.

When I reached the door, he called my name, and then his hand came around my wrist to stop me. As I twisted my head around to look back at him, he scooped my face toward his and crashed his lips back down onto mine.

NICOLE

AKIO—THE skinny, anime-loving geek—lifted me into the air with ease. I wrapped my legs around his torso and my arms around his shoulders, pulling him closer and closer, my lips moving effortlessly against his.

While he might not have been the best kisser, there was *need* behind his lips, a certain desire that I had never felt before from anyone I had been with. Not Jace. Not Carter. Not even my own father.

It wasn't uncontrollable desire or lust, but much softer, much needier.

Something that both terrified me and filled me with love.

Love? I don't even know the meaning of that word.

After walking with me all the way up to his bedroom, Akio placed me down on the bed. He peppered kisses from my mouth to my ear and then down to my neck. I arched my back, my hands gliding across his shoulders.

Akio's hands found the waistband of my pants, and he pulled them down my legs until he could crawl comfortably between them. With Akio nestled between my legs, I gently placed my hands on either side of his face and drew him in closer to our kiss. Our tongues slipped into each other's mouths, and I wanted more. More of him in any way that I could get him.

Once he removed his pants, Akio pressed the head of his cock against my entrance. While my pussy was wet, all I could feel was the searing pain that Dad had caused this morning. He had fingered me so hard that … it still stung.

But I didn't want Akio to stop, so I closed my eyes and wished the pain away.

Akio pushed against my entrance slowly, the pressure building higher inside me.

And not the good kind.

It'll go away once he's inside you, Nicole. Just take it.

An inch slipped into my cunt.

"Ow," I hissed, then immediately bit my tongue.

Akio tensed and stopped immediately. "What is it?"

I rested my head back onto the pillow and arched my back, not wanting him to stop. Because if he stopped, then maybe he'd fall in love with Imani Abara. And I didn't want him to be in love with anyone but me.

"Akio," I whispered, "don't stop."

"You're hurting."

"I can take it."

"No." Akio sat back on his heels. "I don't want you to hurt."

"I like being hurt," I said. "Please, don't stop."

"You like being hurt?" Akio said.

I stared at him for a long, long time because … I had lied. I didn't like being hurt, but I had gotten so used to the pain I felt every day that I could take it if it meant that Akio would choose me over someone else.

Akio brushed some hair off my forehead, eyes softening. "Nicole …"

My lips quivered, and suddenly, a shoulder-jerking sob escaped my throat. "No, I don't like it," I cried, tears bursting down my cheeks.

I held my hands over my face so he wouldn't see me cry off all my makeup. So he wouldn't see the bruises.

But most importantly, so he wouldn't see through the facade I put up every single day.

"I'm sorry. I'm sorry. I'm sorry. I'm sorry. I'm-I'm an idiot," I said.

While I waited for him to spit on my face, to call me weak—like Hannah had been—to punish me even harder for wailing in the middle of sex, Akio wrapped his arms around my torso, pulled me into his lap, and hugged me.

"I'm sorry if I hurt you," he whispered. "Please, don't cry."

"I deserve it," I sobbed.

I deserved every punishment that Dad had given me. I deserved the hate that the entire cheer team had for me for the mess my father had roped them into. I deserved to end up just like Hannah for the hell I'd caused everyone at Redwood.

"I deserved it," I cried, my nails tearing into the skin on my face because I couldn't deal with all the pain anymore. I wanted to rip out my skin, rip out any ounce of pretty, make myself so ugly that Dad couldn't even fix me anymore. "I deserved it."

My nails pierced my skin deeper and deeper, and all I wanted was to stop the pain.

All of it.

How could I go through this for the rest of my life? I had turned eighteen less than two months ago, and I still had no control over my body or my life. I had never had it. But I wanted some—badly. But the only way that I could do that was to …

Hurt myself.

Physically.

Possibly even further than just hurting myself. Maybe even … maybe even kill—

"Nicole!" Akio shouted suddenly, grabbing my hands and attempting to pull them away from my face.

But I sank my nails even deeper because I didn't want him to see me like this.

"Stop it. You're tearing the skin off your face."

"Go away." I sniffled, body trembling uncontrollably against him. "I'm a mess."

Akio held me tighter. "I'm not going anywhere."

I sank my head into the crook of his neck. "B-b-but … look at me."

Nobody would ever put up with me.

Suddenly, he cupped my face in his hands. "Who's hurting you?"

My eyes stung, and I wanted to look anywhere but at him. "Nobody."

"Who, Nicole?"

"Nobody."

Even if I told Akio, what could he do about it? He was the sweetest guy I knew and didn't have a bad bone in his body. He couldn't save me from the torture that Dad and his buddies put me through every night.

"Nicole," Akio said again.

"Please, drop it." I sniffled. "I don't want to talk about it."

While Akio didn't relax, he didn't push it any further. Instead, he gripped me tighter and drew his fingers through my hair in soothing circles. I closed my eyes, my face stinging from where I had dragged my nails across it, but it didn't hurt as bad as my pussy did.

Not even close.

Akio held me and held me and held me until my eyes were so heavy that I couldn't hold them open any longer.

And the last thing I heard before I drifted off into sleep was, "I'm going to protect you."

CHAPTER
TWENTY

AKIO

MY ALARM WOKE me up at five fifty.

I slammed my hand on the Stop button so I wouldn't wake Mom if she had returned sometime late last night and rolled off the couch. After yanking my shirt over my head, I grabbed some cream and bandages from the bathroom and headed to my bedroom.

Once I pressed my ear to the door to make sure Nicole wasn't already up and dressing, I walked into the room and shut the door behind me. She lay in my bed, her head against my pillow and her cheeks still stained with tears.

After tucking strands of Nicole's hair behind her ears, I sat on the edge of my bed and squeezed some cream onto my finger. The cuts on her face from her fingernails were deeper than I'd originally thought they were, and there was blood.

A lot of it.

I gently pulled off the bandages I'd placed on them last night and dabbed the cream on the cuts to moisturize them so they'd heal faster, until each one of them was covered with a glob of ointment. Then, I fastened some new, very small gauze pads over the wounds.

Nicole loved keeping up with her appearance, and I didn't want her to see what she had done to her face last night. It hadn't even seemed like it hurt her. She had sunk her nails into her head and pulled as if she wanted to rip off her face.

My chest tightened at the thought of her wanting to do that to herself.

Of anyone wanting to do that to themselves.

In the middle of me covering her last wound, Nicole fluttered her eyes open. I stiffened for a moment because I hadn't wanted her to see me.

Last time I'd cleaned someone's wounds was when I was five. Mom had come home and passed out on the couch, bleeding everywhere. I cleaned them up the best I could, but accidentally used the wrong cream on her. Instead of Mom being grateful that I'd tried to help, she'd beaten me for using the wrong cream on her face and accidentally making it worse.

"You look tired," Nicole whispered, glancing over at the empty bed. "Did you sleep?"

"On the couch, downstairs."

"Why not with me?" she asked.

"Because."

While I had thought about sliding into my bed and holding her like I had dreamed about doing for years now, I had decided that would be crossing a line. I didn't know Nicole on that level and hadn't wanted to do anything wrong.

After all, I was just the kid she was using to get a good grade.

Her lips quivered, yet she pressed them together. "You really didn't sleep with me?"

"No."

"You're ..."

A wimp. At least that was what Carter would probably say.

"So sweet."

My gaze flickered up to hers. "Respectful."

She didn't have to call me sweet or nice because I would've done that if it were any woman in my bed. It shouldn't be celebrated, but expected. And by the look on Nicole's face, that wasn't what she expected anyone to do.

Which pissed me off.

"Are you hungry?" I asked.

"A little bit." She pushed herself to a seated position and leaned against my headboard. Her gaze raised to the mirror across from my bed, and she lifted her hand to her face. "Did you do this too?"

I nodded.

She slipped off the bed and walked toward the dresser, her eyes widening. "Oh my God. There are so many," she whispered.

Her lips trembled, but she bit her bottom lip to stop it. Then, she leaned forward and peeled off one of the bandages, flinching when she saw the wound underneath it. I shuffled my feet against the hardwood, not sure what to do.

"I'm never going to be able to hide these," she said under her breath.

"What?"

"Nothing."

But I had heard her. Who was she hiding these from? Kids at Redwood?

After she replaced the bandage, she glanced at me in the mirror.

"Why are you so nice to me?" she whispered.

Because I like you.

"Returning the favor," I said, but, God, it was so much more than that. I shuffled my feet across the floor, rubbing my sweaty palms together. "You know, from the other night when you cleaned up my black eye."

"Oh," she whispered. "I thought it was for another reason ..."

My heart raced inside my chest, and I wanted her to say that she thought I liked her the way that she liked me. But she never finished the sentence, and I so desperately needed to hear it. So, I moved closer to her.

"Like what?" I asked quietly, standing next to her but placing the cream on the dresser and keeping my gaze on it. I couldn't look her in the eye … because what if her reasons were drastically different from mine?!

Nicole moved a few inches closer, her body facing the dresser too. "You know …"

I swallowed, heart pounding.

She glanced up into the reflection, those bright eyes burning into me. When I lifted my gaze to meet hers in the reflection, she pulled hers away and gently ran her fingers across her bandages, cheeks reddening.

A moment later, she looked back at me through the mirror. Her gaze dropped to my lips, then lifted to my eyes. I swallowed again, my mouth suddenly dry and my heart so loud that I could hear it in my ears.

I moved an inch closer to her, our arms brushing against each other's.

She leaned closer, brushing her arm against me again.

Does she know what she's doing to me? She has to know the effect she has on guys.

Especially guys like me.

She stared at me in the mirror, her eyes wide and her lips pressed together, as if she desperately wanted to tell me something. And, hell, I wanted to tell her something, too, but it probably wasn't the same thing.

"Akio," she whispered, her cheeks even redder, "I li—"

But before she could finish her sentence, someone banged on the door. "Open up!"

CHAPTER
TWENTY-ONE

NICOLE

I SMACKED my lips closed and stared at Akio through the mirror as someone banged on the front door so loudly that we could hear it from his bedroom.

What is wrong with me?! He cleans me up, and I fall in love with him?!

Not only that … but I almost admit it to him?!

"What were you going to say?" Akio asked.

Turning away, I walked back over to the bed and searched for my purse. "Nothing."

Whoever was at the door continued to bang on it like their goddamn life depended on it, and I glanced out the window and into his enormous backyard.

Akio had been returning the favor because I'd helped him the other night.

Nothing more.

Another bang.

"You should get the door," I said.

Akio stared at me quietly for another moment, then slipped

out of the room. When the door closed behind him, I slumped my shoulders forward and collapsed back onto his bed.

Fuck, that was close.

After lying back on the bed, I stared up at the ceiling and pulled Akio's pillow to my chest, inhaling his scent. I closed my eyes and wished that I could get the courage up to leave Dad and go into hiding for good. I'd bring Akio with me.

It was only a fantasy because that could never happen.

I would always live in fear that he'd find me and take Akio from me.

With the pillow plastered against my chest, I pulled it even tighter and bit back the giggle that had been building in my throat. I thought Akio really liked me. I wasn't sure, and maybe he didn't, but nobody had taken care of me like he had last night.

Plus, no other guy would do that for someone that they didn't feel something for, right?

Maybe?

Another giggle bubbled through my chest. I hoped so.

Once I played through the silly thought a few more times, I rolled off the bed and replaced the pillow so Akio didn't walk in on me rolling all over his sheets like a madwoman just because I wanted him to become obsessed with my scent.

So much so that he couldn't find it in any other woman.

"Nicole!" Akio shouted from downstairs. "It's for you."

For me?

After grabbing my purse, I exited the room and descended the stairs. I hopped off the last one and found my way to the foyer, eyes widening when I spotted Dad standing in the doorway with Akio and his mother.

"What are you doing here?" Dad asked.

I swallowed hard and glanced over at Akio, who was the reason why I was here. He had been out with Imani Abara yesterday, and I so desperately wanted to be the one who he laughed with like that.

"We are working on a project together," Akio said.

"I'm sorry I didn't text you," I said. "I fell asleep."

Dad smiled sweetly, the way he always did to trick people into thinking he was just a worried father who loved and cared about his daughter. But if he cared about me, he wouldn't hurt me every single day of my life.

"What happened to your face?" Dad asked.

"That's my fault," Akio said without skipping a beat. "I had some project supplies out in my car. Nicole was helping me bring them in the dark, and she tripped over a rock on the front stairway and hit her head on the gravel."

Damn, how'd he come up with that on the fly?

Akio had no trouble lying right through his teeth.

"Akio," his mother snapped, grabbing his elbow, "what's wrong with you?"

"I'm sorry," Akio said to Dad.

"Is that true, Nicole?" Dad asked.

Mouth scorched, I nodded. "Y-yes."

If he found out the truth, I feared what he'd do to me.

Dad placed a hand on my upper back, then slid it to my opposite shoulder and squeezed. "We should get you home to clean up before school. Don't want anyone to see those gashes on your face."

"Okay," I whispered.

After nudging me toward the door, Dad held a hand out to Akio for him to shake. "Thanks for taking care of my daughter." He flashed Akio's mother one of his fake smiles. "Yui, you raised a good one."

I wanted to shiver in disgust at how incredibly fake he was, but I held it together and exited the house without looking back at Akio once. I didn't want him to see the fear in my eyes, the agony written in my skin.

A few moments later, the door shut behind us, and Dad caught up with me.

"What're you really doing over here?" he asked, walking way too close to me.

"Getting you information," I whispered.

Lie. Lie. Lie. Lie. Lie.

I didn't have anything on Akio and hadn't even tried to grab anything from his parents' room last night or any other night that I had been over here with him. I really didn't want to hurt him in the process. He had cleaned up my wounds, for fuck's sake.

And had left me to sleep alone—though I wished he'd slept with me.

"Good girl," he murmured. "What'd you get?"

"Nothing yet." I crossed the street and thanked the Redwood gods that we were out in public because he wouldn't do anything to me right in front of Akio's house, right? I stopped in front of my car. "Akio is different. I'm just planting seeds right now."

A low growl left his throat. "Well, plant them fucking faster."

After I nodded, Dad finally left my side and walked back to his police car. I glanced across the street at Akio's house and spotted him in the living room window, watching me. My heart fluttered, and I smiled softly at him.

He waved awkwardly, like he usually did, then disappeared into the room.

I slipped into the car and locked the doors, resting my head back against the headrest and giggling. I'd slept over at a guy's house last night, and for the first time, I hadn't had to have sex with him. Warmth exploded through my chest. And he'd held me so tightly.

Tighter than anyone ever had.

TWENTY-TWO

AKIO

"WOULD you like to tell me why Nicole slept over last night?" Mom asked as soon as I pulled my gaze away from the window. She stood with her arms crossed and that devious grimace on her face, strands of black hair on her face. "Hmm?"

I walked past her and headed for the stairs. "I was doing as you'd asked."

She snatched my wrist. "If you were doing as I'd asked, you would've been back here last night before I left for work. I had something that I needed you to take care of, and you completely blew me off to see Nicole."

Before she could dig her claws any further into me, I ripped her wrist away, tearing my skin, and headed up the steps. "You asked me to get closer to Nicole because you don't trust her father, so that's what I'm doing for you."

Lie. Lie. Lie. Lie. Lie.

Big fat lie.

I wouldn't even think about involving Nicole in my mother's *business*, even if my life depended on it. But now that Mom had seen Nicole at our house, I would have to play along and drag this out for as long as possible.

Because I didn't want anyone knowing that I liked Nicole. I had already let that one slip out around Imani, and I doubted that she would *ever* let me live that down. Everyone at Redwood seemed to hate her. And I understood their reasoning …

Everyone else thought Nicole was a bitch, but she was sweet to me.

"Where do you think you're going?" Mom growled, storming up after me.

"To school," I said blankly and entered my room.

After inhaling Nicole's scent that seemed to linger on everything, I swallowed hard and stopped in front of my dresser. Her bandages from last night lay on the oak wood. I glanced in the mirror and back at Mom, hoping that she'd leave.

"Would you like to tell me how she really got those cuts on her face?" Mom asked.

"No." *I really wouldn't like to tell you anything, so stop asking.*

"Akio, you—"

"What?!" I exclaimed, gritting my teeth. "I'm finally doing as you asked. I murdered someone. I'm sleeping with Nicole to get information out of her for you. So, you should be happy that your son is finally following in your shitty footsteps."

She slapped me across the face and then grabbed my chin. "Don't talk back to me."

"I wouldn't talk back to you if you just listened to me."

After glaring at me for another moment, she shoved me away. "We have business to take care of after school. You'd better fucking be there to replace Joe or else I will let Rick do whatever he cares to do to you."

"I have work."

"Then, you'd better skip it," she shouted.

She stormed out of the room, and then the front door slammed shut.

I blew out a ragged breath, snatched the bandages from the

dresser, and hurled them into the garbage can in the corner of my room.

After pulling on *My Hero Academia* T-shirt and some jeans, I grumbled all the way to my car.

If I could skip town with Nicole and not have to see Mom ever again, I would.

In a fucking heartbeat.

But Nicole would never want to leave Redwood Academy, where she reigned as the most popular, most beautiful, and most powerful cheer squad captain in the halls. She had built too much of a life here for herself.

Meanwhile, I hadn't done anything but maybe make my first friend during my senior year. *Imani.*

After driving to school, I waited in the parking lot for Nicole—though she would never want to be seen with me around here—until the first bell rang. Then, I lugged my backpack out of the car and walked on the sidewalk to the front doors, glancing back at her empty parking spot.

I wished that Nicole's father had never shown up this morning.

I would've even considered skipping school for the first time ever to be with her.

She didn't even show up when I started slowly stuffing books in my locker, dragging it out so I could see her one more time today. I hoped she was okay, but I doubted that she'd be in school today after those wounds on her—

"Watch it," João growled, shoving me into the locker with one hand.

I hit the metal door hard and gently rubbed my cheek, yet he didn't even turn around.

"Your little girlfriend isn't here to protect you this morning, so don't get in my fucking way."

"She's not my girlfriend."

João stopped and turned his head toward me, dark bags underneath his eyes and his Brazilian accent somehow even thicker now. "I smell bullshit. She fucking kicked me in the balls because she'd thought I hit you."

My eyes widened. "She did?"

Without missing a beat, João stormed toward me again. But this time, Imani shouted at him from down the hall, pushing people to get to us.

He cursed underneath his breath and quickly headed in the opposite direction, muttering something like, "I hate this bitch."

When Imani reached me, she placed her hands on her knees, breathing heavily.

"He didn't hit you, did he?" Imani asked.

"No."

"Good," she said, standing up straight. "Don't worry about him. He's an ass."

But I wasn't worried at all about João. All I could think about was that Nicole … had confronted João because she thought that he'd hit me. *And* she kicked him in the balls *for me?!* Warmth filled my chest.

Imani waved a hand in front of my face. "Uh, hello?"

I shoved the daydream of Nicole away and blinked a few times until Imani became clear in my vision. I scratched the back of my head and wiped off my glasses, as if they were cloudy, when all I could think about was her.

Nicole. Nicole. Nicole. Nicole. Nicole.

Lying in my bed. That smile this morning. Almost kissing her.

Fuck, why didn't I just do it?!

The second bell rang throughout the halls, and I shoved the rest of my books into my locker so I didn't have to lug around forty pounds all day. When I grabbed the books I needed for my first two classes of the day, Imani slammed my locker closed.

Students flew through the hallways to get to their classes, but I glanced over my shoulder to the front door and hoped that Nicole would walk in at any second. She had spoiled me by staying over last night.

"Don't tell me that you're daydreaming about Nicole," Imani murmured.

"I am not," I said.

She stopped, crossed her arms, and arched a dark brow. "That's not what it looks like."

Cheeks burning with embarrassment, I walked past her. "We're going to be late."

TWENTY-THREE

NICOLE

SITTING in the passenger seat of Dad's police car, I pulled down the sun visor.

Dad had forced me to stay home from school and from seeing his *friends* all week—because he didn't want anyone to see how ugly I looked from the gashes in my face—but he finally let me go to school on Friday. And I felt so refreshed.

I glanced in the mirror on the sun visor, dabbing some Vaseline on one of my cuts.

"I canceled your breast augmentation," Dad said, one hand clutching the steering wheel so hard that his knuckles whitened. "No sense in making you pretty if your face is all fucked up. Nobody will want to fuck you like that."

While his words stung, I held back the happy tears.

I didn't even believe in a higher being, but *thank fucking God*!

I had bought myself at least a few more months—maybe. If I had that much time left …

"Oh, really?" I asked as calmly as I could.

Because if I even sounded happy about it, Dad would be pissed even more.

"Instead, I scheduled another appointment with Dr. Aldridge to see what she can do about your face." He turned into the student drop-off line and stopped the car behind an SUV. "But you'd better cover those gashes tonight for the game."

"I will."

"With makeup. Not bandages."

"I have my makeup bag in my backpack."

"Good. I'll see you at the game tonight."

After nodding, I exited the car and waved him off. When his police car disappeared down the street, I turned around and held my hands to my chest, a huge grin crossing my face and warmth surging through me.

Dad might not have trusted me—hence him driving me to school—but I had saved myself.

Bubbling with excitement that I didn't have to go through surgery for Dad and his friends, I skipped up the front steps and headed into Redwood Academy. My cheer skirt bounced in the wind, and goose bumps rose on my thighs.

But I couldn't even care how chilly it was here anymore.

The first bell must've rung already because when I walked into the corridor, students were hurrying to class. Imani and Allie—Jace Harbor's stepsister—walked past me to their first class, each shooting me a dirty look.

Still, nothing could damper my mood.

Akio shut his locker and headed toward a back hallway, in the opposite direction of his first class. It wasn't like I had flirted with his adviser to get his schedule so I could know what classes he had or with who or anything …

When he turned the corner, I followed him, slapped a hand over his mouth, and pushed him into an alcove with a recessed door to a classroom that hadn't been used in ages. I pressed him against the wall and pushed my breasts against his back.

"Shh," I whispered into his ear, releasing his mouth and dipping my hand to his abs.

"Nicole," Akio stiffened. "What are you d-doing?"

"Making it up to you," I murmured into his ear. "For making you stop the other night."

"Y-you don't h-have to."

I slipped my hand into his pants.

"Nicole! We're in the h-h-hall."

"The cameras are broken down here," I whispered. "Poison destroyed them last month."

"Where have you been all—" He grunted when I gripped his cock. "*Fuck.*"

I stroked his huge cock, stuffed inside his pants, almost immediately getting him rock hard. My pussy clenched, and my nipples stiffened. I closed my eyes, warmth gushing between my thighs at the thought of him being inside me.

"I've been thinking about you all week," I mumbled into his ear. "About you inside me."

"Nicole …" he said, voice shaking.

"Have you thought about me?"

"Yes."

"How many times have you jerked off this huge cock with me on your mind?"

A low grunt escaped his mouth. "Every night."

Pleasure rushed through me. "Me too."

Another moan from him.

After grabbing his hand, I pulled it behind him and placed it underneath my skirt. He cupped my pussy through my underwear and rubbed my clit in circles through the thin, lacy material, faster and faster and faster.

"I want to be inside you so badly."

"Beg for it," I whispered, seizing the control.

I never ever had control with any guy that Dad forced me to sleep with. They did what they wanted with me, whenever they wanted. But with Akio, I loved telling him what to do. I loved giving him pleasure. It was so easy with him.

"Please, Nicole," he said. "I haven't been able to think about anything else all week."

"Please what?"

"Please, let me be inside you." He breathed heavily. "I wanna make you feel good."

More heat coursed through my body.

"Please," he pleaded. "I need it badly."

Once I released my grip on his dick, I leaned back against the opposite wall. While the hallways were dimly lit, this little alcove was darker and more hidden than some other places in Redwood Academy, so it was a good place to hook up.

Akio turned around, his eyes hazy with lust and his bulge huge. "Please, Nicole."

I entwined my fingers around his belt loops to pull him closer and undid his buckle, unbuttoned his pants, and pulled down his zipper so he could spring out against my stomach. "Fuck me, Akio. Hard."

Lifting my skirt with one hand, he twisted his fingers around my panties, pulled them to the side, and lined himself up with my entrance. I stared up at him through my lashes and lifted my leg, but before I could set my foot on the opposite wall, Akio dropped my skirt and grabbed my thigh.

He pushed himself into me. Pleasure rushed through my body, and I curled my toes.

"Akio," I whispered, my fingers against his chest, "please …"

After gripping his *MHA* shirt in my hand, I yanked him toward me and crashed my lips against his, desperate to feel them against me again. His tongue slipped into my mouth, his needy lips moving on mine. He thrust into me faster.

I clenched around him, causing him to pull back and moan.

I placed a hand over his mouth, muffling his moans. "I know my pussy feels too good for you, but you'd better keep quiet or else someone might hear us." I moved back and forth on his cock. "And you don't want anyone to see me using you for your huge cock, do you?"

None of that was even remotely true. Akio's eyes rolled back in his head, and he moaned louder into my hand. I moved myself back and forth on his dick and stared at his lips, wanting them all over my body.

"Fuck, you're so beautiful," he whispered softly.

I tightened even more.

My face was fucked, and yet he somehow still found me pretty.

"Keep fucking my pussy," I whispered, "as hard as you can."

Akio pulled out of me, turned me around so I pressed my front against the wall, and shoved himself back inside me, grasping my hips as hard as he could. I dug my fingertips into the wall, pleasure surging through me as he pumped into me.

We listened to a pair of heels clack down the hallway, and Akio slowed.

"Even if they come over"—I moaned softly over my shoulder—"don't stop."

He placed his mouth on the column of my neck, his hands gliding up and down my body, touching every inch of me. He finally set them on my breasts and squeezed, and another low grunt drifted into my ear.

I closed my eyes, about to explode.

"Fill me up with your cum." I moaned. "I want to feel it running down my thighs during the game tonight. Don't you want to see how much of a dirty little slut I am for you in front of everyone at Red"—I threw my head back against his shoulder—"wood?"

He slammed into me and groaned loudly into my ear, and the sweet sound tipped me over the edge. My legs trembled, and I plastered myself against the wall and bit my lip so I wouldn't scream out in pleasure.

"G-g-good boy," I mumbled. "Good, good boy."

CHAPTER
TWENTY-FOUR

NICOLE

"YOUR MAKEUP LOOKS GOOD TONIGHT, NICOLE," Dad said after the football game that night, following me to the sidewalk. "Almost like you didn't fuck up your own face, making it so ugly that it's irreparable." He looped his thumb around the gun on his hip. "Why don't you talk to Jace tonight?"

"Why?" I asked, regretting the word as soon as it left my lips.

"Because if you don't work for me, then you're worthless to me." He ground his teeth together. "And you do remember what happened when Hannah became worthless to me, don't you, *sweetheart*?"

I gulped. "Yes."

"Now, invite Jace over tonight. Understand?"

"Yes," I breathed.

Though I had wanted to go see Akio tonight. He had come to the game.

For me. At least, I hoped it was for me.

I hadn't been able to stop thinking about him since this morning and our little hookup in the hallway. God, he had given me so much pleasure.

Once the boys changed out of their gear in the locker room, the cheer squad, the football team, and a group of students chatted in the student parking lot about the game. I walked over to them, scanned the crowd for Jace, and finally made eye contact with him, Dad's gaze burning into my back from the far lot.

Jace offered me a smirk, which was unusual for him. I usually had to work for it.

When he tilted his head to the sidewalk, as if he wanted me to walk over to chat, I excused myself from the other cheer girls who didn't really give a fuck about me anyway. I walked over to him, nipples taut because of this damn cold and not because I actually wanted to do this with him right now.

"Good game." I bit my lower lip to stop it from chattering. "But you looked a bit stressed the entire time." Not that I had actually watched the game, more like I stared at the bleachers, looking for Akio. "Why don't you come over tonight? I can help with that."

I would much rather *not* help Jace with anything.

But Dad had given me the entire week off, so he expected something from me now.

"Party tonight." He slung an arm around my waist. "But what about tomorrow?"

While I stiffened at the thought of anyone except Akio touching me, I forced myself to relax and sprawled my hand across his muscular abdomen. "Mmm, Jacey … why don't we sneak into my car and get it over with?" I peeked over at Dad, who was now looming behind his police car. "I bet you've been aching to fuck me hard, get all that anger out, *hurt* me."

That was all guys liked to do to me anyway. Except Akio.

Jace snatched my jaw in his hand, and I resisted the urge to flinch. "I said tomorrow."

I forced a giggle. "I love when you get all dominant like that. If you want to wait until tomorrow"—I glanced down at my body and pressed my tits against his chest—"for this, then I'll see you at my house at seven." An urge to puke after saying those words bubbled up inside my throat, but I swallowed it down and headed toward my car. "Don't be late, lover boy."

Once I climbed inside the car, I shoved my key into the ignition with a shaky hand and sped off in a hyperventilating fit. I drove all the way around the school to the student drop-off section and parked on the side of the road, just staring at the group of people to calm myself.

Before Dad showed up and asked me what had happened.

Except …

When I looked across the field, Allie Hall—Jace's stepsister—now stood across from Jace and stared at him with a mix of horror, despair, and sadness. I gripped the steering wheel and looked at her through wide, teary eyes because I recognized that pain on her face.

Helplessness.

Loneliness.

Heartbreak.

Jace stared back at her with wide brown eyes, like a deer in fucking headlights on one of Redwood's back roads. They exchanged a few words, and then he stepped toward her, causing her to move backward and wrap her arms around her body.

Pain shot through my chest.

They loved each other, and I … and I … had caused this.

I caused every bad thing to happen in Redwood.

After another few words, she barreled toward him and shoved him back, tears streaming down her cheeks. Through my slightly rolled down window, I listened to her scream at him, the pain in her voice unbearable.

"What was that? What was it? Tell me! Are you fucking sleeping with her again?"

My hands tightened around the steering wheel, manicured nails digging into my palms. I bit back a cry and tried desperately to pull my gaze away from them, but I couldn't do it. They loved each other—it had been obvious to me since sophomore year—and I had destroyed their relationship.

Twice.

Jace grabbed her wrists and said something quiet to her.

"No! I'm not going to drop it. This is *my* business, Jace. So, tell me. Fucking tell me!"

While I didn't want her to cry because this was all my fault, her sobs muffled mine in the car. I placed a hand over my mouth, tears stinging my eyes. Why couldn't I do anything right? Why did I have to hurt everyone?

"What do you want me to say?" Jace shouted. "That I'm sleeping with her? Is that what you want to hear, Allie? Do you want to hear all the fucking things I'm doing with her that I used to do with you? Why are you making such a big deal out of this?"

But Jace was lying.

We hadn't slept together. Ever.

We had gotten close—so close. Multiple times. But we had both stopped each other.

"Because I love you, Jace!" Allie shouted.

Pain flooded through every inch of me, my body in tingles. I cried out loud, not caring anymore, and shook my head. This was my fault. Allie's pain. Jace's pain. My fucking pain. I had caused it all when I was just trying to survive.

Jace's features softened—in a way that was similar but different from when I used to say *I love you* to Hannah and she'd stare down at me in awe. Something about having someone to care and love you, no matter how terrible of a human being you thought you were, no matter how hard life became, it was nice.

And that look ... was the most precious thing to me.

Now, I had broken the trust between them.

Imani suddenly enveloped Allie in her arms and pushed her into a car. After slamming the door, Imani twirled around, said something snappy to Jace, then drove off with Allie in tow as Jace stood there, defeated.

I wiped my tears with the back of my hand and wished people at Redwood could mind their business instead of now gossiping about Allie and Jace, but the people surrounding Jace were whispering tensely with each other.

Jace and Allie might've been stepsiblings, but before their parents married … they had been together. And I had been the one to rip them apart. All because of Dad. All because I hadn't been strong enough to stand up to him.

All because I feared that he'd kill me if I didn't listen.

Aimlessly looking around in the crowd, my gaze locked on to Akio, who stood by himself on the sidewalk on the outskirts of the mob with his hands stuffed into his coat pockets, his body turned toward me and his glasses all foggy from the cold, but somehow, I knew he was looking right at me.

Akio turned on his heel and headed in the opposite direction, shoulders slumped forward.

I had seen him at the game tonight, had forced myself to be extra loud with the cheers, to hit the stunts perfectly so he'd notice me out of the rest of the girls.

And now … I had betrayed his trust too.

I exited the car, slammed my door, and ran across the parking lot to the pack where Akio had disappeared. "Excuse me. Excuse me!" I pushed through the horde, elbowing people so they'd get the hint. "Move!"

After I finally made it through the herd of students, I glanced around in the dark in hopes of finding Akio, to explain myself, to promise that I wasn't doing this because I wanted to, but because I had to.

But he was already gone.

TWENTY-FIVE

AKIO

TEN AT NIGHT ON SATURDAY, I sat in Imani's car, driving around Nicole's block.

I didn't want to be here with Imani, sitting with my thoughts and imagining what Nicole was doing with Jace in her living room. I balled my hands into fists by my sides and stared at her house as we passed, wishing that she were with me.

The only reason that I'd actually gone to the football game last night was to see her cheer. I usually didn't do school activities, but Nicole had made me feel things that I had never felt before at my house … then in the hallway the other morning.

"Fuck," I whispered under my breath.

Imani glanced in the rearview mirror at a car parked a little ways down the street, and then she clutched the steering wheel tightly and looked back at Nicole's house. She had told me that we were here to spot Jace Harbor in the act with Nicole so she could protect her best friend, Allie. But with that look on her face …

"Are you okay?" I asked Imani. "You look like you saw a ghost."

"Not a ghost," she said. "But maybe my death …"

I peered into the rearview mirror to get a better look at the car Imani had spotted and saw João, Landon, and Kai from Poison sitting inside it. What the hell were they doing here? This late at night and two doors down from Nicole's place?

"Fuck it," Imani mumbled to herself and parked across the street.

Why are we stopping?!

After she cut all the lights, she pulled out a pair of binoculars from the center console.

"Why do you have binoculars in your—"

"Bird-watching, Akio," Imani snapped, zooming in with the dial on the top, "aka none of your business." She nodded to the glove compartment. "There is another pair in there for you if you want to snoop. I know you like her, so you might as well see how big of a bitch she is."

When I opened the glove compartment, sure enough, there was a pair of binoculars.

"Why do you care that I like her so much?" I asked, putting the binoculars to my face.

"Because friends don't let friends make bad decisions," she said.

First of all, I didn't know we were friends. And second …

"You let Allie fall for Jace again."

She paused. "That's different."

I zoomed in with the dial to get a better view of Nicole's dining room. The light from the living room flooded in and hit the glassware stored in the china cabinets, which meant that Nicole and Jace were in there, doing God knew what.

And it pissed me off.

Last night, *Nicole* had been the one to come on to Jace, unlike all the other guys she had been with. To my understanding, they all came on to her, touched her, used her for their pleasure. I was still trying to piece it all together.

But … this didn't make sense.

Why Jace? And why had she been crying yesterday in her car *after* she flirted with him?

Suddenly, Imani pulled the key from the ignition. "Come on."

"Come on?" I asked, glancing over at her.

Imani snuck out of the car and shut the door quietly behind her. Then, she sprinted across the street and slipped between Nicole's house and her hedges. I stared at Imani with wide eyes from the passenger seat of her car.

What is she doing?!

If Nicole saw me with Imani *and* saw me stalking her, I'd be screwed!

But I ran across the street after Imani because I didn't want her getting into trouble.

"What are we doing?" I asked. "We can't stalk someone. It's against the law!"

Though ... I wasn't about to tell Imani what I did in my free time with Nicole.

"Yeah, yeah, yeah," Imani said, waving me off. "There is a better place to see into her house around the back."

"How do you know this?!" I asked, hurrying after her. "It's Poison, isn't it?"

Stopping on her heel, she whirled around and poked a finger into my chest. "No, it's not Poison. I did this far before I ever met them, so stop thinking that I'm such a good girl, and let's have fun, snooping on Jace Harbor and the girl you like ... and Poison."

After slumping my shoulders forward because she wasn't going to budge, I followed her around to the back. We pressed our bodies flat against the house and inched closer to the back door that led to the pool.

"Are you sure this is okay?" I asked.

Desperate to persuade her to leave ... but also desperate *not* to see Nicole and Jace.

Together.

"No, but we're doing it anyway." She glanced over her shoulder at me. "You ready?"

"Uh ..." I scratched the back of my head. *No!* "Sure?"

She crouched and glanced in through the back glass door. I looked over her shoulder and gritted my teeth. Inside, Nicole sat on her knees in front of Jace Harbor, who smirked down at her.

Suddenly, Imani pulled back and hit her hard head into mine. "Jeez, Akio," she said, rubbing the spot. "You have a hard-ass head. Now, do you see who Nicole really is? Look at how uncomfortable she's making him, and she—" Imani glanced back into the room. "Wait."

Uncomfortable? Jace didn't look uncomfortable.

If anything, Nicole did.

Or at least ... I could tell that she did because when she was really comfortable, her smile wasn't as tight, her shoulders weren't as stiff, and her eyes weren't stricken with as much fear as they were right now.

We both peered back into the house, only this time, my gaze drifted behind Nicole and Jace to Poison, who had snuck through a back hallway. Imani cursed and shoved me back so I stumbled into the bush.

Is this all some kind of setup? For what?

"Go, Akio!" Imani shouted, pushing me around the house and making a beeline for her car.

I stumbled along in front of her, trying to regain my footing.

"They're going to see us if you don't get your ass in gear!"

Behind us, the front door opened.

After we reached the car, I glanced through the passenger window. Imani fumbled with the keys in an attempt to turn on the car, terrified of Poison, then slammed her foot on the gas pedal to speed the hell out of there.

I gripped the seat to steady myself and gazed at Kai, who pulled off his ski mask and stared at us as we peeled out into the road. Kai already didn't like me because I kept hanging out with his girl.

Now, he *really* wouldn't.

"Fuck!" Imani whispered. "He saw us."

"Why are you so scared?" I asked. "I thought you didn't take Poison's shit."

"Ha-ha," Imani said, still peering into the rearview mirror. "Funny. But you don't understand … Kai will …" She took a deep breath, cheeks reddening, even in the darkness. "Let's just say, he'll do to me what you hope to do to Nicole one day."

I furrowed my brow. "What?"

"He'll *punish* me."

"I don't want to punish Nicole."

"You know what?" Imani said, turning on the music. "Forget it. They're not following us anyway …"

I didn't want to punish Nicole, but maybe I wanted to punish Jace Harbor for touching her. Maybe later tonight, I would pay him a visit. Maybe … maybe I would show him and the rest of Redwood Academy that Nicole was my girl.

CHAPTER
TWENTY-SIX

NICOLE

AFTER SUCKING in a quiet but long breath, I reached up to the button on Jace's pants and undid them. I didn't want to do this, but I honestly didn't have much of a choice anymore. As soon as Jace left, Dad would be home.

Once I pulled down Jace's pants, I swallowed the bile in my throat at how disgusting I was for doing this to Allie Hall and to Akio. Then, I ran my manicured fingers over Jace's cock pressed against his briefs.

Sometimes, Dad told me why he forced me to sleep with the guys he did. Sometimes, I could easily figure out his reasons. But other times, like this one, I had no fucking idea. I didn't know what he wanted from Jace Harbor, Redwood's football prodigy.

I squeezed my eyes closed and placed my mouth on Jace's underwear, sucking lightly on his dick through them, all the way up until I reached the head of his cock nearly peeking out around his waistband.

I'm sorry, Akio, but I have no other choice.

My tongue traced his head near his waistband, and suddenly, Jace's dick softened.

Pausing, I pulled away and looked up at Jace. "Why is your dick getting soft?"

I wasn't complaining, but I really, really didn't want to do this, especially if *he* didn't want to do it either. He loved Allie, and I didn't want to ruin what they had. Hell, I refused to do it. I would rather take the punishment from Dad than ruin another relationship permanently.

Jace's eyes snapped open, and he zippered up his pants. "I need to use the bathroom."

When he slammed the door closed, I sat back on my heels and stared up at the ceiling through teary eyes. *Thank God.*

If Jace hadn't pulled away, then I might have. Because all I could see in my mind was Akio's expression last night.

Those sad eyes. His frown.

A tear fell from my eye, and I quickly pushed it away before Jace came back.

I couldn't have him see me like this. I couldn't have *anyone* see me like this.

After twisting around to sit on my ass and lean against the couch, I stared emptily at the wall and wrapped my arms around myself. All I wanted was to be normal. For once. Allow myself to be happy with Akio.

Yet I would never get to be normal. I would never get to go on dates. Never be happy.

Twenty minutes later, Jace emerged from the bathroom with puffy, bloodshot eyes, as if he had been crying. I pressed my lips together, not knowing if I should comfort him or ... maybe make him something to eat?

"What do you have to do?" he asked.

My eyes widened, and I looked around in an attempt to figure out what he meant. He wasn't going to go? If he didn't want to have sex, then why the hell would he stay here with me any longer?

"Huh? Anything fun?" he asked.

What do normal people do together?

The only normalish thing I did was do makeup. But that was to hide bruises.

"How about you practice your makeup on me?" he suggested, almost as if reading my goddamn mind.

"What?" I asked, completely confused.

He scratched the back of his neck. "At lunch, you keep saying how none of the other girls on the cheer team let you do their makeup. So, why don't you practice on me? Until, uh … my dick gets hard again."

I slightly arched my brow because Jace Harbor would *never* get caught in makeup and headed to my room to grab my makeup bag. He was doing this to pass the time, and I was completely fine with that.

I didn't want to fuck him anyway.

After returning to the couch, I sat beside him and pulled out some concealer. Jace turned on a football game on the television as I blotted some cream on his skin to cover one of the bruises on his face from the game last night.

Jace would never be a friend, but this was the closest thing I had to normal.

"How are your tremors?" he asked.

My eyes widened. He'd remembered?

I had told him about my hand tremors right after Hannah died a couple of years ago, after he asked me to meet him at the Overlook, where he staged a whole scene between me and him in front of Allie, his girlfriend at the time.

"They're better," I said.

Around Dad, not so much. But around Akio … I didn't feel any anxiety.

"Hmm," he hummed. "Your dad still have them too?"

"What?" I asked.

"Does your dad still have tremors too? I think you mentioned a couple of years ago that they ran in your family."

"Oh." I cleared my throat and remembered that I had lied and told him my tremors ran in the family even though they didn't. I *thought* mine were caused by the constant state of stress and anxiety that I was in because of Dad. "Um … no. His went away."

"Cool."

"Yeah, cool," I repeated because what else could I say?

A while later, after an unbelievable amount of small talk that led nowhere, Jace gathered all his things from the coffee table and headed to the front door. "It's getting late. I should get going."

"Jacey," I whined, desperately clutching his arm, "why don't you stay the night?"

As soon as Jace stepped out of the house, Dad would see the security cameras and would race back over here to see what I had gotten out of him. But I didn't know *what* Dad wanted me to get out of him.

And if I didn't have anything, he'd punish me because I was useless to him.

Like Hannah.

Jace curled his finger around a lock of my hair and tugged. "You know I don't stay over."

I frowned. "We didn't even do anything fun."

Which I am so grateful for because it wouldn't have been fun for me.

"You caked me in makeup, Nicole." He took a deep breath, as if he was pushing his frustration away, then presented me with a smile that I knew was fake. "Isn't that what you wanted? You never get to do that."

Game recognized game.

Liars recognized liars.

Actors recognized actors.

And I recognized that Jace Harbor didn't want this either, so I wasn't going to push it.

I'd already semi-ruined his relationship with Allie, and I wished to take it all back. I wished to explain everything to him, *to her*. I just wanted a friend that I could tell everything to. A friend who'd hold me, like Imani had held Allie the other night. A friend who would tell me that every story had a happy ending.

But life didn't have happy endings for everyone.

Sometimes, life gave those with the brightest smiles the most horrific endings. Sometimes, a soft giggle that calmed every one of my nerves turned into a washed-up body at the Overlook. Throat slit and eyes gouged.

And I'd be a fool to hope that my life would be any different.

CHAPTER
TWENTY-SEVEN

AKIO

MONDAY MORNING, I stood by my locker and watched the front doors. I had gone over to Jace Harbor's house twice this weekend to *talk* to him, but every time I showed up, the maid had answered the door.

I rearranged the books in my locker, desperate to appear busy. All I wanted was to talk to him to see what Nicole had wanted, to ask why he had shown up at her house … but I already knew the reason—he'd wanted to get his dick sucked.

Teeth gritted so hard that I nearly chipped them, I slammed a book deep into my locker and hit the metal backboard.

What the hell was wrong with me?! I shouldn't like Nicole. I shouldn't care about Nicole. She was using me.

Yet it'd felt so real with her.

But maybe that was because she was my first everything.

I wasn't her first anything and definitely wouldn't be her last.

After grumbling to myself, I caught Jace walking through the door. I slammed my locker closed and followed him down a few hallways to his locker. He opened it up and stuffed some books into it.

"Jace," I said.

"Look who it is," João said from behind me.

Jace glanced over his shoulder at me, then João. "What's up?"

João wrapped an arm around my shoulders, in a much better mood than he had been the last time I saw him in the halls, and pulled me tight. "Akio is here to warn you to stay away from his girl *or else*. Fucking nerd."

Jace shook his head at João. "What's up, Akio?"

After shoving João away, I straightened myself out. "I, um …"

Why'd João have to ruin it?

João leaned against the lockers and lit up a cigarette. "That's why you're here, isn't it?"

I pressed my lips together and looked at Jace, who seemed just as curious. "No."

"Then, what're you doing here?"

"I came to tell *you* that I had a good time with Imani on Saturday night."

Jace chuckled.

João slammed me into the lockers. "The fuck did you just say?"

"You heard me."

His forearm slid up my chest and to my throat. "You fucking want to say that—"

Jace shoved him back. "Lay off the guy, João."

After shooting João a glare, I turned on my heel and headed back down the hallway. I had wanted to confront Jace, but he seemed like a decent guy … at least from my one-minute interaction with him.

But that didn't mean I liked him.

"Akio!" someone shouted from down the hall. "Akio, wait up!"

After readjusting my glasses, I glanced over my shoulder and spotted Nicole. With her heels clacking on the tiles, she ran down the corridor toward me, her hair thrown up into a messy bun and her eyes soft.

I didn't know whether to continue walking to class and ignore her or wait.

The closer she came, the harder it was to pick up my feet or even drag them.

"Can we talk?" she asked, pushing a strand of her blonde hair around her ear.

"I have class," I said.

"Screw class."

"School is important to me."

"You're right." She looked at the ground between us. "I'm sorry."

"Nicole, I didn't …" I started, unsure how to finish. "I mean … we can still talk. We have—"

"No. No, you're right." She fidgeted with her fingers. "Maybe we can talk after school."

"I didn't mean it," I said, shaking my head. "I mean, I did, but—"

"It's okay, Akio." She smiled, but it didn't reach her eyes. "School is important to you."

"Yeah, but you're important to me too."

As soon as the words tumbled out of my mouth, I wished that I could take them back. *You're important to me too?!*

All Nicole cared about was getting a passing grade so she could graduate and go off to live as a trophy wife to Jace.

She didn't give a shit about me.

"You what?" she asked breathlessly.

Warmth spread throughout my chest. I opened and closed my mouth a handful of times, not knowing what to say. Whether I admitted it again or not, I was screwed. One way, she would laugh in my face at how stupid I was. The other, she'd brush it off like I hadn't said anything.

I didn't know which was worse.

"I, um …" I whispered, mouth parched. "I …"

"I'm important to you?" she repeated.

After waving my arms, I cleared my throat. "I—Nicole … I didn't mean it."

A long pause, and I couldn't stop myself from screwing up.

"Oh," she whispered, wrapping her arms around herself and turning. "Never mind then."

Before she could walk away, I grabbed her wrist and twirled her back around. "I'm sorry. That's not what I meant. Please, don't be angry or upset with me, Nicole. I just …" I swallowed hard, unsure about what to say. "I …"

"It's okay," she said, pushing me away. "I'm just some … pussy to you."

My chest tightened, and I squeezed her hand tighter. "No, you're not."

She plastered the fakest smile on her face that I had ever seen —one she had given Jace the other night—and laughed. "Come on, Akio. It's fine. That's what everyone uses me for. I'm used to it. No need to be so uptight about what you—"

I didn't know how to get her to stop talking nonsense, so I kissed her.

Fingers laced through her hair. Mouth on hers. Body pressing her into the lockers.

"I'm sorry," I said, pulling away, suddenly hyperaware that there were other students around and potentially watching the nerdy kid kiss the head cheerleader. I wiped my lips. "I shouldn't have kissed you here …"

Nicole leaned against the lockers, cheeks flushed and breathing heavily. "Akio—"

"Come on," I said, grabbing her hand and leading her down the hallway. "We need to talk, but not here. Somewhere more private."

CHAPTER
TWENTY-EIGHT

NICOLE

AKIO BROUGHT me to the library, where a couple of students lounged around during their free period. We sat at a table off to the side and away from the door, near the computers. Akio fumbled with his fingers.

"Nicole," he whispered, an expression full of anguish crossing his face, "I didn't mean what I said back in the hall. I … you're …" He paused again and looked at my hands, as if he wanted to grab them. "I …"

I waited impatiently for him to finish his sentence, for him to *explain* what he didn't mean.

Was it *you're important to me* or *I didn't mean it*?

All I wanted him to say was that I wasn't just someone he only wanted to hook up with, that I meant more to him than a couple of blow jobs at school, that he wanted me to be in his life because he cared about me.

For once, I wanted to be important to someone. And not for my body.

"Akio, it's fine," I said to get this over with and to stop feeling so upset about my shitty life. Nobody was coming to save me.

Nobody would ever care about me for more than just my body. "I don't mind hooking up with you."

"You don't mind?" he repeated.

I shrugged. "I don't mind."

Suddenly, Akio tensed and looked away from me. "I know that I'm not as good as Jace Harbor at stuff, but I don't want to be pitied."

Akio had always been soft and sweet, and I had rarely ever seen this side of him. The side of him that snapped.

"I don't want you to hook up with me because you feel like you need to so I'll do our project."

My eyes widened. "No, Akio, that's not what I—"

He pressed his lips together. "How was he?"

"What?"

"How was Jace on Saturday night?" Akio asked. "I saw you two together."

H-how does he know? He saw me talking to him, but how does he know I was with him Saturday night?

"Akio, I don't know what you're talking about," I said, curling my finger around a strand of my blonde hair and tugging on it nervously. *How the hell does he know?!* "I wasn't with Jace on Saturday night."

Akio clenched his jaw. "Why are you lying?"

"Where did you see us?"

"At your house!"

As soon as the words left his lips, Akio snapped his mouth shut and cursed underneath his breath. The librarian shushed us, and a couple of students looked over, including Sakura Sato, the class valedictorian.

I grabbed Akio's hand and yanked him toward the back of the library, my mind racing.

Akio was at my house on Saturday night? Did he see ... everything that happened between Jace and me?

It hadn't been anything, but from an outside point of view ... it could've looked like a whole lot more than what actually happened.

The bell rang through the library, and Akio tried to leave, but I tightened my grip.

"Forget I said anything," he mumbled, pulling on his wrist.

Instead of releasing him, I continued to march to a secluded area with hundred-year-old encyclopedias, and I cornered him, standing between him and his escape route. If he wanted to get past me, he'd have to push me out of the way.

And Akio wouldn't do that.

"You were at my house?" I asked, nerves bubbling up in my stomach.

He stared at me so harshly for a few moments, and then his gaze softened. "Sorry."

"Were you at my house?"

His lips turned into a frown, and he dropped his head. "Yes."

Oh my God. Oh my God. Oh my God.

"For how long?" I whispered, tears building in my eyes.

Because I desperately hoped and prayed—not that there was actually anyone listening—that he had left way before Jace Harbor left. I drew my fingers over the bruises on my legs that I had hidden with makeup and some tights. If he had seen what Dad did to me that night …

Akio shook his head. "I didn't see anything."

"How. Long?"

"Long enough to see you with Jace."

I placed a hand on my forehead to ease the tension between my brows. Too much stress led to wrinkles, and wrinkles led to getting needles jammed into my face. I had to be picture-perfect for Dad and his friends.

When I blinked, two tears slipped down my cheeks. I wiped them with the back of my hand and stared at the center of Akio's chest. So many questions ran through my mind, but all I could think about was that …

He hadn't seen anything.

At least not between Dad and me.

And, *fuck*, that gave me so much relief.

"I'm sorry, Nicole," Akio said, grasping my face and pushing away the tears. "I should've never come over or confronted you about Jace. It's none of my business what you do or who you're with in your free time."

A sob escaped my mouth, and I pressed my hand over it.

He didn't see. Thank God. Thank fucking God.

"I won't ever do it again," he whispered, drawing me closer. "I'm sorry."

I wrapped my arms around his torso and placed my head on the center of his boney chest. If he had seen Dad fucking me on Saturday and me pretending that I liked it, he would think that I was disgusting.

He wouldn't want to talk to me ever again. And I needed him.

Nobody else in this school or this town liked me.

Nobody else cared.

Everyone had it out for me, like Allie and Imani, and rightfully so.

But Akio had been the only person that I could lean on these past few weeks. And if he saw me with my own blood-related father, if he saw him inside me, I would've killed myself from straight-up embarrassment and guilt.

"Why were you at my house?" I asked between sniffles, unable to look up at him.

"I was"—he paused—"with Imani."

My chest tightened, and I lifted my gaze. "With Imani?"

Jealousy pooled throughout my body.

Why was he with her again? Last time, he told me that she meant nothing to him. But if he willingly decided to hang out with her on a Saturday night, that had to mean something, right?

"What is she to you?" I asked.

Akio paused. "What is Jace to you?"

"Jace means nothing to me," I said honestly. "He's just someone ..."

"Who can fuck you'd better than I can?"

"No, that's not it." I grasped his shirt in my weak fists. "He's just a friend," I said.

Because how could I explain anything to him? Where would I even begin?

"So is Imani," Akio said. "But I don't sleep with her."

"I don't sleep with Jace," I said, my voice dropping. "Not willingly."

Akio tensed. "What did you say?"

"Nothing," I reassured. "Nothing. I said nothing."

But Akio didn't seem convinced.

"I promise," I said, setting my hands on his chest. I moved them up to his shoulders, then to his neck, and then I gently grasped his face to pull him closer so our lips were millimeters apart. "You mean more to me than anyone in my life right now. Please believe me."

Akio blew out a shaky breath.

"Please, Akio ..."

CHAPTER
TWENTY-NINE

AKIO

AFTER STUFFING some books into my locker, I kept my gaze on the hallway for any sign of Jace. He hadn't been alone all last night. But if he had been, I would've shown up at his front door, like I had with the other two men who had fucked Nicole, and taken care of him.

Nicole had explicitly said that she wasn't with him willingly.

Which meant that he must've threatened her.

Kai Koh, the third member of Poison, stormed up to me. While Kai stayed on the quieter side, he terrified me the most, more than João and Landon. I shut my locker and pulled my books to my chest, knowing *exactly* why he was here.

"I told you to stay the fuck away from Imani," he said between clenched teeth.

"I-I did."

Out of all the members of Poison, Kai was the most protective of Imani and the most dangerous. I had heard rumors that he had killed many people with his bare hands. Unlike Landon and João, who were loudmouths who intimidated their *business* partners, Kai actually took action.

He'd *definitely* take action against me. He'd already told me to stay away from her once.

Especially after I'd taunted João about being with Imani on Saturday night.

Kai grabbed my collar and shoved me against the locker. "Don't fucking lie to me. You were at Nicole's house on Saturday night, spying on us, weren't you?"

"How do you know that? Did she tell you?"

"No," Kai said. "Imani didn't tell me anything. I saw you with her."

"Look," I said, shaking my head and spotting Jamal Simmons, who was Jace's best friend, walk down the hallway. "Nothing happened. We were hanging out. I … I don't even like Imani like that. She's not my type, and I … I just wanted a friend …"

And I needed to get out of this conversation now so I could pester Jamal about Jace's whereabouts. He hadn't shown up yet today. Not only was it a few minutes before the bell rang, but there was a sudden uproar of whispers, Allie Hall's and Jace's names being thrown around in the halls. Something must've happened.

"It's not my fault you guys wouldn't hang out with her this weekend," I said.

Kai's grip on my collar tightened as he gritted his teeth. "We were doing a fucking job."

"What do you want me to say, Kai?" I asked, looking over his shoulder at Jamal, who was staring at his phone with wide eyes.

I glanced around to see cliques of students giggling at their phones. What was going on?

"I want you to tell her what your parents did to mine, and then we'll see if she still wants to be your fucking friend," Kai growled, so much anger and rage boiling up inside him, more than usual, all because of Imani.

My parents did so much shit to everyone that I couldn't keep it straight anymore.

What had they done to Kai again?

Kai released me and reached into his black cargo pants to pull out his phone. On the screen was a picture of Allie Hall with a stack of *Playboy* and *Mayfair* magazines and porn DVDs falling out of her locker. It looked like it had been taken moments ago, and it was already circulating social media.

"You're fucking lucky that I have other shit to deal with," Kai said to me.

The first bell rang, and Kai shot me one last warning look. Students rushed down the hallways, scrambling to get to their first period while gossiping about Allie and Jace. My phone buzzed, and an image popped up on the screen of Allie standing in front of a thick-as-fuck ten-inch dildo, suction-cupped to her locker.

Well, Imani was about to be livid. I should probably find her.

Curiously, I followed Kai down the hallway and toward Allie's locker because Imani was bound to be around. I stopped at the end of the hallway and glanced around the corner, watching Carter—the quarterback of the football team—mess with Allie.

"Your date with Jamal go good?" Carter asked Allie, leaning against the locker and crossing his muscular arms over his chest. "You finally let him hit it after those soggy Saturday night fries?"

"Fuck you, Carter," Allie said through clenched teeth, scrambling to get her books for the day without the DVDs and magazines falling out of it. Her cheeks were red and blotchy, and her eyes were filled with tears.

"Akio," someone said from behind me, tugging on my wrist, "it's not safe here."

"What's not safe?"

Nicole looked over my shoulder at Carter and Allie with Kai storming toward them. "That."

Carter pulled the dildo out of her locker. "You buy this because Jamal wasn't big enough for you, baby?" He stepped closer to her and rested his hand on her shoulder, leaning in. "You wouldn't have to worry about that with me. I'd fill your tight little ass up until you screamed."

Allie punched Carter in the jaw, who stumbled back and smirked.

"Feisty," he said, licking the blood off the corner of his lips. "Just how I like them. You'll fucking learn to be a good little"—he placed a single finger on her thigh, beneath her skirt—"whore—"

Kai pulled a gun from his waistband and stuck it against the back of Carter's neck. "You fucking move your finger a fucking millimeter up her thigh, and you'll get a bullet in your skull."

My eyes widened, and Nicole tugged on my wrist again.

"You see. Now, come with me."

We headed down the hallway.

"What happened with Allie?" I asked.

"I don't know," she said. "But you shouldn't associate yourself with Poison or Imani."

"Why not?"

She stopped at the corner of the hallway and looked over. "Because they're into her and they will do anything to protect her, just like—" She cleared her throat, cheeks reddening, then lowered her voice. "Just like I'd do anything to protect you."

Warmth spread throughout my chest, but I wondered exactly what she was trying to protect me from. Was it Poison? Maybe Jace was involved in some bad shit somehow? Did she even know who my mother was?

The second bell rang, and I realized that I was late for class *again*.

"Get to class." She turned on her heel, her blonde hair bouncing around her shoulders. "But stay out of trouble and meet me in the library at lunch." She threw me a wink. "I have something for you."

"Wait," I said, taking her wrist and pulling her back.

Before I could stop myself, I kissed her on the mouth because something felt different about *us* today. Maybe it was my imagination, or maybe it wasn't. But she had come up to me, told me that she'd protect me. And I wasn't going to let her slip through my fingers.

Not this time.

I pulled away and tucked some strands of hair behind her ear. "I'll see you at lunch."

CHAPTER
THIRTY

NICOLE

"NICOLE?" Akio said from behind me.

I snapped the manga shut and twisted my head. Akio walked my way with his cute gray lunch bag in hand and a shy smile on his face. After slipping the manga inside my purse, I stood and grabbed his hand.

"Where's your lunch?" he asked.

"In my bag."

"Where are we going?"

"To the encyclopedias," I said, warmth raging between my thighs. Between that kiss earlier that had come out of nowhere to the smutty story that I had just been reading, I couldn't keep it together today. "For privacy."

When we reached the books in the back of the library, behind rows and rows of bookshelves, I sat in one of the oversize beanbag chairs and patted beside me so he'd sit with me. He glanced around, then placed his lunch bag on the ground and sat.

"I thought you wanted to eat."

"I have something for you."

His lips curled into a wider smile that made me all warm and fuzzy. "What is it?"

"I might or might not have found these in the library yesterday after you left," I murmured, pulling the erotic manga with explicit pictures out of my purse. "I don't know why the library has these, but"—I wrapped my hand around his biceps—"I thought you'd enjoy them."

Akio took the manga from me and flipped it open, gaze landing on the illustration of the woman with her tits out, getting rammed by a huge cock. Akio snapped the book shut and looked over at me, his dick hardening inside his pants.

"Nicole," he said quietly.

I moved my hand down his arm to his bulge and cupped it. "Open it back up."

He opened and shut his mouth a handful of times, then reopened it to the same page. I stroked his huge dick through his jeans as we looked at the illustrations inside the book. My pussy grew warm, clenching hard.

"It's really good," I whimpered. "I read the whole thing."

"Fuck, Nicole," he cursed under his breath.

"Read it," I said, undoing his pants and reaching inside them to pull out his hard cock. I leaned over and let a wad of spit drip from my mouth and onto his head, and then I drew my thumb across his pre-cum and my spit. "For me."

He sucked in a breath and turned the page, glancing between me and the manga.

After fastening my mouth around his cock, I swirled my tongue around his head. He grunted softly, gaze lingering on me, and aimlessly turned the page. I sucked more of him into my mouth, down my throat, desperate to make him feel good.

"Don't stop reading," I gargled, strings of spit hanging from my lips to his groin.

Akio turned back to the book, looking at the woman's tits bounce. He gently grabbed one of my breasts and squeezed. A wave of heat rushed through my body, and I swallowed his entire dick in my mouth.

"Fuuuck," he grunted.

"Tell me what's happening," I said when I came up for breath.

"She's bouncing on his dick."

"Mmm," I hummed, licking from the base to the head of his cock. Then, I crawled up into his lap, my back against his chest and my pussy under my skirt hovering over the head of his huge dick. "Just like I should be doing."

Another groan. "Nicole …"

I slid down on his dick and tightened, my pussy forming to his huge cock.

"Someone will see," he said, placing the manga down.

"Keep reading it, Akio," I ordered, slowly moving my hips all the way to the head of his cock to tease him. *God, he is so big!* "Don't worry about anyone seeing us. Nobody will as long as you stay quiet."

"Stay quiet?" he asked, dick twitching inside me. "How can I do that when you're riding me?" He placed one hand on my hip to help me along and picked up the manga in his free hand. "When your pussy is gripping me from the base all the way to the tip."

"What's happening now?" I asked, bucking my hips faster.

"She's moaning his name," he murmured into my ear.

"Akio," I whimpered, moving my hips up and down on his dick. "Akio!"

"Nicole." His voice shook, but his hand was still helping me move on his dick. "You're being so loud."

"Your dick is so big," I cried softly, pussy pulsing. Then I looked back at him. "I can't help it."

Warmth exploded through my pussy at the sound of his soft groaning.

"Now what?"

"She's—" Akio tightened his grip on the book and closed his

eyes, taking slow, deep breaths, as if he was trying to hold himself back from busting inside me.

"What is she doing?" I urged, knowing exactly what was already happening. I had read this manga three times last night and had come all over my fingers multiple times to this specific scene. "What is she saying?"

"S-she's b-begging him to bre-breed her."

"Breed me," I whispered, mirroring the words she cried in the manga. "Breed me!"

"N-N-Nicole," Akio grunted, slamming deep inside me.

"Fill up my pussy with your thick load, Akio," I cried. "I need it so badly."

"Fuuuck," he hissed, hand tight around my waist.

As he pounded up into me, my tits bounced around in my shirt, coming out of my bra. I grabbed one of his hands and pulled it up to my breasts to let him squeeze. He grunted even louder and slammed deep into me.

My pussy exploded around his cock, and I bit my bottom lip to stop myself from screaming out in pleasure. His cock twitched inside me. I dug my nails into his thigh, eyes rolling back in my head as wave after wave of pleasure coursed through my body.

"B-b-breed m-m-me, Akio," I whimpered. "I want every last drop."

CHAPTER
THIRTY-ONE

NICOLE

AT THE MED SPA, Nurse Lucianna shoved a needle into my upper lip. I winced and stared ahead at a pristine painting on the wall. After injecting filler into my lip, she pulled the needle out and found her next spot.

Dad sat to our right, staring so intensely at me that it gave me chills. My plans to stay happy all day after my adventure with Akio in the library had been cut short by a text from Dad, telling me that I was getting *prettied* up tonight for his friends.

"Beautiful," Lucianna murmured in a thick Italian accent.

"Thanks," I said with a forced smile, hopping off the bed.

Before I could make it to the door, Dad placed a hand on my shoulder and pushed me back down onto the bed. I sat with ease because I didn't want him to be too hard on me tonight and stared down at my trembling hands. I intertwined my fingers so Dad wouldn't see.

"We're also getting filler in her nose," he said. "I despise that bump in it."

Your mother had the same thing …

"Your mother had the same thing," he finished, just like I'd expected.

"No problem!" Lucianna said, swooping her finger down my nose. "We can smooth out the bump and make her look so much prettier." She smiled at me. "You'll look like an irresistible goddess, my dear."

I pressed my lips together. *Great.*

Exactly what I don't want to look like.

"How's that sound, Nikki?" Dad murmured, as if he *wanted* me to complain.

"Great," I said with another fake smile. "I would love that."

Lucianna walked to the closet and pulled out another needle. I blew out a shaky breath and closed my eyes, thinking about taking that goddamn needle from her and slamming it into my eye and going blind so I didn't have to see half the shit that Dad did to me.

"Don't be scared." Lucianna laughed. "It'll just be a pinch."

After a slight pinch below the bridge of my nose, Lucianna pulled the needle out of my face. She stabbed me with it a few more times, then held up a mirror in front of my face and beamed at Dad.

"How does it look?" she asked.

While Dad grunted in approval, I stared at a woman that I could barely recognize anymore. The innocent girl who used to cling to Hannah, giggle in her lap, and watch anime and cartoons early every morning ... was gone.

Completely wiped away.

New hair. Lips overdone. Eyes dull.

Innocence faded.

Dead on the inside.

"Beautiful," Dad said to Lucianna, slipping her some cash. "Thank you."

"Thank you," I repeated to her, trying my best to sound grateful.

It wasn't Lucianna's fault. Dad had done this to me. If I didn't have to be a dick, like I did in school, then I wasn't going to. Maybe … just maybe … one of these days, Lucianna would see that I was here against my will.

Or maybe she already knew it but turned a blind eye because of Dad's money.

"Come on, Nicole," Dad said, shrugging on his jacket. "We need to stop at Henry's house before heading home." Dad flashed Lucianna his signature *I'm such a great dad* smile. "You've done wonderful yet again, Lucianna."

After hopping off the bed, I ignored their flirting and grabbed my coat. I pulled it over my shoulders and slouched down into it, my lips and nose tingling. Then, I quietly followed Dad out of the building and to his car.

"How was your day?" Dad asked after he slipped into the car.

"Great."

Most girls would've been ecstatic that their father had brought them out to the salon and spa so they could get whatever they liked. But I didn't have a say. If I did, I wouldn't look *anything* like this.

No blonde hair. No lip fillers. No Botox at eighteen. And, God, especially no bangs.

Before starting the car, he tucked some hair behind my ear and smiled softly at me. "I love your new hair, Nikki. You look just like your sister."

He is sick. Absolutely sick. He probably thinks about her when he fucks me too.

He reached into his pocket and pulled out Hannah's necklace that he had stolen from me weeks ago. He held it out for me to take, and I hesitated because I didn't know if this was some kind of joke or not. Was he *really* giving this back to me?

"Here," he said. "You've earned it."

"I've earned it?" I whispered, letting the pendant rest in my palm.

"You let me take you to get a makeover without complaining once," he said.

I curled my hand around the pendant and gently pulled it away from him, heart pounding because I'd finally gotten it back. Tears welled in my eyes. I hadn't thought I would ever get it back. Not willingly. I'd thought I'd have to steal it and hide it.

Or pay Poison to steal it for me.

"Thank you," I whispered.

He placed a hand on my inner thigh and squeezed. "Anything for you, Nikki." After I fastened the necklace around my neck, Dad's hand moved up my inner thigh. "You know that I would do anything for you, right?"

"Yes," I said stiffly.

"Like I would have done anything for Hannah, if she had listened to me."

"I know."

But I didn't.

I couldn't.

How could I?!

My skirt bunched as he trailed his hand higher and higher up my inner thigh. "We're going to Henry's, so a couple of my buddies and I can play poker. You're going to be a good girl for me tonight." He moved his fingers against my underwear. "Aren't you?"

"Yes," I whispered.

"And?"

"And I'll make them all feel good."

"How?" he asked, still moving his fingers.

"However they want me."

He chuckled and lifted my chin with his opposite hand. "You're so much better than your sister ever was. You make me a *very* happy father, Nikki. I don't know if I tell you this enough, but I'm so proud of you."

AKIO

MOM STABBED the knife into Duncan's ribs. "I told you to get me the fucking money."

I leaned against the farthest wall and scanned the room to find an exit strategy without looking like I was finding an exit strategy. Mom had been stabbing and torturing him for about three hours now, and I wanted to go home.

Why did she insist that I watch this? She knew I wasn't going to do anything for her.

And I sure as hell wasn't going to be her puppet that she could use and throw away.

When another scream left Duncan's throat, I glanced over to see him convulsing. Two guards held him steady, their arms around his to keep him upright. I didn't ask how they had stood like that for hours on end, but they were loyal dogs for her.

Hell, I didn't even know *why* she was torturing him or who he was to her.

"Akio!" Mom shouted. "Come here."

"I don't want my clothes to get blood on them."

"Here. Now!"

After growling under my breath, I crossed my arms and walked over to her, making sure to keep a good few feet away. This was now my all-time favorite shirt, especially after Nicole had ground her pussy all over it at the library. I didn't want to ruin it.

Mom held out the knife. "Your turn."

"No."

"Take it."

"No."

"Akio!" she growled, pressing the knife against my neck. "Take the motherfucking knife."

Blood dripped off it, rolled down my neck, and stained my shirt. I snatched the blade from her and clenched my teeth together. Now, I would definitely have to clean this tonight. Curse that wo—

"Now, kill him."

"No."

"You've killed my men before," she snarled. "So, kill him."

"He didn't do anything to me," I said. "No."

She stalked around me and nodded her head, not breaking eye contact with me once. "Oh, so you only kill men who betray you. Tell me, *son*, what did Santos do to you? Because the only thing that he had been doing that night was Nic—"

I sliced the knife into Duncan's throat, killing him instantly.

I didn't want her to continue talking. I didn't want her asking questions. I didn't want to get Nicole involved with my mother and her dogs in the slightest. If they found out that she was the reason I'd killed Santos, God only fucking knew what Rick would do to her.

Duncan's legs gave out, and the guards dragged him out of the room.

"Are you happy?" I asked, shoving the grip of the knife at her.

After taking it from me, she narrowed her eyes. "Get out of here."

I twirled around and grabbed my coat from the table by the

doorway. My phone buzzed in my pocket, and I snuck a peek at it while Mom shouted at one of her men to bring the next guy she would torture into the room.

Nicole: I know it's late, but wanna meet up?

Eyes widening, I stared at the message. Nicole wanted to meet up with me at this time. It was nearly one in the morning, and we had school tomorrow. If she wanted to meet this late, it was either something serious or she wanted to hook up.

Me: Are you sure you have the right number?

Nicole: Yes, I'm talking to you, Akio.

While I thought she would've been off calling Jace Harbor, I wasn't going to pass up the chance to see Nicole. So, I slipped out of the building and headed for my car parked a few buildings down.

Me: I can be at the Overlook in ten minutes.

Nicole: See you then. <3

A heart? My eyes widened even more that I thought they would burst out of my head.

Nicole: SORRY, I MEANT :)

As I slipped into my car, I ignored her last message and pretended like she had meant to send me a heart. It hadn't been a slip of her fingers, accidentally hitting an emoji on the keyboard. She'd actually had to type the less-than symbol and the number three.

Warmth spread throughout my chest.

But even if it had been a mistake, maybe, one day, she'd mean it.

CHAPTER
THIRTY-THREE

HEADLIGHTS SHONE on me from behind. I anxiously sat on the rocks with some food for us beside me and stared at the sea, hoping that Akio wouldn't think I looked *too* bad after Dad's stupid little makeover today. Every time he brought me to Lucianna, I felt more and more like a bimbo.

But I didn't want Akio to think any differently of me.

I wanted him to like me for me. Not because of how I looked.

When the car door opened, I pushed some tears off my cheeks and clutched Hannah's necklace. Still, I couldn't believe that Dad had given it back to me. Based on how he'd treated me in the past, it should've been gone forever.

"If I knew you had picked us up something to eat, I would've —Nicole, what's wrong?"

After shoving away a few more tears, I wrapped my arms around my torso and burst out into cries. "I'm sorry."

He sat down beside me and pulled me into his arms. "Did someone hurt you?"

"No." A lie that I'd always tell to protect him. "I'm just

thinking about my sister." I clutched the necklace harder. "I miss her."

"Is that her necklace?" he asked.

"Yes."

"You haven't worn it in a long time."

"My dad took it away from me," I whispered.

But how had Akio known that I'd even had it to begin with? He had said it like he had seen me wear the necklace a million times now, yet it hadn't been around my neck in weeks, before we started hanging out.

After completely wiping my tears away, I smiled at him and handed him a McDonald's bag with burger and fries—the only place that had been open this late at night. "Here. I didn't ask you to come so you could watch me cry."

"It's okay, Nicole," he said. "I don't mind."

My smile trembled for a moment. Who wanted to watch someone cry?

Only Hannah had done that for me.

Akio stared into my eyes for a few moments, and then his gaze drifted up to my bangs, then down to my nose and even lower to my lips, which were plumper than plump. I shifted uncomfortably beside him, hoping that he liked how I looked.

That was one of the reasons I had invited him out. Not only did I want to spend time with someone who wasn't trying to face-fuck me every moment, but I wanted him to tell me that … this didn't look as bad as I thought it did.

"I like your bangs," he commented.

Warmth spread through my chest. "You do?"

He nodded. "Are you wearing lipstick?"

"No, I …" I paused, thinking that this was a horrible idea to tell him. What would he think of me? I wasn't naturally pretty, and as soon as he found that out, then he'd think less of me. Maybe he wouldn't like me as much as he did. That was assuming *if* he did. "I got lip fillers today."

"Oh."

I kept my gaze on my food. "What do you think of them?"

"Did you get some in your nose too?"

"Maybe …"

"Why?"

I opened and closed my mouth a handful of times, not sure *how* to respond. If Akio said he liked it, then I would feel bad because I didn't look like this in real life, and I didn't want to *keep* going to her, even if—by some miracle—Dad released me from his grasp. But on the other hand … if Akio said he hated it, then I would be self-conscious of it for the rest of my short, pathetic life.

"Huh?" I asked, hoping that he'd forget it.

"Why'd you get fillers?" he asked again, smiling softly at me.

Waves crashed along the rocks a few rows down, the sound actually calming.

"I mean, I think they look really good, but I don't think that you needed them."

"I just wanted to," I lied. Again.

I didn't know how—in whatever fantasy world that I was living in—we'd ever work if all I did was lie to him.

We sat in silence for a few minutes while we ate and stared out at the ocean.

"So, is this, like …" He paused and readjusted his glasses. "Never mind."

"Is it what?"

He shrugged and looked out at the waves. "You know …"

"What?" I asked because I surely didn't.

"A date," he asked, his voice barely above a whisper.

Was this, like … a date?

My head didn't know what to think, but my heart started beating like crazy.

I never thought that I'd ever have a normal life, and while eating McDonald's at one in the morning at the Overlook with a guy I liked wasn't the ideal first date, I couldn't stop thinking that this was one step closer to normal. That, with Akio, I might get a glimpse at a simple life.

Even for a couple of hours a week. I'd be happy with that.

"And if it is?" I asked because I didn't want to overstep. If Akio just wanted to be friends that hooked up sometimes, then I sure as hell didn't want to ruin what we had. Because I would rather be friends than be nothing. "How'd you feel about that?"

With his cheeks tinting red, he shrugged again and looked away. But I caught a small smile on his face that he tried to hide from me. I popped another fry into my mouth and smiled softly, my lips still a bit tingly.

"I've never been on a date before," he said after a few moments.

"Me neither."

He snapped his head in my direction. "Y-you haven't?"

"Not one that I actually wanted to be on."

His smile seemed to stretch even more. "You want to be here with me?"

I gently knocked my shoulder into his. "If I didn't, then I wouldn't have invited you."

He fidgeted with his hand, moving it toward his face and then back, pulling his jacket zipper up and down a few times, as if he didn't know what to do. I moved closer to him until our legs were nearly touching and waited for him to do something to show me that he also wanted to be here with me.

His gaze flickered down to my knee, and warmth spread through my body. Then, he lifted his hand, hovered it over my knee for a few moments, and placed it down. Although I was wearing sweatpants, his touch still drove me insane.

"Is this okay?" he asked nervously.

Unlike Dad and all of his buddies, who shoved their hands up my skirt without questioning their goddamn morals, Akio was respectful enough to ask if placing his hand on my knee—*on top of my sweats*—was okay with me.

My heart swelled at how simple and … thoughtful it was.

"It's perfect," I whispered, glancing at his lips.

All I wanted to do was reach over and kiss his pretty mouth.

So many feelings were rushing through me, and I felt like nothing —*nothing*—could ruin this moment. Until … suddenly, thunder rolled overhead, and a sheet of rain fell from the sky.

Akio went to stand. "I'll get us an umbrel—"

I wrapped my hand around the back of his neck and pulled him into a deep kiss.

Maybe this was normal. And maybe, one day, I could be normal too.

CHAPTER
THIRTY-FOUR

NICOLE

"STAY WITH ME," I whispered.

My hands tightened around his collar as I pulled him closer to me. I never wanted to let go. I never wanted our kiss to be over, these feelings to fade, my life to end. With Akio, I felt more alive than I ever had.

"Please, Akio," I begged, and while he might've thought that I wanted him to stay with me for the night ... I wanted more than that. I wanted him to stay with me until the day Dad killed me, the day I'd get to see Hannah again. A crushing pain came over my chest, and another tear fell from my eye. "Stay with me."

"I'll stay," he said against my mouth.

"Promise me."

Promise you'll stay even when ... you find out what my own father does to me.

Promise you'll stay when I come crying to you with black eyes and broken ribs.

Promise you'll find it in yourself to love me because nobody ever has.

All the promises I wanted him to make rushed through my head, but I couldn't speak.

Not even one of them.

"I promise, Nicole," Akio said, tucking some hair behind my ear and pulling away slightly to look me in the eye. "I'm not going anywhere. But if we stay out here, you're going to catch a cold." He took my hands and stood. "Come on."

Once he pulled me up, I wrapped my arms around his torso and hugged him as tightly as I could, my forehead on his chest and my fists clenching his shirt, like if I didn't, then he would disappear into thin air.

Rain poured down on us, but he stayed with me until I felt … okay.

I would never feel good, never feel better. But I felt okay, and that was something.

At least I still could feel.

"Come on," he said, tugging me to his car. "You're going to get sick."

While nobody else was at the Overlook tonight, we had both parked near the far edge of the round roadway toward the more private areas of this side of town. Akio opened the door for me, and I slid onto the leather backseat with my wet clothes.

"Sorry about—"

He slipped in beside me and shut the door behind him. "It's okay."

"But you don't even know what I was going to apologize for."

"I don't need to," he said, shaking off his coat. Underneath, his graphic tee was soaked through from the rain. He reached over his shoulder and pulled his shirt over his head. "You don't need to apologize to me for anything."

I opened and closed my mouth a handful of times, my wet shirt clinging to my body and making me feel so sticky. When he had pulled off his shirt and dropped it at his feet, I gulped and averted my gaze so I wouldn't stare at him.

But, God, every time I was with him, he became more and more attractive to me.

Maybe it was because of how sweet he was, how safe he felt.

"You don't have to sit in your wet clothes," he said, peering over the center console into the front seat. "I think I have a spare sweatshirt around here somewhere." He reached his skinny arm between the seat and the door, making a face. "Here it is."

Once he gave me the *Jujutsu Kaisen* sweatshirt with the infamous Satoru Gojo on the front, I set it on my lap and played with the button of my shirt. Bruises covered my body from this evening, and I didn't want him to see.

The thought of him finding out about what had happened scared the hell out of me.

But it was dark.

So, I quickly tugged my shirt over my head and yanked on the sweatshirt before he could even say a word. And luckily, Akio hadn't noticed as he took my shirt and tossed it at his feet with his wet clothes.

"I can wash it tomorrow for you."

"You would do that?" I asked.

His lips curled into a small smile. "For you."

Warmth spread through my body, and a giddy feeling rose in my chest. I didn't know how to react in this kind of situation, so I giggled behind my hand and watched water droplets drip off his hair and onto his face.

"Do you want me to take you back to your hou—"

"No!" I exclaimed, then cleared my throat. "I mean, no."

He scratched the back of his head. "I'd suggest coming back to my place, but I think my mom will be home soon."

"I don't mind."

"I do." He opened and shut his mouth. "I mean, I … she …"

"Nobody likes their parents," I whispered. "I get it."

"We can go if you want. I don't mind."

I placed my hands on his shoulders. "Let's stay here."

Suddenly, two sets of headlights shone in through the rear windshield. Rain pounded down on the glass, but I squinted enough to see Mr. Avery, one of Redwood's Literature professors, step out of the farthest car with an umbrella.

Akio peeled off his foggy glasses and wiped them. "Is that Mr. Avery?"

"Yes."

Once Akio pushed his glasses back up his face, he moved closer to me. "What do you think's going on?" he asked. "I've seen him do some business with my mom, but business doesn't happen down this way because it's usually busy at the Overlook."

Mr. Avery stopped next to the driver's side of the nearest car.

After exchanging a few words with the driver, the car lights turned off, and Sakura Sato stepped out of the car. Akio and I both gasped, turned around, and sank down in the backseat of his car so they wouldn't see us.

"Is that Sakura?!" Akio whisper-yelled. "She's the valedictorian of our class!"

"I know!" I whispered back. "What is she doing with him?!"

When he shrugged, I peeked my head up over the edge of the seat to look back out the window. Mr. Avery had Sakura pressed up against the car, her chin in his hand and his head buried into the crook of her neck.

My eyes widened even more, and I sank back down in the seat. "Oh my God!"

Akio peered over the seat, then widened his eyes and sank back down. "Oh my God!"

We both looked over again to see Mr. Avery now setting Sakura on the hood of her car and kissing down her body to her open legs.

"Oh my God!" we said in unison.

Sakura Sato and one of our teachers.

One of our *married* teachers?!

"Do you think they can see us?" Akio asked.

"Of course not," I whispered, heart racing. I clutched his hand. "If they saw our cars, then they wouldn't have stopped."

"I can't believe this is happening."

"Akio!" I exclaimed. "Stop looking."

"They're having sex in the middle of the road! How can I not?"

A giggle bubbled up my throat. "Because it's private."

"But they're doing it in public."

When Akio peeked up again, I tackled him until we fell back on the seat, him lying down and me on top of him. He wrapped his arms around my waist and smiled as that pretty mouth laughed. I playfully slapped his shoulder.

"Why do I get the feeling you wanted me to do this all along?" I asked.

"Hmm ..." His grin widened, the moonlight glimmering off his brown eyes. "I don't know."

Once my laughter died down, I rested my head on his chest and closed my eyes, listening to the constant pounding of rain on the car and the fast racing of his heart.

I'm declaring this the most normal thing I've ever done.

I didn't care what anyone said.

Sleeping at the Overlook with the guy I am falling in love with seems pretty normal to me, right?

CHAPTER
THIRTY-FIVE

NICOLE

THE CRASHING of waves woke me from my sleep. I blinked my eyes open to the blazing sun on my face and shifted in the backseat of Akio's car. He gently moved his hands through my hair in soothing circles, and all I wanted was to doze back off.

But we had school, and I didn't want him to be late.

I lifted my head off his bare chest, only to see him already awake.

His eyes widened, as if he had been caught doing something that he shouldn't, and he pulled his hand away. "Sorry, I didn't mean to wake you."

"You didn't," I said. A pink imprint of the seat belt covered the right side of his face. I turned onto my belly and reached up to draw my fingers against it. "How long have you been awake?"

"Not that long."

"How long?"

"Like, thirty minutes."

"Akio, why didn't you wake me?" I asked. "This has to be uncomfortable for you."

Again, his lips curled into a small smile. "You were sleeping."

"So?"

"It's not every day I wake up with a pretty girl lying on top of me," he said, nervously gazing toward the windshield and scratching his neck. "Besides, you looked so peaceful that I didn't want to wake you."

Pretty? Peaceful?

Those were two words that I rarely ever felt.

Gently, I cupped his chin and turned his head toward me. A smile made its way onto my face, and I pressed my toes against the opposite door to give myself a push toward him until my lips met his.

Truthfully, I never woke up with a guy that I actually liked, a guy who thought I was pretty and didn't hate me for ruining his life. But today, I had … and my heart was so, so happy that I could think of nothing else … but to kiss him. For as long as I could.

When I pulled away, our lips were still touching. The sweet taste of him, the way his hands rested on my hips, how gentle he had always been with me …

I closed my eyes and breathed him in.

"I think I love you," I whispered.

As soon as the words left my mouth, both of us tensed.

What the fuck was that, Nicole?! I think I love you?!

"Wh-what?" Akio asked.

"I …" My mouth was parched. "I said that … that I'd love to get … breakfast with you!"

We both knew goddamn well that hadn't come out of my mouth.

I sat up in the seat, grabbed my pants that were still a bit damp from last night, and yanked them onto my body. My bangs were flat on my head and a bit frizzy from the rain. I ran my fingers through them, trying to distract myself.

Why did I say that?! And aloud?!

With his cheeks bright red, Akio sat up and tugged on his damp shirt. "Y-yeah, we can g-get some breakfast before school."

He averted his gaze and climbed into the front seat, grabbing his keys with a shaky hand. "Where do you want to go?"

Once I climbed up there with him, I looked out the window. "Anywhere."

My knees were bouncing uncontrollably, and I tried to force them to stop with my hands, but they only shook with them. My mind was going about a million miles a second, and I still couldn't get over myself.

What is wrong with me?!

If I ruined my friendship with Akio forever, then everything would go back to the only life that I knew—living in hell, with the only escape being death, whether it was from Dad's hands or my own. We sat in complete silence all the way to Dunkin' until we reached the speaker post.

"What do you want?" Akio said, his hand tight on the steering wheel.

"Just a, uh … a sandwich is fine."

After he ordered, he pulled up to the window.

"It's twelve dollars and eighty-seven cents."

When we both reached for the center console—me for my purse and him for his wallet—our hands collided. We paused for a few moments, neither of us moving for the money, and then I yanked my purse into my lap to find my wallet.

"Here."

"No," Akio said, already pulling his card out.

I held out my hand in front of him. "Here, Akio."

He ignored my hand and gave his card to the cashier, who looked at us weirdly.

"Akio," I said after they gave back his card and our food, "take it."

"No."

Instead of taking my money, he turned right onto the road to head to the school. After grumbling to myself that I had messed everything up, we sat in silence for the rest of the drive. When we reached the high school, he parked in the student lot.

Neither of us had gone for the food yet.

I peered over at him, only to see him staring at me.

Both of us looked away.

"Akio ..." I whispered. "I'm sorry. It was just ... I ..."

My heart pounded in my chest, and I wanted him to say something first. I wasn't used to all these feelings and especially not having as much control as Akio gave me in whatever kind of friendship that we had.

Akio stared ahead and swallowed hard, his shirt sticking to his scrawny shoulders.

Another awkward silence fell upon us, and then the bell rang over the intercoms.

"I don't want to be late," Akio said, grabbing his backpack from the back and exiting the car without taking his food. "I'll see you later."

CHAPTER
THIRTY-SIX

AKIO

LATER, I sat at the dinner table at Imani's house with Mom, unable to get the words Nicole had said to me out of my head. I swore she had said that she loved me. *Me!* And like the idiot that I was, I'd completely frozen up and not known how to respond.

So, I had run away from her. I had blown it.

After groaning to myself, I turned back to the dinner in front of me.

Usually, Dad had dinner with Imani's parents and always tried to set us up. But tonight, Mom was here, and something felt … off. Or maybe I was feeling this way because Nicole had told me that she loved me out of nowhere, and I hadn't said it back …

Even though I might love her too.

Imani's mom laughed at something my mother had said, smiled tensely at Imani, then elbowed her. Imani gently rubbed her ribs and cleared her throat. That glint in her eye was the same one she'd had when we snuck over to Nicole's house the other day.

Which meant that Imani was about to say something she shouldn't.

And I'd have to clean it up.

"What'd you do to the Koh family?" Imani suddenly asked.

My eyes widened.

Koh, as in Kai, the third member of Poison? Why would she ask that?!

After her parents sucked in a collective breath, an awkward silence fell heavily over the room. I stared at her in hopes of getting her to look at me, to get her to apologize for even bringing it up because Imani didn't want to know what my parents had done to Kai's parents.

Imani pursed her lips and looked between my mother and father, who was pale.

"So?" Imani asked, eyebrows arched. "What happened?"

Once my mother regained her composure—because *nobody* talked to her like that, except me—Mom smiled too widely at Imani and continued eating her steak. "Nothing, sweetie." She sent daggers my way with her pointed gaze. "Why do you think something happened?"

"Because Kai Koh's parents are both dead," Imani said.

Fuck, Imani! Why can't you keep your mouth closed?!

"Why do you think we had something to do with it?" Mom asked her.

Imani's nostrils flared.

"Imani," her mother said harshly, "stop it."

Pissed off, Imani pushed out of her chair and leaned over the table with her hands posted on it. "People like you won't get away with everything. Whatever you did to them, you will pay for it one day."

"Are you threatening me?" Mom asked her, wiping her lips.

Imani held her intense stare. "Yes."

Oh my fucking God. I can't have one normal day of my life, can I?

Mom gave a shrill laugh as Imani walked out of the room and into the kitchen.

"Akio, why don't you take care of your *friend*?" Mom said, smiling like she wanted to finish with, *Before I have to.*

After pushing back my chair, I hurried into the other room and shut the door behind me. "What are you doing?! You can't say stuff like—"

Before I could finish my sentence, Imani grabbed her keys from her purse and walked to the back door like she hadn't just said what she said, like she didn't fear the punishment that my mother would give her. "Come on."

Because there would be consequences.

After groaning, I shrugged on my coat and followed after her. I wanted to meet Nicole tonight, to apologize for freezing up and to tell her that I might possibly feel the same way as her, but that wouldn't happen if I stayed at dinner any longer with Mom. She'd probably want me to do something for her after this. Then, I'd have to watch her splatter blood everywhere.

I shoved my hands into my pockets and grabbed something large and—

As Imani headed toward her car, I stopped and pulled a gun— *a fucking gun*—out of my jacket pocket. Mom must've placed it there when she got here this evening. I opened it up to see one of the bullets was gone and gritted my teeth.

That damn woman had probably killed a man and stuffed the weapon in my jacket.

I hated her.

Once I shoved it back into my jacket, I climbed into Imani's car. Instead of chatting it up like she usually did, Imani stayed quiet the entire ride around Redwood. Never once opening her mouth to ask any questions.

She knew that I knew what my parents had done to Kai's. That was why Kai had especially had it out for me lately. Not only was I friends with Imani—the girl he and his crew liked—but my parents had caused that motorcycle accident that killed his father. And the drugs his mother bought after it to cope with the pain ... Mom had sold them to her.

After taking a spin downtown, Imani drove around Main

Street and looked out at the dark ocean. Restaurants and shops were filled with the Redwood rich. I stared out the window and scanned for Nicole.

I needed to apologize.

But instead of Nicole, I saw a woman walking with a big, burly man.

Suddenly, like she wanted to kill us, Imani slammed on the brakes. My body moved forward, but the seat belt caught me before I could fly through the windshield. The car behind us laid on its horn, and Imani finally turned on the blinker and pulled to the side of the road.

"What the hell are you doing?" I asked, yanking on my seat belt.

"João's mother," she said, like I was supposed to know what the hell that meant.

Suddenly, Imani jumped out of the car and began following the woman and the man. I cursed underneath my breath and exited the car, an uneasy feeling in the pit of my stomach. Poison was doing nothing but corrupting Imani, making her more insane than she was.

Maybe being friends with her wasn't my best idea.

I could've picked Sakura … but she was sleeping with Mr. Avery.

I could've picked Allie … but she had her stepbrother drama.

Hell, I even thought that Vera Rodriguez—one of the sweetest girls at Redwood Academy—was banging the billionaire, bad-boy punk who skateboarded around Redwood and pissed off Principal Vaughn.

Nobody in Redwood was normal.

"Imani!" I called after her as she turned a corner and stopped in an alleyway.

Fuck!

I raced toward her, my heart pounding and shoes hitting the pavement.

"You're Poison's friend, aren't you?" a man's voice asked.

"No," Imani said.

She crossed her arms and stared down the alleyway at who, I would guess, was the burly man, though I couldn't see him yet. But I told myself that I really needed to start working out and push myself harder.

"Yeah, you are," he said, stepping toward her so I could see him now. Towering over her, he curled his upper lip into a snarl. "And João murdered my boss last week. It looks like it's time to return the fucking favor."

When the man reached for a gun in his pocket, I yanked mine out and pulled the trigger twice as fast. Imani screamed and ducked. The man dropped his gun and was clutching his bloody hand that I had shot a hole into.

I had aimed for his chest, but his hand worked too.

With her hands shaking, Imani grabbed the gun he had dropped and turned around to see *me* with my gun. My eyes widened because *nobody* was supposed to know that I even had the capability to hurt someone, never mind maybe kill them.

Imani ran toward me and pushed me to the car before any of the man's friends could come out a back door and shoot at us.

I stared through the windshield, my eyes heavy and stinging. "I-I'm sorry. He … he was going to kill you. He had a gun. I didn't think …" I continued rambling.

Imani sped to the Overlook, checking in her rearview mirror about a hundred times for any followers, then parked. Then, she took both our guns and shoved them into her glove box. "What the hell was that?!" she exclaimed. "Where did you get a gun?! Where did you learn how to shoot like that?!"

But I was terrified.

I had never shot anyone so quick, especially not in front of people who weren't my family. I had never allowed anyone to see what I was capable of, especially not the one friend I had at Redwood. And for the first time, I was … thankful that Mom had forced me to go to the shooting range with her.

That was the only thing she had ever been good for.

Only problem now ... I needed to make sure Imani kept her mouth shut. If word got around that I'd almost killed a man and Nicole found that out ... I might lose her forever. She couldn't know what I'd done to those assholes she'd been with.

CHAPTER
THIRTY-SEVEN

AFTER CHEER PRACTICE, I sat in my car at the end of my street and stared at Akio's contact. I didn't want to go home yet. All I really wanted to do tonight—and every night—was be with him like I had been last night.

Falling asleep on his chest had made me feel so safe … and I had to ruin it.

Before I could talk myself out of it, I pressed the Call button. My heart thumped so loudly that I could hear it in my ears. I waited and waited and waited for him to answer, only for my call to go directly to voice mail.

"Hi, Akio. It's Nicole." I chewed on the inside of my cheek. "I just, um …"

I sputtered out a few more words that didn't make sense in the same sentence, then immediately ended the call before I could embarrass myself more.

What was I thinking?! I'd sounded so desperate.

And I totally was.

Last night, Akio had given me a taste of what normal could feel like. It wasn't walking on eggshells. It wasn't hiding my tears when I thought about Hannah. And it surely wasn't living in fear of anyone who might like me.

My fingers tightened around my phone.

I wanted a normal life more than anything now.

I wanted to be happy.

I wanted to *live* …

Three things that I never thought I'd get or want. Dad stood in the way of all of them, and now … right now … I needed to find a way to get rid of him or maybe to run away. I wanted out of this situation.

Once I wrapped my fingers around Hannah's pendant, I closed my eyes. "I'm going to get out of this for you," I whispered, tears pricking the corners of my eyes. "I didn't think that I had a chance, but I … I'm going to do this for us. Soon."

My phone buzzed on my lap, and I snapped my eyes open, hoping that it was Akio.

Instead, Dad's name flashed on the screen.

Dad: Where the fuck are you?

Stomach tightening into knots, I placed the phone back down onto my lap and decided to ignore him—at least for the next few moments because now was my time with Hannah. I didn't get many moments with her anymore.

I closed my eyes again and rested my head against the headrest. "I miss you."

And I swore I heard her say, *I love you too.*

I could see her smile and those pretty eyes that had always been clear of tears for me because she wanted to stay strong. I tightened my hand around her necklace.

"I'm going to make you proud," I whispered.

Again, my phone buzzed on my lap.

Dad: Get back home now. We have a problem.

After sighing, I picked up my phone once more and scrolled to Akio's contact.

Me: Sorry about earlier. 😌

Me: I didn't mean to make you feel awkward or uncomfortable. It just slipped out.

Me: Totally get if you don't want to see me.

I typed my next message and hovered my finger over the send button.

Another message from Dad popped up, and I slammed my finger down on the screen to send one last message to Akio for the night, before I went home and had to listen to God knew what from Dad.

Me: But I meant every word.

Warmth spread through my chest at the thought of admitting it again to him.

Even if he hated me for it, even if he never wanted to talk to me again, it was the first step at being normal. Admitting my feelings to my crush … was such a rush of adrenaline, of terror and excitement.

Once I set my phone back into my purse, I started my car and headed back home. I pulled up the driveway with a smile on my face, feeling so fucking giddy. When Hannah had been alive, I hoped that she'd had a chance to experience this feeling …

Being in love with someone …

After shutting off my car, I grabbed my purse and backpack from the passenger seat and walked up the front walkway in the rain to the front door to get a few more moments of peace to myself for the night.

I didn't know what Dad had in store with his buddies tonight, but if I got to see Akio tomorrow and the next day and the day after that, if he responded to my messages with *anything*, all this pain would be worth it.

Because I would be leaving soon.

Hopefully.

When I made it inside, I dropped my backpack by the door. "Dad, I'm home."

A bottle shattered in the kitchen, and I glanced over at the walkway to the kitchen, where Dad emerged, dressed in an alcohol-stained white wife beater with a brown bottle of beer in his hand.

He snarled at me, "Where were you last night?"

I opened and closed my mouth a handful of times and shook my head. "I … I was …"

Come on, Nicole. Come up with something believable!

Yesterday, I had told him that I would be home in a few hours. But once I got to the Overlook, I didn't want to leave. I'd thought Dad wouldn't notice. I'd thought he'd be conked out on his recliner in the front room.

"At home," I whispered, mouth drying. "In my bed."

"Bullshit!" he growled, taking the side table and throwing it across the room. It hit the door and clattered against the floor. He stalked closer to me, his lips in a snarl. "You were out with Yui's son at the Overlook."

"Only for a little bit," I whispered, shuffling back. "I p-promise that I was only—"

"You promised me that you'd be back, but instead, I got a call from the station that your car was parked at the Overlook and *you* were sleeping on that boy's chest." He stalked even closer. "You're not getting out of this."

"I'm not trying to get out of anything," I said, my heels hitting the door. "I swear, I—"

Dad seized my throat. "By the end of the night, you're going to know who owns you."

CHAPTER
THIRTY-EIGHT

NICOLE

BEFORE HE COULD START SQUEEZING my throat, I pushed Dad away.

He reached for Hannah's necklace on my chest, but I stupidly covered it with my hands. I didn't even realize what I had done; I just didn't want to lose it again. It was the only piece of her that I had left, and I had just gotten it back.

After Dad shoved me hard, I reached behind me to catch myself, and Dad took the chance to snap the necklace right off my neck. The chain broke, and the pendant fell off it and at his feet.

"You don't deserve this."

Tears welled up in my eyes. "Please, give it back. I didn't mean it. I should've come—"

Instead of listening to my pleas, he stomped on the pendant. The sound of metal snapping echoed through the quiet house, followed by one of my sobs. He ground it into the floorboards with the toe of his boot.

"Please!" I cried, grabbing his wrist. Tears stung my eyes, but I couldn't lose her. I couldn't lose my sister. "I'm sorry! Don't break it anymore. Please don't break it. It's the only piece of Hannah that I have left!"

"Fucking pieces of shit," he growled. "Both of you."

I yanked at his wrist. "Stop it!"

Once I finally moved him away from the pendant, I grabbed the broken pieces from the floor and desperately tried to piece them back together. *This can't be happening. I need Hannah. I fucking need her!*

"She's dead!" Dad roared, dropping his bottle and hurling himself toward me.

When his fist collided with my jaw, I collapsed. My shin scraped against a side table, the edge slicing apart my skin. I grabbed my leg as blood gushed between my fingers, yet I bit back a cry … because Dad would get even angrier if he saw my tears.

He straddled my waist, wrapped both of his hands around my neck, and squeezed harder than he ever had before. Stars danced in my vision from the sudden pressure, and my head was woozy. I reached up and tugged on his wrists.

But he only squeezed harder.

I opened my mouth in an attempt to gasp for air. He took one of his hands off my throat and punched me right in the mouth. My head bounced off the floorboards, and the iron-like taste of blood filled my mouth.

"P-please s-s-stop," I sputtered out, my vision blurring. "I-I-I'm s-s-s-orry."

In a weak attempt, I reached for something that I could use as a weapon, as a piece of defense. My fingers feebly wrapped around Dad's baton that he'd left on the coffee table. I smacked him upside the head with it and scrambled out of his hold.

I need to get out of here. Now.

My head pounded as I crawled away. I used the couch to pull myself to my feet and give myself a running start to the front door. If I could just make it out of the house and scream at the top of my lungs for someone to help … maybe I could escape.

Dad grabbed me by the shirt. I whipped around and went to smack him with the baton again. He caught it halfway to his head and ripped it away from me. I stumbled back onto my ass and tugged on the side table to pull it in front of me.

After tripping over it, he cursed and grabbed my ankle from underneath it. I kicked him in the face with my free leg. Once. Twice. Three times. But he didn't let go. Instead, he pulled me underneath the side table, taking out one of its legs and making it tip over.

The lamp shattered beside me.

I turned onto my hands and knees and crawled. Glass from the lamp sliced into my palms.

But I continued until Dad's grip on me tightened. And even then I tried to move forward to the front door, thinking about Akio, about having a normal life. If I didn't get out of here right now, Dad would kill me.

Dad pulled down my cheer skirt. I reached behind myself to pull it back up, to stop him from touching me, from hurting me, from killing me. I finally had something to live for, and I wasn't going to go down without a fight.

Blood seeped out of my wounds, the glass in my palms piercing me. "Get off me!"

When I kicked back again, Dad captured my ankle in his hand and yanked it all the way back so I fell on my belly. Glass lodged into my stomach and my upper thighs. He crawled up so he straddled my waist with his hips, doing what he could to rip open my clothes just enough…

I struggled underneath him. Desperate to get out. Desperate not to die.

"Dad, stop!" I screamed. Blood covered my thighs. "Please stop!"

Instead of feeling any ounce of remorse for hurting his own daughter, Dad drove all his weight into me. I cried out in pain as his cock stretched out my dry pussy. He began thrusting fast and rough, every single time. My dry pussy stung with every pump.

"Please," I sobbed, throwing my elbows back. Doing anything. "It hurts."

He spit in my hair. "You worthless and pathetic bitch."

After grabbing a fistful of my hair, he slammed my head against the ground over and over until my vision darkened. The last thing that flashed through my mind before I blacked out was that I would never see Akio again.

CHAPTER
THIRTY-NINE

AKIO

IMANI SPED down the road toward the slums. I stared through the windshield with wide eyes, unable to believe that I had done that in front of *anyone*. If Imani told Nicole what I was capable of …

My phone had been buzzing in my pocket, but I couldn't look at it.

Too many thoughts and fears raced through my mind about what had gone down.

"We need to get out of here," I said, glancing into the rearview mirror. I readjusted my glasses and breathed heavily, chest heaving while I nervously rubbed my hands together. "We can't stay in this car. We have to ditch it. They'll be coming."

"We don't have time!" Imani said, cutting a corner a bit too sharply.

The right tires came off the ground by a couple of inches, and I grabbed hold of any handle I could find, shrieking and still in shock from what I had done. Imani slammed her foot to the floor, making the car accelerate.

After a few more moments, Imani finally pulled up to João's

house. Once she parked, she literally dragged me from the car and marched up to the front door, banging on it with the side of her fist.

I stood beside her with wide eyes and muttered, "No. No. No. No. No. No."

"Stop it, Akio," she snapped, banging on the door again. "You're giving me anxiety."

When João didn't answer, she searched under the doormat and in the bushes for a key. I ran a hand through my hair and shook my head. If that man worked for Mom and Mom found out that I had shot one of her guys *again*, she wouldn't be happy.

"Imani, we should go," I said again, desperate to get out of the slums and back home to clean up my mess before Mom could hear about it. I wrapped my arms around myself and rocked back and forth on my heels. "We should go, get out of here. You're not saf—"

Before I could finish my sentence, the door swung open. A middle-aged woman that resembled João's mother stood inside with a cheap plush robe on and tired eyes. Imani furrowed her brow, then stepped into the house, uninvited, and pulled me along with her.

Imani and the woman exchanged a few words in Portuguese. The more they chatted, the more Imani seemed to get pissed. I didn't know what the fuck was wrong with her, but we needed to go.

Now.

I needed to get back home, and so did she.

Suddenly, Imani stomped off into a back room while I stood in the front with João's mother. She returned a moment later with her arms crossed and steam nearly smoking from her ears while continuing to grill João's mother about something.

Then, because she had lost her sanity ever since she'd started hanging out with Poison, Imani walked right out of the house. I forced a smile at the woman, muttered an apology, then followed Imani back to the car.

We were going home. I wasn't going to fight with her.

When she started the car, I climbed in and clicked on my seat belt.

"I'm dropping you off," she said, starting back toward the ritzy part of Redwood. She tapped her fingers on the steering wheel. "I need to find out what's going on, but I can't bring you to Landon's house. Kai's probably there."

God, Kai was the *last* person I wanted to run into right now.

Instead of dropping me off at my own house, she parked in her driveway, which was fine by me because I could walk home and I really didn't want Mom to confront Imani, especially after what had happened during dinner.

"Sorry, I'm not going to drop you off at your house. I don't want to see your mom."

Good.

"But I'll get you an umbrella."

After blowing out a breath, I followed Imani up the front walkway to her house. She shoved her key into the door and then pushed it open, tugging me into the house and out of the rain.

"Mom!"

No answer.

Once Imani locked the door, she released me and turned on the foyer lights. "MOM!"

Nothing.

She muttered something under her breath and turned the corner into the living room, freezing. A piercing scream escaped her lips, and she suddenly collapsed onto the hardwood floor. "Akio! Akio! What did your parents do?"

I scrambled to the living room and spotted Imani's parents lying on the couch—beaten, bruised, and bleeding. Blood drenched their floor. Without thinking, I ran toward the bathroom and rummaged through their closet for medical supplies.

Fuck, this is my fault.

I had been pissing Mom off more and more lately, killing one of her men and spending time with Nicole instead of getting information from her. And then Imani had had to open her big mouth today at dinner.

"Fuck!" I growled, running back to the living room.

While I wasn't a doctor, I did what I could to stop the bleeding and treat them. I couldn't let them die because of me or Imani. Mom had done this to piss me off, to scare Imani, to keep her parents in place. Imani didn't know it, but her parents worked for mine.

Blood drenched my hands as I wrapped the last bandage around her mother's stomach. I sat her up next to her husband and gave them a couple of pills to ease the pain. Imani sobbed next to them, shaking her head uncontrollably and asking why my mom would do this to them.

"She sent them a warning," I said, swallowing hard because I knew that Mom wouldn't stop there. "To keep their daughter from getting in their business."

Next would be Nicole. Mom would hurt her to get me to obey.

I would do anything to protect my girl. She loved me.

CHAPTER
FORTY

AKIO

AFTER I HELPED Imani clean up her parents and bring them to bed so they could rest, she dragged me to another house in the slums, probably one that belonged to either Landon or Kai from Poison.

I didn't want to go, but felt obligated to because of what my parents had done to Imani's. The last thing I wanted was for her to be driving through Redwood with tears blurring her vision and her getting into a car accident.

That would definitely weigh on my conscience.

"Come on!" Imani exclaimed after squealing into the dirt driveway.

I exited the car to follow her.

Once she burst through a door, she hurried down a set of steps that led into a basement. When I reached the bottom stair, I spotted João with a cigarette hanging out of his mouth, Kai glaring at me, and Landon with his arms crossed. Allie—Imani's best friend—also sat on a couch.

"They ... they beat my parents up. I found them almost dead." Imani cried hysterically, like she had been while we drove over here. "I ... I didn't know what to do. I bandaged them as much as I could, but I ... I don't know if I did it right."

"Slow the fuck down. What happened?" João asked.

After glancing over her shoulder at me, she turned back to Poison and shook her head. "Over dinner, I asked Akio's parents what they did to Kai's. They were being assholes, so I left with Akio. We went down to Main Street, and ... and I swore that I saw your mother talking to someone. I went to confront him to make sure she was okay, and he tried to kill me. Then—"

"Who the fuck tried to kill you?" Kai asked, standing up and tucking his gun into the waistband of his cargo pants.

Tears ran down her cheeks, but she quickly pushed them away. "Some guy on Main Street. The same place João had found his mother. Akio ..." She looked over her shoulder at me. "Akio saved me." Imani sat beside Landon, wiping the blood from her hands with a wet towel.

Kai growled and dragged me by the back of my jacket, all the way back up the stairs and through the basement door. After slamming the door behind us, he threw me up against the side of the house. "If I find out that you touched a hair on her fucking head, I will kill you."

I shook my head. "I didn't. I swear."

After shoving me into the street, Kai nodded toward the road. "Walk home."

If he wanted me gone, then I would leave, but ...

"You have to protect her from my parents," I said, turning back toward him. I wasn't going to plead because he already knew what my parents were capable of. They had killed his father. "You know how violent they can be to anyone who disrespects them. Imani ... she told my mom off during dinner. My mom will want me to kill her for it, and if I don't do it, they will. Please, keep her safe."

"Get the fuck out of here," Kai said through gritted teeth. "You're not welcome."

"Please, Kai. I can't protect her," I whispered. "They'll kill me if I don't."

With his jaw twitching, he stared emptily at me. "Leave."

So, I left because there was nothing more I could do. I couldn't protect everyone.

I needed to make sure my parents wouldn't do anything to her.

On my walk home in the rain, I decided to take a detour because I knew Mom couldn't wait to gloat about what she had done to innocent people. And I wanted absolutely no part in that. I hoped she was gone by the time I got home.

Hands stuffed into my pockets, I walked up Nicole's street toward her house. Rain splattered on me, wetting my hair and making it stick to my forehead. I yanked off my glasses and tried to wipe them off, only for more raindrops to decorate the lenses.

After walking up her front steps, I sucked in a breath and knocked on her door.

I only saw her car parked in the driveway, so I hoped that she was home.

My chest tightened at the thought of how stupid I had been by not telling her what she meant to me. I had frozen up, and … and I didn't know what or how she would react to me showing up at her house this late at night.

But I wanted to apologize … and I needed someone after what I just did.

For Nicole, I'd kill anyone. But for Imani?

She was my friend and all, but that was Kai's job.

When nobody answered the door, I knocked again. Rain continued to pound down on me, and I didn't even have an umbrella to keep me dry. Another moment passed without the door opening, and I decided that she must be sleeping.

After all, it was late.

Yet when I went to turn around, the door swung open, and Nicole's father smiled at me.

"Son, what can I do for you?"

NICOLE

"SORRY FOR DISTURBING you so late, sir," a familiar voice said. "Is Nicole home?"

"You're Yui's boy, aren't you?" Dad asked.

Eyes fluttering open, I tilted my head to the side to get a better view of the door, yet I could barely see out into the hallway. What was Akio doing here this late at night? Something must've happened.

And something definitely *would* happen if he didn't leave soon.

Still, I wanted to get to him. I wanted him to see me, to hold me, to tell me that everything would be okay and that his parents would take care of Dad for me … even though I knew they never would. Not without payment, and I didn't have a penny to my name.

"Akio!" I screamed.

But my voice was hoarse, and not even a whisper came out.

My body ached all over, and I could barely feel my lower half from how much Dad and his friends had used me in the past few hours. Someone grabbed my waist from behind, moving my body back and forth.

Get up, Nicole!

I pressed my hands into the puddle of blood underneath me and pushed as hard as I could. I pushed. And I pushed. And I pushed. Only to barely get a centimeter off the ground before Pick, one of Dad's friends, flattened his hand across my lower back and I smacked down with a thud.

"Nicole's not feeling too well right now," Dad said to Akio.

"Can I see her?" Akio asked.

"She's cooped up in her room. Puking."

"I don't mind."

God, I don't know whether I want him to leave before he gets hurt or to come get me …

If he tried to protest with my father any longer, I could only freaking imagine what would happen to him. Dad would snap at any minute from being pulled away from punishing his own daughter … and I would be left to suffer and watch as Dad killed him.

"She's not available now," Dad said. "Give Yui my best wishes."

And with that, Dad slammed the door in Akio's face.

A stray tear slid down my cheek, and I bit back a sob as Pick grabbed a fistful of my hair to pull my head back. I stared into the camera that Dad had set up earlier as a sort of blackmail—to make sure that I didn't step out of line again or else everyone would see the whore that I was.

After listening to loud footsteps, I lifted my gaze higher to see Dad stopping at the door.

He unbuckled his belt and whipped it off himself, then crouched by my side. "Look at you, so fucking sexy that the nerdy kid comes to say hello to you."

"I … I didn't know he was coming over," I tried to say.

"Let me tell you one thing, my girl," Dad said to me, cupping my face and pulling my head a few more inches off the ground.

"If I see you hanging out with that boy ever again, I will kill him in front of you."

Tears welled in my eyes, and I nodded, knowing that he would kill him.

There was absolutely no question in my mind that Dad would chop him up into small, tiny pieces for me to find weeks after he murdered Akio. I didn't know what I would even do. I didn't know how I would think. I didn't know how I would *live* after that.

Truthfully, I wouldn't.

"Do you understand me?"

"Yes," I whispered. "I understand. I understand!"

CHAPTER
FORTY-TWO

AFTER STARING into the car mirror, I dabbed a bit more concealer on my cheek. I hadn't come to school for almost a week because my entire face had been swollen to basically twice its size.

I stared at my dull eyes for a few more moments, then slammed the visor up and exited the car. Akio had come back to my house a few more times these past few days, only for Dad to give him the excuse that I was sick.

Every time he came over, it only pissed Dad off more. And I braced myself many, many times for another punch to the face after the front door slammed, but it never happened. I wished that boy had just stopped coming over.

He was putting himself in danger, showing Dad that he cared about me … when nobody was supposed to care about me.

As soon as I stepped into Redwood Academy, the second bell rang, signaling that I was late for class. I hurried to my locker to drop off some books and decided that I needed to flirt with the teachers to get out of all the work I'd missed because I didn't have it in me to do the work.

Why did it matter anyway?

When I turned the corner, I spotted Akio at my locker. He looked up when he saw me, his eyes wide and a stack of papers in his arms. I paused for a moment to gather myself, then strutted to my locker as if his presence didn't bother me.

"Nicole," Akio said. "How are you feeling?"

"Fine."

"Here," he said, handing me the papers.

"What's this?" I asked, staring down at the one-inch stack.

"All your work that you missed while you were sick," Akio said. "I did it for you."

Be rude to him. Show him how much you don't want him. Protect this precious boy.

After snatching the papers from his hand, I shoved them angrily into my locker. "I didn't ask you to do my work for me, nor did I ask for you to get the work from any of my classes. I've been sick, not incapable of doing things for myself."

"I know, but I thought it would be a nice gesture."

"Well, it's not."

Fuck, I hate being rude. Especially to him.

"Nicole," he said softly, taking my wrist.

Pain shot up my arm from the bruise that I had covered up underneath my long-sleeved shirt. I winced and snatched my hand back, biting back the pain and not looking at him once. I didn't want him to know or even *think* that anything had happened.

A moment of silence passed.

"You're hurt." Akio pushed some hair off my cheek. "You're covering up bruises."

I twirled around to face him, pissed. "Can you leave me alone?"

"Who did this to you?" he pushed.

"Akio," I snapped, "drop it."

He widened his pretty brown eyes, brows knitting together like a puppy dog. All I wanted to do was grab his face and tell him that I took it all back, that this wasn't how I felt, that I was trying to protect him.

If Dad found me with Akio anymore, Dad would kill him.

"Tell me who did this to you."

This time, it wasn't a question. He wanted answers.

"I don't have to tell you anything," I growled, hating to hurt him. "Leave me alone."

While I hurried down the hall, getting away from anyone else, Akio followed after me. I jogged a bit more, my heels making it extremely hard to run any faster. When I looked over my shoulder, Akio was still following me. So, I slipped into the girls' restroom.

"Nicole, just tell me," he said, shutting the door behind him.

"Why do you want to know so badly?!" I exclaimed, throwing up my arms.

"Because I love you too."

My eyes widened slightly, and a warm yet terrifying feeling spread through my chest. I opened and closed my mouth a handful of times, then … tears burst from my eyes, and I choked on a sob. He grabbed my hands, but I pulled them away.

"Why'd you have to say that?" I asked.

"Because it's true."

"It only makes this all harder," I whispered. "I wish you hated me."

Then, I wouldn't feel bad about bullying him, about ignoring him like he meant nothing to me, just like he hadn't before this stupid science project. I wouldn't care about what he thought about me or trying to protect him.

"Why?" he asked, his voice filled with pain. "Why do you wish I hated you?"

I turned my head to the side. "It doesn't matter."

"It does to me," Akio said. "*You* matter to me."

"Stop talking, Akio. I don't matter to anyone."

It was easier that way to protect him. Hell, I didn't care

anymore about what Dad did to me as long as he didn't touch a hair on Akio's head. If I had to hurt Akio myself, then I would do that to protect him from being murdered.

"Tell me who hurt you."

After pressing my quivering lips together, I dropped my gaze to the ground. "I can't."

"Why?"

"Because you can't get involved in this. You can't be involved with *me*."

I would find a way out of this, but I had to do it myself. Once Akio got involved, I would be too distracted by trying to protect him.

"I'm already involved in this. I've already—" Suddenly, Akio stopped short and smacked his lips together. After a few moments of silence, he shook his head and looked away from me. "Just tell me."

"What did you do?" I whispered.

Akio glanced back over at me, brows knotted together. "It was nothing."

"Akio ..."

"If I tell you, you're either going to be angry or feel bad about it." He readjusted his glasses. "All you need to know is that I did what I had to do to protect you, and I will continue to protect you. Whether you tell me who hurt you or not, I will find them."

"Stop with the crazy ideas. Don't get yourself killed because of me."

"Caring about you isn't crazy," Akio said, holding my gaze. "So, you can either tell me who did this to you or I can find out myself. And if you love me the way that you said you did last week, then you'll give me a name. At least one."

My heart pounded in my ears. "But ..."

"Just give me a name, and I'll do the rest."

I stared at him for a few moments, not wanting to get him involved, but knowing that he would get himself killed if he tried finding out for himself. So, I dropped my head and blew out a breath of frustration, mixed with defeat.

"Pick," I whispered. "One of them is nicknamed Pick."

NICOLE

BEFORE AKIO COULD RESPOND, I hurried out of the bathroom. I didn't want to talk anymore about it. I didn't want to even think about it.

When I stepped into the hall, Principal Vaughn's door swung open. Jace Harbor pulled Allie, whose eyes were filled with tears, out of the office and slammed the door behind them.

"Don't say anything to my father," he whispered to her. "We're staying here for now. It's the only place that's safe. As soon as school ends, meet me by my car. We'll go home once I know my dad is gone. Don't leave with anyone."

"We're just going to let him continue to video innocent people?" Allie asked.

My eyes widened as I wondered what the hell Allie could be talking about, especially after leaving Vaughn's office. Who was videoing innocent people? What were the videos about? Clearly, I had missed something during the time I hadn't been in school.

Jace stopped a little ways down the hallway, obviously not having spotted either Akio or me yet. "My dad is far more of a threat than Vaughn. Let me take care of him, and then we can take Vaughn down, along with the rest of Redwood's most corrupt. Okay?"

Allie balled her hands into fists. "Jace, we can't let him get off. He's ruined my life."

I looked between her and Principal Vaughn's door, wondering what that pedo had to do with this. He and Dad were good friends, and he had touched me for the first time in the summer before ninth grade.

If he had hurt Allie in any way—or touched her—I would … do something to him.

I didn't know what. I didn't know how. He could hurt me all he wanted, but when he touched Allie—one of the sweeter and more innocent girls at Redwood—then I had a problem. It was bad enough he had already slept with most of the cheer team.

Jace took her face in his hands and stroked his thumbs against her cheeks. "He won't. I promise that I'll take care of him. Redwood is about to be blown to pieces and crumble. We just have to give it a little more time."

Her lips trembled, yet she held out her pinkie. "Pinkie promise me."

Jace curled his pinkie around Allie's. "I promise you that I'll make everything right again."

And with that, they disappeared down the hallway toward their class.

"What happened?" I whispered to Akio, watching them depart.

"Jace and Allie's sex tape was leaked."

"Their sex tape?"

"Sorta …" Akio paused. "Someone recorded them in the locker room."

My lips quivered. "My God. That's terrible. Who did that?"

Akio shrugged. "I don't know."

But I would bet my soul that it was Principal Vaughn. Dad had gotten him into recording young girls getting fucked, had shared his fair share of his own recordings with me with Principal Vaughn. They all used it for blackmail because this town was screwed to hell.

My stomach growled, and I placed my hand over it. "I didn't get a chance to have breakfast," I said. "I'm going to the cafeteria to see if they have anything left before I head to class. I'll see you later."

Before I could head down the hall, Akio grabbed my hand. "The librarian has muffins."

He guided me to the staircase that led up to the library with his hand tightly squeezing mine and a pissed expression on his soft face. He had always been so nervous around me, always stuttering and fiddling with his shirt.

Never had I seen him so furious. Hell, Akio hadn't stopped grimacing since I had told him about what had happened … or at least part of what had happened. As much as I liked him—*loved* him—I would never tell him the true extent to how Dad treated me. I had so much shame for allowing my own blood to fuck me.

More than once.

Akio would look at me so differently. Maybe even think I was disgusting.

When we made it up to the library, some girls sat in the back room for their free period. Akio marched us right up to the librarian herself, who smiled sweetly at him and readjusted her glasses.

"Akio, what can I do for you?"

"Can Nicole have one of your muffins?" Akio asked her. "She's hungry."

"Akio!" I scolded, not wanting to force her into giving me any of her food.

"It's okay." Without even a pause, she pulled out a plate of freshly baked muffins from underneath the counter and held them out for me. "Take as many as you'd like, my dear. I usually bake these for the girls in the first period, but they're not hungry today."

I glanced over at Akio to make sure it was okay, and he nodded.

After just taking a blueberry muffin, I thanked her. People were never so kind to me.

"Take another," she said. "I can't eat all these myself."

"Are you sure?"

She extended the plate further toward me. "Go on."

Once I took another muffin, she turned to Akio, who shook his head. He guided me to the back of the library and to the big beanbag chair where we had fucked last week. I sat down on the seat, finally feeling relaxed for once.

I slumped my shoulders forward and stuffed the muffin into my mouth. "Thank you."

Akio nodded and stayed quiet.

When I finished my first muffin, I folded the wrapper. Akio held out his hand and took it from me. I smiled softly, my chest so warm and tight at the thought of people actually being nice to me for once. Most times, I didn't deserve it.

But after what had happened this past week, I thought I did.

"What happened to your necklace?" Akio asked.

"What?"

"Your sister's necklace," he continued. "You're not wearing it anymore."

"Oh," I whispered. "I accidentally broke it."

He paused and crouched down in front of me. "Why are you lying?"

I tucked some hair behind my ear, flustered. "I'm not lying."

"Nicole," he said softly, taking my hand, "you can tell me anything."

"No." I shook my head. "I can't."

Pain crossed his face. "I'm not going to hurt you."

But that was what everyone said before they did. The only person in my life who hadn't hurt me was Hannah, and she had been gone for more than half a decade now. I had been all alone, and I didn't know *how* to be with someone else. I didn't know how to let them in on all my secrets. I didn't know how to let them help me.

"One day, I'll let you in on everything," I whispered, gripping his hand. "I promise."

I just hoped that I lived that long.

CHAPTER
FORTY-FOUR

AKIO

AFTER SCHOOL, I walked into the house at a time when I knew Mom would be home and dumped my backpack on the couch. She chatted with someone in the next room about a guy named Jett Harleen and paused when she heard my footsteps.

"Akio, is that you?" she called.

I blew out a low breath and walked toward the dining room. "Yeah, it's me."

Before I stepped into the room, I prepared myself for the worst possible punishment for what Imani had done to her. I had been avoiding Mom, very successfully, since that dinner and hadn't had a chance to confront her about it. Or vice versa.

But I needed to suck up today. I needed information.

When I entered the room, Rick Santos glared at me from Mom's side. I ignored him and leaned against the doorframe, my arms crossed over my chest in a way to protect myself from everything she was about to explode on me for.

"Where have you been all week?" she snarled.

"Working at the pharmacy," I said. "At school. What kids my age do."

"We need to talk." She looked over at Rick. "Leave us."

"What do you want me to do with Harleen?" Rick said to her.

"Clean up the mess."

After nodding, Rick headed in my direction to leave the house, shoving me hard into the wall on his way out. I balled my hands into fists, wanting to unleash on him the way I had with his brother. I had wanted to kill someone since this morning, when Nicole had told me what had happened.

She had been holding back information, but at least she'd opened up to me.

One day, I would get to the bottom of it. All I had to do was gain her trust, show her that I would do anything for her, and maybe she would trust me enough to tell me everything that was going on, without hiding any secrets.

Once the front door closed, I sidestepped Mom's lunge at me. Her fist collided with the wall beside me with a thud. Her knuckles split, blood trickling down her fingers. I waited for her to lunge at me again, but she never did.

"How could you do that to Imani's parents?" I asked.

Mom clutched her hand. "I did it because her parents hadn't taught her respect."

"So, you almost killed them?"

"No," she said, jaw clenched. "I gave them a warning."

Fury rushed through me, and for a moment, the thought of killing Mom crossed my mind. She was a threat to Imani and Nicole … except if I did that, I would have an even bigger target on my back. Rick would try to kill me. Everyone in the mob would have it out for me.

Plus, Mom had connections. She had information.

"If you think Imani will back down because you hurt her parents, you're wrong," I said, thinking about the pure anger I had seen on her face every single day since that night. "Believe me, I've tried to talk her down from hating you for what you did."

After a pause, Mom walked to the kitchen and turned on the sink. She washed her knuckles underneath the water. I followed after her and stood at the door so I could find an easy escape if she tried anything else.

"Imani has some balls, talking back to me," Mom said. "I wish you had the same."

I flared my nostrils and took the jab. "We need to talk about—"

"She would be a good leader," Mom continued. "Much better than you would be."

"For what?" I snapped. "To lead your stupid mob?"

She tightened her hand into a fist underneath the flowing water. "Yes."

"She won't be interested in it."

"Maybe not now," Mom murmured. "But I can be quite convincing."

After I bit back a sour response because Imani would *never* be interested in any shit that Mom had to offer, she turned off the water and grabbed a towel from the drawer beside the sink to wipe off her hands.

"Do you know anyone nicknamed Pick?" I asked, not wanting to draw this out any longer.

Mom peered over at me, one brow arched. "Why?"

"Do you?"

"Is this about your little girlfriend?"

"No," I exclaimed. "It's not about Nicole."

Even though it one hundred percent was. But I didn't want her thinking that I cared about Nicole. She would use Nicole against me. She'd hurt her to hurt me, to force me into doing shit for her. And I couldn't let that happen.

"Then, why do you wanna know?"

"Because I need to talk to him."

Mom placed down the towel and grabbed her gun on the counter. "About what?"

I gritted my teeth and turned around to leave. "Forget it."

"How about I make you a deal?" she said, stuffing her gun into the waistband of her pants and stalking toward me the way she always did to try to intimidate me. "You do a job for me, and I'll give you information on Pick."

I clenched my jaw and glared at her, knowing that this was a shit idea. "Deal."

CHAPTER
FORTY-FIVE

AKIO

"OH MY GOD." I stuck my head into the toilet and puked up the remainder of my dinner. Another wave of bile rose in my throat, burning the back of it. I gripped the toilet bowl. "This is sick. This is fucking sick."

In the other room, Patty O'Neil lay dead. He was the job that Mom had given me to do in order to get information out of her about Pick. And I suddenly wished that I had gotten that information someplace else.

When I finished puking up the only contents left in my stomach, I walked to the sink. I wiped my mouth, cupped my hands under the running water until they filled, and then splashed it on my face to wake myself up.

This had to be a dream—a nightmare. What I had seen in here was …

Sick. Repulsive. Nauseating.

Those words didn't even cover how I felt right now.

After turning off the water, I opened the bathroom door and walked out of the room, through the hall, and to the back door. Droplets of water ran down strands of my hair and onto my face. I needed to get out of here, and I needed to get out of here fast.

With Patty's body lying in a puddle of his own blood in the middle of the living room, I exited the house and slammed the door behind me. Shit in Redwood was more messed up than I'd thought, and usually, I had a front-row seat to what Mom was a part of, what she forced me to watch, what she forced me *to do*. And yet ... I still didn't even know everything.

Once I slid into my car, I slammed my finger on the button to start it.

Fuck!

I had come here to do a job so Mom would tell me about Pick. I had come for Nicole.

And now, I knew more about Redwood than I wanted to know. I had learned that the unthinkable was happening on the streets, with girls I went to school with, with girls who smiled in the hallways as if nothing bad was happening to them.

As if they weren't being sex-trafficked.

I slammed my foot on the accelerator to get the fuck out of here. I needed to talk to Kai, to tell him to keep Imani safe from my parents, from Principal Vaughn, from everyone that he didn't trust ... and maybe some people that he did trust because she wasn't safe.

But I doubted he'd even talk to me.

Once I made it to Mom's place down the beach where she did most of her work, I parked my car and stormed into the building, following the sound of her voice to her office. I opened the door, not caring what meeting I was interrupting.

Mom sat at her desk, on the phone, and clicked it off when I walked in. "Akio."

"I held up my end of the deal. Now, who's Pick?"

She raised her brows at me. "You did it?"

"Yes."

"I don't believe you," she said. "Prove it."

"He was sex-trafficking women."

"So, that's all it takes to motivate you to do shit for me." She smirked. "Interesting."

"Did you know about this?" I asked.

Mom clenched her jaw, her eyes hardening. "Found out about it yesterday. Terrible, isn't it?"

"It's worse than terrible," I growled.

If Patty had been sleeping around with some cheerleaders at Redwood, there was a possibility that Nicole was involved in this. A possibility that her bruises and tenderness were from some sex trafficker raping her.

Did she know about this? Was she involved? Was that why she wanted to keep it a secret from me because she was embarrassed? Or maybe someone was blackmailing her, threatening to embarrass her and her family.

"So, now, you see how fucked up this town is, Akio," Mom asked. "You understand that I'm not the bad guy here, don't you? That I do what I have to do, not what is right? You've always despised me, but I'm here to help you."

I clenched my jaw and stared blankly at her because I didn't believe her. She had been selling me lies since I had been a child. Why should—or would—I believe her now? She didn't care what happened to girls here, only that she controlled the town, that she had the money.

"Now, I want my information on Pick."

"A deal's a deal." Mom nodded. "Pick will be at the football game on Friday night."

AKIO

"GO REDWOOD!" Allie Hall screamed next to Imani on the bleachers.

I stood beside Imani with my arms crossed and scanned the stadium for any sign of Pick. Mom had given me the vaguest description of him, but it was something that I could work off of. At least, I knew that he was a police officer.

Along with the rest of her team, Nicole waved her pom-poms in the air to cheer up the already-excited crowd. When she caught my eye, she smiled softly and cheered even more loudly, as if she wanted me to hear her.

Warmth spread through my chest at the sight of her. All these years, I'd had a crush on the cheer captain, and I was finally dating her … *sorta*. Until I took care of Pick, she would never trust me with her secrets, and she would never truly tell me what was wrong.

Jace Harbor paced the sidelines—not dressed to play tonight—and walked past Nicole, but she didn't even spare him a glance. Her gaze was set on me as her blonde hair in a high ponytail.

Imani bounced on her toes next to me, shivering in the late fall air.

I leaned closer to her. "You're lucky. My mom hasn't said a word about you since the dinner." Well, she had said something, but it was because I'd brought it up. "I expected her"—I glanced over her shoulder at Allie—"to want me to kill you."

"My mom said to drop it," Imani said, referring to how my mother had brutally tortured hers. She nudged me with a sassy and bratty attitude that she had to have picked up from hanging out with Poison too much. I wondered where they were tonight. "But you know that I won't."

"It would be smart if you did."

"Your mom nearly killed my parents!" she whisper-yelled. "Have *you* killed anyone?"

"No!" I exclaimed, glancing back toward the game that I had absolutely no interest in. A couple of policemen walked around the track that surrounded the field, but none looked like the description of Pick. "I would never do that. You know I wouldn't."

"Touchdown!" Allie cheered beside Imani, jumping up and down.

Imani side-eyed me, as if to say that we'd talk about this later. Instead of pretending to be part of the Bird's Nest—which was what Redwood Academy students called the fandom that sat on the right side of the bleachers during every game to cheer on the Ravens—I made up some excuse about getting drinks and hot dogs for us at the concession stand.

After walking down the wobbly steps as the students jumped up and down on the metal bleachers, I made it to the bottom, closer to the cheer team. Nicole was the bubbliest of them all with a huge smile that didn't meet her eyes.

She hadn't told me much about what had happened, but I could gather from how she'd reacted to my touch that Pick—and possibly others—had raped her. And yet, here she stood in the middle of the stadium, acting like everything was perfect.

"Let's go, Redwood!" she cheered, scanning the Bird's Nest with her gaze. "Woohoo!"

My hands tightened into fists by my sides, and I continued down to the concession stand. After ordering a soft drink and a hot dog because I had a feeling that tonight would be a long night, I waited for my food to come out.

Once I grabbed my food from the counter, a buzzer rang through the stadium. I walked to the fence that surrounded the field to keep fans and family members out and leaned against it, my glasses fogging slightly from the cold.

Bright white lights on the scoreboard read 14 to 6. The teams retreated to their sides of the field, packing up to head to the locker room for halftime—or at least that was what a couple of guys to my left said. I didn't know much about football.

Across the field, a tall policeman stood with his hands on his hips and a tattoo peeking out from underneath his uniform. My eyes widened, and I stood up taller to see if I could get a better view.

Is that Pick?

Just when I thought I spotted him, the stadium lights turned off.

Every single one of them. Even the scoreboard.

A sea of buzzing echoed through the stadium, and then my phone vibrated in my pocket. With my hands full, I decided not to pull it out and kept my gaze on Nicole—or at least what I thought I could see of her.

"What the fuck is this?" the guy standing next to me asked his buddy.

I peered over for a brief moment to see a video of Principal Vaughn sitting naked in an abandoned warehouse. Vaughn trembled in fear as someone shot a bottle of water off his head, then a couple of trophies. Then, a masked man came on the screen.

My eyes widened, and I returned my gaze to the field to try to spot Nicole again. But it was too dark. I dropped my hot dog and soda on the ground and jogged toward the bleachers. Something was about to go down.

With a voice enhancer to block the real sound of their voice, someone came over the intercom. "Redwood Academy, your principal has been jerking off to hundreds of recordings of naked Redwood students in the locker rooms."

Throat drying, I scanned the field. Nothing.

Where is Nicole?

I had a bad feeling about this. I didn't know the first thing that was happening—maybe something that had to deal with Allie and Jace walking out of Principal Vaughn's office the other day … maybe something Nicole was a part of. Fuck if I knew.

"Is this who you think is fit to lead your school? Is this who we're giving thousands of dollars to every year? Is this someone you think deserves to live?" the man said, every word growing angrier.

Whispers erupted through the stadium. I didn't know what was happening on everyone's phone screen, but I could tell that it wasn't good as everyone sucked in a collective gasp, a couple of students in the Bird's Nest muttering inappropriate things about Vaughn's dick.

"That's not the only punishment that the Redwood rich will receive for their sins. Over the course of the next few months, all the lies, all the secrets, all the scandals that have run this town will be exposed. Nobody is safe from the truth!"

The lights turned back on, and my eyes slowly adjusted to light.

I finally spotted Nicole standing alone to the right side of her team, arms crossed over her chest and eyes wide. From out of nowhere, a ball bounced to the right of Nicole and onto the field. Once. Twice. And then she began screaming at the top of her lungs.

My eyes widened slightly as my gaze followed hers.

It wasn't a ball, but Principal Vaughn's head.

"Welcome to the end, Redwood."

CHAPTER
FORTY-SEVEN

NICOLE

AFTER GRABBING my purse on the side of the field, I sprinted toward the exit. Panic erupted in the bleachers, and football players ran to the locker rooms. Except Jace. He ran toward the panic, desperately scanning the stands for Allie.

My phone buzzed, and I fished around for it.

Dad: Get out of there now.

Dad: If I find out that you had something to do with this …

Anxiety rushing through my body, I stopped and scanned the crowd, spotting Jace.

"Jace!" I shouted, wiping my tears with the back of my hand. "We have to get out of here, Jace. My father is—"

When I grabbed his hand, he pulled it away. "Stop it, Nicole! We're not dating. We were *never* dating. Learn your fucking boundaries and don't fucking touch me again. I don't have the patience to deal with your fucking ass."

While it stung to hear those words—because I had never tried to make him uncomfortable, though I knew that I had—I grabbed his wrist tighter and pulled him toward the exit. "My dad texted me and told me to leave. I think he's going to blame you for this.

He knows that you hate Vaughn because of how much he hated you."

But Jace wasn't even listening to me.

"Jace, listen to me!" I shook him. "We have to go!"

"I need to find Allie first." He shoved me to the side. "When I find her, we can talk."

"Jace!" I shouted again.

Once I decided that he wasn't leaving, I continued my sprint to my car. Thankfully, because I hadn't been in the Bird's Nest, I got to my car in the student parking lot before many people made it there. After fumbling with my keys, I slipped into the car and reversed it at full speed.

My tires squealed against the pavement as I blew through the Stop sign before the main road. I headed around the back side of Redwood Academy and found my way to the main entrance of the stadium.

Students poured out of the gate that led into the bleachers and spilled out onto the sidewalks, running to their cars parked on the side of the road, behind the school, and in the lots. I spotted Allie clutching Imani's hand, looking around as if they didn't know where to go.

I pulled to the side of the road a few feet ahead of them and rolled down the passenger window in an attempt to get their attention. Allie might've hated me, but I didn't want to see them get trampled in this mess, or worse …

Like let the Redwood Police take advantage of them during this situation.

"Get in!" I shouted at them. "You'll freeze out there."

Allie stopped, almost tripping over her own two feet into Imani, and widened her eyes. Then, her surprised eyes turned to anger, and she continued hurrying down the sidewalk with Imani, away from Redwood—not even toward Imani's car, parked in the lot.

"We're not going anywhere with you," Allie said.

I sped up enough to catch up with them, barely dodging students. "Get in, Allie. Jace is looking for you."

Alarms and sirens blared behind us. Allie took one last look at the stadium, then at Imani, and then she yanked open the passenger door and slid into the front seat with me. Imani took the back.

"This doesn't make us friends," Allie said.

"Fine by me," I said, slamming my foot on the accelerator. "Poison's place it is."

It was the only place that I thought would be safe.

"I am literally going to kill them!" Imani exclaimed from the back. "Murder!"

"Who?" I asked, looking in the rearview mirror at her pouty expression.

"Who do you think?!" Imani flared her nostrils. "Poison, obviously."

"You think they did it?" Allie asked, looking over her shoulder.

"Of course! Do you know how big of a target they've put on our backs now?!" Imani crossed her arms, gritted her teeth, and glared out the window. "It's bad enough that I have to deal with Akio's parents. Now this?!"

"Akio's parents?"

"His mom is crazy! She almost killed my parents the other day."

"What?!" Allie and I exclaimed at the same time.

Imani widened her eyes and smacked her mouth closed. "Nothing."

When I pulled up to a red light, I glanced back at Imani. "She did?"

"No!" Imani said. "It was nothing. Just drive!"

After arching my brow, I stayed silent and continued to dodge the crazy students and worried parents all through Redwood. Roads were blocked off for some reason with police cars, so I took the long way around Redwood in order to avoid Pick or any other officer tonight.

Especially Dad.

Usually, Dad worked on nights I cheered, which meant that I sometimes had the night off. And I really didn't want to be dragged in the middle of this during an off night. I wanted to find Akio and try to talk him out of doing whatever he was planning to do to Pick.

Allie tried to get more information out of Imani, who decided to zip her lips closed. I pulled up to another stoplight and took out my phone from my purse to text Jace to meet us at Poison's place.

But there were more messages from Dad.

Dad: Did you have anything to do with this?

Dad: Was this Jace's doing?

Dad: He stole files from my house when you had him over a few weeks ago, then leaked them. Now, that punk killed one of my business partners. If I find out that you knew about this, you're going to be in so much fucking trouble, Nicole.

After forcing myself to ignore his messages—because I didn't know what the hell he was talking about anymore—I texted Jace. Someone laid on their horn behind me, and I dropped my phone in my lap to continue driving. My mind wandered to Akio. I had seen him halfway through the game, and then he'd vanished.

Right before everything happened.

Where was he? I hope he didn't get trampled in the herd.

Once I dropped off Imani and Allie and ensured they were okay, I would go back to Redwood to find him. It was the least I could do for him, even if that meant possibly seeing Dad or Pick on the way there.

FORTY-EIGHT

NICOLE

"LANDON'S PLACE is up there to the right," Imani said, cracking her knuckles.

The moment I pulled into the small dirt driveway, Imani jumped out of the car and went barreling toward a back door. I parked, grabbed my purse, and hopped out after her, walking with Allie toward the door. Imani swung the door open.

"What the hell was that?!" she screamed, halfway down the steps.

When we reached the bottom stair, I spotted Imani shoving João, who had a cigarette between his lips, against a wall. "Are you guys dumb?!" Another push. "You are the stupidest fucking people I've met!"

Allie left my side and hurried to Jace, wrapping her arms around his shoulders and melting into him the way I wanted to melt into Akio. "I lost my phone in the crowd. Everyone was going crazy. Sorry for making you worry."

After kissing her forehead, Jace guided her toward a stained couch.

The basement was larger than I had expected, but still fairly small with a heavy stench of weed. I glanced around, noticing holes in the walls, glass scattered in the corner, and crayons and a coloring book on the coffee table.

João grasped Imani's hands and shoved her off. "Don't push me."

Yet Imani continued to scream at all three of the Poison boys now. "What's wrong with you guys?! You can be thrown in jail. You can't just send out a video to everyone around! Then throw a head into a football game?! Are you serious?!"

"Relax, Imani," João said.

"Nobody is going to jail," Landon continued, taking the pack of cigarettes from João and lighting one up. He puffed on it once and blew out a cloud of smoke, slumping down on a couch and sighing. "Nothing will happen."

"You don't know that!" Imani continued.

Kai placed a hand on her shoulder and glanced at Allie for the quickest second. I pressed my lips together, kinda wishing that Akio were here with me, comforting me like that.

"We've done this before," Kai said. "We know how to clean shit up and hide the evidence. Don't make a big deal out of it."

Imani widened her eyes, shook her head, and backed away. "All three of you are insane." She looked at Allie and me. "Why aren't you both freaking out more?! We just saw our principal's head in the middle of the football field."

Instead of freaking out like I'd thought she would, Allie blew out a long breath and shrugged her shoulders. She looked tired, and I didn't blame her. From what I had gathered from the video released tonight and from her and Jace's conversation in the hallway the other day, it seemed like Principal Vaughn had been using Allie to get off.

And I was glad that Poison had killed him.

One last guy who would bother me.

Imani huffed. "You guys can't just—"

"Calm the fuck down!" João shouted, putting out his cigarette. "You know what we did when you got involved with us. I gave you a chance to leave. You didn't. So, sit down and keep your mouth shut before someone hears you screaming at us for what happened."

Imani marched right up to him and smacked him right across the face, leaving a big fat red handprint on his cheek. João clenched his jaw and narrowed his eyes at her as she muttered something under her breath.

"You want to say that a little louder?" he asked, gritting his teeth in annoyance at her. "Because you're one more mistake away from me teaching you a fucking lesson on how to behave, Imani."

Imani turned on her heel, walked to the other side of the room, and sat against the wall. "Fuck you, João. I hate you."

When the room finally went quiet, I cleared my throat and sat next to Allie, unsure if she would let me. But she didn't say a word.

"Well …" I started, explaining what Dad had texted me earlier. I didn't partake in Jace's or my father's drama, but Jace had a right to know that the police chief was blaming him for this mess tonight. I didn't know why, nor did I know much about the supposed files that Jace had stolen from my house.

But I cared.

Even if Jace hated me. Even if Allie hated me. Even if Redwood hated me.

I still cared about them.

Landon waved his hand dismissively. "Don't worry about the police chief. We're taking care of him next. He's the only person standing in the way of Redwood's fall. All the other police officers don't know shit about all the blackmail your father has been doing throughout the years."

I teetered back and forth on the sofa and toyed with the ends of my skirt.

Kai and Jace began chatting tensely about something that I couldn't care less about, so I let my mind wander. If Poison took care of my father like they said they would, then maybe I could be with Akio without him getting himself in trouble with Pick.

Akio didn't know what Pick looked like, and I had made sure not to give him *any* more details than just his name. He was too cute and small, too sweet to get in the middle of any of my crazy drama. Plus, I didn't want him to find out the truth.

Pick would surely spill it if put in a life-or-death situation.

"Will you really take care of my father for me?" I asked Landon.

Jace, Allie, and Kai were still chatting. João and Imani had disappeared upstairs, screaming at each other like an old married couple. And I was so, so alone with nobody to lean on, nobody to talk to. I had even lost Akio tonight.

"I don't know when," Landon said. "But that's the plan."

"Good," I whispered, tucking some hair behind my ear. "That's good."

CHAPTER
FORTY-NINE

AKIO

WHILE THE WORLD burned around me, I stayed glued to my spot and scanned the stadium. Someone–and my prediction: Poison–had released the video thirty minutes ago, and the crowd had trampled a handful of students and parents while trying to leave.

My hands tightened into fists as I watched EMTs tend to wounds and broken bones. Other victims were driven off in ambulances to the hospital. And three of Redwood's finest police officers stood around Principal Vaughn's head on the field.

I leaned against the fence to get a better view. None of the cops on the field were Pick, but Pick had been here tonight. I knew that I had seen him a moment before the chaos. Yet now, he wasn't even on campus anymore.

"Akio, right?" someone asked to my left.

After peering over, I stiffened and stood up taller, spotting Nicole's father. I didn't know whether or not I should tell him about Pick—because if he had known, then surely, he would've done something, right?—but I decided to keep my mouth closed.

"What're you still doing here?" he asked. "Yui is probably looking for you."

Yeah, right. Mom doesn't give a fuck about me.

"Is everything all right?" I asked.

The police chief looked onto the field. "Just great. What are you doing here?"

"I didn't want to be trampled," I lied, nodding to the others. "Like the rest of them."

Once he peered at the last few victims being treated, he placed his hands on his hips and rocked back on his heels. "Have you seen Nicole? You and she have been getting pretty close lately, haven't you?"

I paused. "No. We're just working on a project together."

He clenched his jaw. "That'd better be all that it is because she's taken."

As the words left his mouth, my chest tightened. My first instinct was to ask *who* she was taken by because Nicole had never mentioned anyone else to me, but she kept a lot of secrets to herself. And I still didn't think she wanted anyone to know about us.

So, I nodded. "Okay."

After eyeing me for a few more moments, he turned around and headed toward the entrance to the field. "You should get out of here for your own good. I doubt Yui would like to know that her son is hanging around a crime scene. Makes you look suspicious."

When he was at least fifty feet away from me, I reached into my pocket for my keys and walked out of the stadium and to the student parking lot. A single light flickered over my car. I walked through the nearly desolate lot and spotted Nicole's parking space empty.

Which meant that she'd made it out.

Imani's car was still parked in her normal spot, and while I hoped that she and Allie had gotten out alive and were safe, I didn't have time to go looking for them. I had missed my goddamn chance to prove to Nicole that I could be a different man than who she thought I was.

If I had just kept my eyes on Pick…

I slipped into my car and turned it on, the soft hum of the engine coming to life. After readjusting my rearview mirror, I caught sight of a police car driving around the campus, as if to check the perimeter for any stragglers.

The whole purpose was to be undercover, but undercover Redwood Police cars were sometimes even more obvious than the regular ones, with tinted windows and even blacked-out plates. Not legal, of course, but this was Redwood.

I started after him and drove about thirty feet behind him, lights completely off so it wasn't obvious, and I stopped far behind him whenever he came to a streetlight or a Stop sign. Instead of circling Redwood, he headed back toward the police station.

When he came to the light before Fitz Road, he rolled down his window, hung his arm out of it, and looked into his rearview mirror, his gaze locking on to mine. Pick. Knowing that I had been caught—and that I had caught him—I flashed my high beams, blinding him for a moment.

He parked and stepped out of his car, but I was already out of mine, running toward him. I didn't have my gun—I'd left it in Imani's car—but I didn't need it tonight. If he'd hurt Nicole the way that she'd said he had, I wasn't going to let him off with a single bullet.

No easy death.

Before he could seize hold of his gun, I snatched him by his jacket and hurled him to the ground. I dropped my shins onto each of his shoulders, straddling his back and then grabbing fistfuls of his hair. I smashed his head into the pavement over and over and over.

Until he stopped struggling.

Until blood was splattered everywhere.

Until I could pick him up off the ground and throw him into the back of my car.

While I took off down the road with Pick in my backseat, I listened to the rev of an engine behind me, and then a motorcycle flew past me. The only person in Redwood that I knew had a bike like that was Kai Koh from Poison, the guy who hated me the most.

And he had just seen that I had kidnapped a cop.

NICOLE

AFTER CHEER PRACTICE the next Monday, I walked to my car in the parking lot. Thankfully, I hadn't seen Dad all weekend. I didn't know where he had been, but Redwood had gone fucking crazy after what Poison did on Friday night.

I was honestly surprised that there was school today.

My phone buzzed, and I yanked it out of my bag, hoping that it was Akio. He hadn't been in school today—and that kid had nearly perfect attendance—and he hadn't been great at responding all weekend.

At least, he'd told me that he was safe. I had driven around Redwood all night on Friday, trying to find his car. But he hadn't even been at his home, or at the Overlook, or at any other place a nerdy kid might hang out.

When I reached my car, I spotted a ripped sheet of paper, from what looked to be from a science textbook, stashed between my windshield wipers. I pulled it out, slipped into my car, and locked the doors.

I wasn't about to get jumped.

Once I set my belongings on the passenger seat, I unfolded the note and saw Akio's handwriting: ***Overlook. 11 p.m. Tonight.***

Eyes widening slightly, I glanced toward his parking spot to see it empty. Where was he, and when had he stuffed this in here? It had to have been within a few hours ago because when I got to cheer practice tonight, there hadn't been anyone here.

After stuffing the note into my backpack, I turned on my car and headlights. It was nearly eight o'clock and dark at Redwood. I had a few hours to kill before I met Akio—no way in hell was I missing that—so I headed home for a quick dinner.

———

Halfway into cooking some leftovers in the microwave, the front door slammed open.

"I'm going to fucking kill that kid," Dad growled, clutching his side.

What happened to him?

Bloody bandages were wrapped around his bare torso. He hobbled into the house to the kitchen and pulled out a beer from the fridge. After popping it open, he put it to his lips and walked right out of the house without saying a word to me.

I released a breath—thankful that he either hadn't noticed me or hadn't cared to touch me tonight—and I snatched a quick bite to eat before heading out to the Overlook to meet Akio, though … I didn't know why he hadn't just texted me to meet him there.

What was with the note?

Ah, whatever. At least I get to see him tonight.

An hour later, Dad still hadn't returned, so I headed out before he got back and could stop me from seeing Akio tonight. I didn't know who had shot Dad or stabbed him, but I didn't care. He'd deserved it.

After driving around Redwood to kill some more time, I found my way down by the beach. While this place was popping during the summer, it was dead in the late fall, early winter. And way too dark for my liking. It gave me the creeps.

A couple of kids had drowned down here last summer in the middle of the night, and their families had found them the next morning. All I remember was being at the police station when it'd happened and listening to the cries of their mother.

Memories of Hannah had been increasingly hard since that night.

When I reached the end of the road, I turned right and headed down to the Overlook. Mansions with views of the Atlantic Ocean sat to my left, the ocean to my right. I drove on the desolate road until I came to another curve—the Overlook.

I drove through it once to make sure that nobody was perched outside and waiting for me, then I parked on the side of the road, waiting for Akio. The last time I had been here with him, we had seen Sakura Sato and Mr. Avery fuck, and I had spent a nice night with Akio in the back of his car.

Tonight … I didn't know what would happen.

Fifteen minutes past eleven, and Akio still wasn't anywhere to be found. A couple of cars had driven past to admire the views, but nobody had parked in front of or behind me. I didn't want the company anyway.

Needing some fresh air, I shut off my car and stepped out into the chilly fall breeze. I tasted the salt from the ocean on my tongue as I walked over to the rocks, leaning against one at the top. Moonlight glimmered off the water.

I gazed down at the waves hitting the rocks and noticed something smashing against the shore. My eyes widened slightly, and I looked around to make sure nobody was watching before I descended a few more rocks to get a better view.

When I reached the rock before the water, my mouth dropped open.

Bruised in multiple places on his face and neck, Pick's corpse was being thrown against the rocks repeatedly. He still had on his police uniform, but it was ripped from what looked to be a knife, and a sheet of paper stuck out from his shirt pocket, drenched in salty water.

Warmth spread throughout my chest, and I didn't even have to pull the paper out to know that ... Akio had had his family do it to protect me. To prove himself to me. To show me that he really wanted this, wanted *us*.

I pulled the paper from Pick's pocket and unfolded it.

I told you I'd protect you.

—A

CHAPTER
FIFTY-ONE

NICOLE

TWELVE THIRTY THAT NIGHT, I banged on Akio's front door. I didn't know what had come over me, but I couldn't stop myself. His car was parked in the driveway, and it didn't seem like his mother or father was home.

When nobody answered on the first knock, I knocked again. This time louder.

"Akio!" I called.

Another moment passed, and then I heard footsteps descending the stairs. I sucked in a breath and stared at the door, waiting for him to answer it.

Nobody had protected me like that. Ever.

I didn't care if he'd had his parents handle it since they were part of the mob. All I could think about was that he really, truly cared about me and he wanted to show me that he wanted me … that he wanted *us*.

The door swung open, and Akio stood in the doorway with his hair disheveled and dark bags underneath his eyes. I stepped into the house without being invited, kicked the door closed behind me, and then kissed him hard on the mouth.

"Nicole, did you—"

"I saw him," I murmured against his lips, slipping my hands underneath his black Goku graphic tee and running them all over his body. I stalked closer to him, causing him to move back into the living room, his legs hitting the arm of the couch. "I can't believe you did it for me."

I didn't have any money to give him, but I had one thing that every guy seemed to want.

Dropping to my knees, I grasped the waistband of his pants.

"Nicole," Akio said, his voice shaky, "you don't—"

"Stay," I murmured, sprawling one hand across his skinny abdomen and undoing his belt with my other hand. Warmth exploded through my pussy, and I pressed my thighs together. "Let me do this for you."

"You don't have to—"

Before he could say another word, I pulled out his huge cock and wrapped my lips around the head. I didn't have to do anything for him—he had always made that clear to me—but this was the only way I knew how to repay him.

After swirling my tongue around the tip of his cock, I sucked more and more of him inside my mouth. His hips jerked, and he sank a hand into my hair and threw his head back, grunting softly to himself.

"You don't have to do this for me, Nicole," he murmured. "I would've … *fuuuuck.*"

A gush of pleasure rushed through me, and I whimpered on his cock, loving the sounds of his grunts and groans. I sucked more of him into my mouth until I reached the base of his dick, and then I swallowed around him.

His hips jerked forward again, his balls smacking against my chin. I slipped a hand between my thighs and into my leggings, rubbing my clit because I couldn't handle this pressure rising in my core any longer.

Nobody had thought about me like this before. Nobody had cared enough.

"I love you," I mumbled on his cock. "God, I love you."

Akio laced another hand into my hair to hold me in place. "I love you too."

My eyes rolled back into my head, and a burst of pleasure exploded inside my core. I moaned around him and rubbed my swollen clit faster to ride out my orgasm. I pressed my lips against his pelvis and stared up at him, choking and loving every moment of this.

The first time I had told him I loved him, he hadn't said it back right away.

This time, there had been no hesitation in his voice. Not even a pause.

"Say it again," I whispered, my hand wrapped around the base of his dick but my head now pulled back so I could watch him say it. I stroked him back and forth, desperate. "Please, say it again for me, Akio."

"I love you."

I knitted my brows together as another wave of pleasure coursed through my body. My toes curled, and I stroked him faster. Akio took my hand and stopped me, but I wanted to please him. I *needed* to repay him.

"Let me," I pleaded. "Please."

Yet he pulled my hand away and pulled me up to my feet. After tugging up his pants, he took my face in his hands and drew the pads of his thumbs across my cheekbones. I sucked in a sharp breath, admiring the way the moonlight hit his face.

"You don't have to repay me for anything," he whispered.

"Yes, I do," I said. "Your family got rid of Pick for me, just like you'd promised."

"My family didn't do anything," Akio said.

My eyes widened, and I furrowed my brow. "B-but I saw Pick's body …"

Confusion rushed through me. What was going on? I swore I had seen Pick's corpse, and Akio was the only person that I'd told about—

"My family didn't do anything to him," Akio said again. "I did."

"B-but he ... he was mutilated," I whispered. "Y-you did that?"

"I told you that I was going to protect you," he whispered. "You don't have to repay me for keeping a promise."

CHAPTER
FIFTY-TWO

NICOLE

"WHO ELSE HURT YOU?" Akio whispered, tucking some hair behind my ear.

With my head resting on his chest, I chewed on the inside of my cheek and stared at the wall opposite of his bed. While my heart felt like it was being torn to shreds from the inside out, I kept quiet. Akio had proven himself to me, but ...

I wasn't ready.

Not for the world to know.

Not for Redwood to know.

Not for Akio to know.

Squeezing my eyes closed, I tensed beside him and hoped he didn't notice.

"Who else?" he murmured, gently rubbing my shoulder in circles. "You can trust me."

When I opened my mouth, nothing but a breath came out. After Akio had admitted to doing this all himself, it had taken me almost an hour to really grasp that this hadn't been his family, but had been *his* doing.

"I know I can trust you," I whispered. "But ..."

"But what?"

"I'm scared."

"If you're scared about them finding out and hurting you, then I can take care of—"

My eyes burned with tears. "No, I'm not scared about that."

"Then, what is it?"

"You'll think less of me," I said. "I know you will."

He turned onto his side and cupped my face in his hand, his brows knitted together. "You know how much shit I've seen because of who my parents are? How much I had to put up with? I wouldn't even think less of you if I knew you'd killed someone."

Still …

"You don't get it."

While I knew that I shouldn't feel shame about this—because Dad had done this to me—that was all I could feel. I had never asked for this life, yet I'd accepted it because I didn't know any other way.

"I wish I were ugly. It would make everything easier," I admitted.

"Nicole," Akio scolded. Well, it wasn't so much of a scold, more like a tone change in his voice. But coming from him, it felt like a scold because he rarely raised his voice. "Who made you feel that way?"

"All the guys who've touched me," I whispered. "If I were ugly, then they wouldn't have."

"People who do stuff like that don't care what a woman looks like," he said, drawing me closer. "Don't feel ashamed over any of this because you didn't cause it. Now, please, tell me who hurt you. Just another name."

"If I tell you, you won't believe me. Nobody does."

"Yes, I will."

I curled my fingers against his chest. "No, Akio, you won't."

Even if there were a chance that he would believe me, I couldn't take it. I was just pushing, stalling, waiting for him to give up. Nobody gave a fuck about me, and Akio wouldn't one day either.

"Nicole," he said, his voice softer this time.

"Stop, Akio!" I cried, tears streaming down my face. "Please, stop."

"I just want to protect you," he whispered.

"If you knew everything that I'd done and with whom, you'd think I was nothing more than a dirty slut." I shook my head and wiped my tears with the back of my hand. "I'm disgusting and gross and not someone that *you* should want to protect."

Akio sat up, fury painted across his face. "You don't get to tell me who I should and shouldn't want to protect, Nicole. You don't get to tell me how I feel about you. I don't care how many times I have to tell you, but I love you for you. Not for what others have put you through."

My lips quivered, and I shuffled up the bed, grasping the blankets in my hands and pulling them to my chest in an attempt to shield myself from him, to protect myself. I wanted a relationship so badly, and yet I couldn't stop pushing him away.

"Do you understand me, Nicole?" Akio asked, his eyes softening. "I love you."

I stared at him for a few long moments, feeling so many emotions inside me and yet none at the same time. I thought I loved him, but I didn't even know what love felt like. I had only gotten a taste with Hannah, but that had been so long ago.

Akio grasped my face and moved closer. "I love you."

Chin trembling, I bit down on my lower lip to suppress a whimper. "If you love me, then let me tell you what has happened to me whenever I'm ready because I'm not ready now, Akio. I'm scared and nervous, and I don't want to think about all the bad things when I'm with you."

After relaxing his features, Akio swallowed and nodded. "Okay."

My eyes widened slightly because I'd expected to fight with him, just like Dad fought with me on *everything*. I hadn't expected him to give in, to show me respect—though I should've expected that from Akio.

"Really?" I whispered.

"Tell me when you're ready, but please," he pleaded, taking my hands in his and pulling them between us, "don't let that be long. Whoever is hurting you, I don't want them to get another chance at it."

AKIO

"WAS THAT GIRL IN MY HOUSE?" Mom growled a few days after Nicole had slept over.

I grabbed my keys from the front room and opened the door. "No."

"Akio! Don't you leave this fucking house. You have some explaining—"

Before she could finish her sentence, I slipped out the front door and ran to my car. I didn't want to deal with her trying to convince me to do her dirty work *again*. She had barely said a word to me all weekend, and now this?

Once I locked all my doors and started the car, I pulled out my phone to text Kai.

The one person who hated me the most in Redwood.

Me: Can we talk?

Me: It's important.

While I wanted to protect both Nicole and Imani, I didn't have time to teach Imani how to behave around my mother. And I really didn't have time to keep up with Mom's bullshit. Nicole was still hiding the truth from me, and I had a suspicion who was hurting her.

But I couldn't act on it until I knew that Kai could handle Imani and my mother.

Me: It's about Imani and my parents.

Me: Please.

A moment later, my phone buzzed.

Kai: Warehouse. In forty minutes.

Me: Which warehouse?

Kai: Guess.

After gritting my teeth together, I peeled out of the driveway and headed down the road. Darkness lay like a blanket on Redwood tonight, and I was so thankful for it. It was barely six o'clock, and everyone was already at home from school and work, the biting cold too intimidating for anyone to come out.

Once I circled Redwood like a madman for thirty minutes, not wanting to be late, I spotted a motorcycle parked behind one of the abandoned warehouses in the slums. I rolled up beside Kai's sportbike and shut off the engine.

I hopped out of the car and knocked on the back door, not knowing if he wanted me to just come in or wait out here. I glanced up to see a camera posted above the door, no doubt Poison's property.

The door swung open, and Kai stood on the other side. "I can't believe you're fucking here," Kai said through gritted teeth.

"Me neither."

"Get in before someone sees you."

With caution, I walked into the warehouse and stomped the light snow off my boots near the door. After stuffing my hands into my pockets, I walked through the spacious warehouse and stopped where there was a small puddle of blood.

No doubt Principal Vaughn's.

This must've been where they had beheaded him.

"This is where it went down, huh?" I asked myself. "Where you killed him."

Instead of answering me, Kai pressed his lips together and walked over to me, his hands suddenly reaching into my jacket, running down the seams, probably to check if I had a wire or a hidden camera on me.

When he didn't find anything, Kai stepped back and nodded. "It's where I'll kill you one day if I find out that you've touched Imani. One wrong move, one fucking finger on her body, and I'll make sure your death is far worse than Vaughn's."

I nodded and swallowed hard. "I know."

"Let's get one thing straight." Kai stepped toward me, arms crossed over his chest, and clenched his jaw. "I'm only here this one time because you saved Imani the other day. If it wasn't for you, she'd be dead."

"She would be," I said, which meant that I had some leverage on him.

"What do you want?" Kai growled.

I paced back and forth in front of him and rubbed my palms together. "You shouldn't have recorded killing Principal Vaughn. People know that you guys did it. They know, and they're going to target you."

"They would've known anyway," Kai said. "Nobody has the balls to do shit like that."

"You don't understand," I said, pushing up my glasses. "People are going to target you. And by you, I mean that they won't target *you*, but the people you all care about. Who does that leave?"

"Imani."

"Yes, Imani, and I—"

"Who is targeting her?" Kai asked.

After tightening my jaw—because he *had* to know that my mom and her posse had it out for Imani ever since that day Imani had told her off—I nodded. Kai flared his nostrils and tightened his hands into fists.

"Your parents gave you that," Kai said, nodding to my face. "Didn't they?"

I reached up and touched the slightly swollen eye that Mom had given me this afternoon because I hadn't returned one of her calls yesterday. But I didn't care. If she was preoccupied with me, then she wouldn't have time for Nicole or Imani.

"Listen … you can't tell anyone that I told you," I said, thinking about the conversation I had overheard after she sucker-punched me. "They were talking about getting rid of her and her family if things get much worse. They know you have shit on them, and they don't want to risk anything with the Feds."

Kai grabbed me by the collar. "If you find out that they plan on killing her, you tell me. I don't care how the fuck you do it. You make sure that I'm the first fucking person to find out. Do you understand me? You get me anything you can on them."

I nodded. "They don't have any plans that I know of yet, but I will let you know. I don't want Imani to get in the middle of this. All she's trying to do is get out of Redwood. If she can get through the rest of this year alive, then she'll be safe."

"Why are you fucking doing this?" Kai asked.

"Because I don't want Imani to get hurt."

"Why?"

"Because I care about her."

"Do you like her?"

"As a friend," I said. "Nothing more, Kai. I swear. I like someone else."

"Who?"

I furrowed my brow, not wanting to tell him because he had seen what I did to Pick the other day. That was his bike speeding down the roadways, and if he found out that I liked Nicole, I didn't know what would happen.

"Nobody," I said. "You don't even know—"

"Who?" Kai asked, hand behind his back, probably clutching his gun.

"Nicole," I said, turning away. "Okay? I like Nicole."

Kai scrunched his nose. "The cheerleader?"

"Yes, the cheerleader."

Suddenly, he curled his lips into a smirk and laughed. And then just as quickly as he chuckled, his expression dropped. "If you withhold any information about your parents, I'll torture Nicole in front of you." He glanced down at the blood by my feet, then back up at me. "And you know I'm not fucking around. Get me information, Akio."

Now, I was off to find Nicole.

CHAPTER
FIFTY-FOUR

NICOLE

"JUST LIKE THAT, NIKKI," Dad grunted behind me. "Arch your back."

Fuck, what is wrong with me?! Why didn't I just tell Akio?

With tears burning my eyes, I gripped on to the couch cushion and took the pain of every one of Dad's rough thrusts inside me. He smacked me hard on the ass over and over until I could almost feel the welts.

The day after I had returned from Akio's, Dad had told me that he'd found Pick—one of his lifelong friends—dead. And since that day, he hadn't let me go to cheer practice. He hadn't let me stay after school. He picked me up, brought me home, and took his anger out on me.

"Pick always told me how much he loved your pussy," Dad sneered in my ear, pounding into me hard and fast, hitting so deep that I could feel him against my cervix. I bit back a scream. "So, this is for him."

I should've told Akio when I had the chance, but the thought of him knowing about this ... made everything in me hurt so badly. I wanted someone to know, but did that someone have to be Akio? Yet if it wasn't Akio, nobody else would help me.

"Dad," I whispered.

"Shut the fuck up, bitch," he growled, lacing his hand into my hair and slamming my head down on the cushions repeatedly.

I gasped for air every single time he pulled me back up, the glue from my fake lashes loosening and the lashes falling into my eyes.

"Please," I cried whenever I could. "Stop."

"That's it." He shoved my face against the cushion and did not pull back. "Beg to live."

In a weak attempt to breathe, I opened my mouth as wide as I could, only sucking in the cushion. I flailed my arms back, the pressure making it harder and harder to breathe. I shoved back against him as hard as I could, still not getting anywhere.

"Beg me to let you live," Dad snarled. "Just like your sister did."

Tears burned my eyes as my throat closed up. I pushed one last time with everything that I had, but I still wasn't strong enough. Stars danced in my vision. When my limbs went limp at my sides, Dad pulled my head up.

Pain shot through my head, and I looked around in a daze, trying to grasp hold of my surroundings and to breathe. Dad slapped me hard across the face to wake me out of the daze he had put me in, and I blinked a couple of times.

He smacked me again, then slammed into me.

Smack. Slam. Smack. Slam. Smack. Slam.

My head fell forward. I didn't have the strength to keep it upright anymore. I placed my hands back on the couch in front of me and drew my fingers against the soft material, using it as a way to center me back in the room. I needed to find a way out of this, or he'd kill me tonight.

"Dad," I grumbled, "p-please."

Dad slipped his hands around my throat and squeezed harder every time he pounded into me. "I love hearing my girls beg for their lives. So, beg, Nikki. Beg for me." He squeezed harder. "Beg me better than your sister did."

My eyes burned, and I opened my mouth, but I couldn't physically say anything. I grasped at his wrists and dug my nails into the flesh as hard as I could, drawing blood. "P-please, s-s-s-sto-o-o-p."

"Tell me what you want to live for," he growled. "Tell me that you want to live for *me!*"

I squeezed my eyes closed and saw Akio staring down at me with those soft eyes, begging me to tell him who had hurt me so they would never hurt me again. His laugh drifted through my ears. His smile replayed in my mind.

"I want to live," I cried, but it was getting harder and harder to breathe. "But not for you."

"What?" he roared. "What the fuck did you just say?!"

Ripping my nails into the cushion, I forced my eyes open. I feared that if I closed them, then I would pass out, and if I passed out, then I didn't doubt that he would kill me tonight. I glared at the window ahead of us.

"I want to live for you," I corrected. "I want to live for you! I want to live for—"

Just as his name was about to leave my mouth, I spotted the bushes on the side of the house rustling against the window. It was subtle, and it could've just been from the snow and wind outside, but then Akio peered into the window.

My eyes widened.

"Akio ..."

FIFTY-FIVE

AKIO

IN LESS THAN A SECOND, I stood at Nicole's front door and yanked on the handle with all my might. When the door didn't budge, I slammed my shoulder into it repeatedly, shouting nearly at the top of my lungs.

My suspicions had been fucking correct. I should've come over sooner.

Adrenaline rushed through my veins as I banged even harder. Yet neither Nicole nor her father answered. So, I stepped a few feet back, found a rock the size of half a melon, and flung it through the front window.

I raced forward, but before I could get more than a couple of feet, someone clamped their hand over my mouth from behind and hurled me to the ground. My head bounced off the pavement, and suddenly, a bag was forcefully pulled over my head, plunging me into darkness.

Another pair of hands restrained my arms, tying them behind my back. I kicked upward, trying to make contact with someone, but I was unsuccessful. Nicole raced through my mind, and I did everything I could to try to get away, to rescue her.

The scent of dirty, old fabric filled my nostrils as the rough material scratched against my face. I knocked my shoulder back, hitting someone hard in what felt like the chin. Images of Nicole's tear-streaked face only pushed me harder.

With a jolt, the world around me shifted, and someone hoisted me upward, the bag still obscuring my vision and becoming tighter by the moment. I jerked my arms and legs as hard as I could.

But whoever this was … they were much stronger than I was. And I didn't have a weapon to defend myself. I honestly hadn't thought that I would need one. All I knew was that I wasn't going down without a fight, and whoever was dragging me hadn't wanted me to walk in on the police chief raping his daughter.

For a moment, the man's grip on my arm loosened. With a burst of desperation, I twisted and writhed, my muscles straining and aching. However, his grip tightened on me. Fury raged through me, and I did what I could. Which wasn't enough.

The man punched me in the ribs, cracking them in three different places. I cried out in pain and sucked in a breath, but there wasn't any more oxygen in the small, tight bag around my head. Stars danced in my vision.

Finally, he stopped, and my throbbing body collided with the cold sensation of metal. A door was opened, and suddenly, I was thrown into what felt like a trunk. Ropes bit into my wrists, the tight bindings so painful.

The trunk lid slammed shut, and then a moment later, the car started.

Breathing shallowly, I tried squirming out of the bag placed around my head. But the more I moved, the tighter it became. My chest tightened, and my eyes filled with hot tears because I couldn't save her.

I couldn't fucking save her.

Her father had been abusing her all this time, and I hadn't put it together until now.

Why couldn't I see it before? What was wrong with me?

Seconds felt like minutes and minutes like hours. I screamed and kicked and jerked my body in every direction in a mere attempt to get the hell out of here. But it was no use. Every bit of energy I used up only made me dizzier.

When the engine turned off, I calmed myself down and tried to come up with a plan of escape. Using my energy like this was pointless. I couldn't get out of these binds and could barely breathe. At this rate, I wouldn't be able to think.

After a moment, the trunk opened. A gust of frigid air rushed through me, and strong hands yanked me out of the car. With a heavy thud, I slammed down onto a solid surface. The air carried a distinct salty tang, and the rhythmic crashing of waves drifted through my ears.

I was by the beach.

And I only knew one gang in town that had a place down by the beach …

Someone grabbed my shoulders, and another man grabbed my feet. They carried me up some steps, then into a building much warmer. My fingers twitched, and I couldn't stop thinking about Nicole looking so helpless.

Once we made it into a room, they hurled me onto a chair. My body missed it almost entirely, and I smacked hard against the ground. Then, in a jarring movement, the bag was ripped off my head. I forced my stinging eyes open.

Standing before me was the bitch herself.

Mom.

CHAPTER
FIFTY-SIX

NICOLE

I DIDN'T KNOW what burned more—my eyes or my pussy.

Whimpering to myself and feeling undeniable shame, I stood in front of Akio's door and lifted my hand to knock. I had been standing here for ten minutes, and yet I couldn't get myself to do it. My worst fear had come true.

Akio had seen my father rape me, and he hadn't done anything about it.

In fact, he had been so pissed off at me that he … threw a rock through the front window.

"I'm sorry, Akio," I mumbled to myself and repeated my apology, tears burning my eyes. "I'm sorry. I should've told you sooner. You should've never found out this way. Please forgive me. I … I don't have anyone else."

Summoning all my courage, I knocked on his door. The sound echoed through the night, my heart pounding inside my chest. I bounced on my toes and wrapped my arms around myself to try and stop the nerves.

"I'm sorry, Akio. I'm sorry. I'm sorry. I'm sorry. I'm sorry."

Seconds stretched on and on and on with no response. My

heart sank, but I was determined to beg for his forgiveness, to show him that I … just wanted to be that normal girl he had hung out with all night, that I wasn't just a whore like everyone thought I was.

So, I knocked again.

My heart pounded in my ears, my thoughts racing. What did Akio think about me? Did he find me disgusting? Gross? Just another slut?

Doubts clawed at my insides. What was I doing here? It wasn't like he actually wanted to see me. If he had wanted to see me or to stop it, he would've done to Dad what he had done to Pick. My fingers trembled as I debated my next move—knock again or go back home to Dad. Neither sounded like something I wanted to do.

Should I leave a note, maybe text him?

A gust of wind rustled the leaves in the trees. I tightened my hands into fists. I couldn't leave without knowing that he was okay. I wanted to at least apologize.

Just as I peered through the window, the door opened.

But instead of Akio, an older man with a stern expression etched into his face stood before me. He narrowed his pointed gaze, eyeing my disheveled appearance. "You're that girl that my wife was telling me about, aren't you?"

"What?" I asked breathlessly. "No, I'm here to see Akio. I-is he home?"

"What do you want with my son?" he asked.

"We're, um, working on a science project together."

A low, gruff laugh escaped his throat. "A science project, huh? He should be working with Imani Abara, a smart girl, and not someone like you. You're the police chief's daughter, aren't you?" Another empty chuckle. "You have nothing to bring to our table."

I opened and closed my mouth a handful of times, a mix of hurt and anger swirling within me. I knew that I wasn't as smart as Imani, but I … I didn't have much time to try. But of course, like he'd said, I had nothing to give Akio.

That was apparent.

"Please," I whispered. "I just need to see him."

He scoffed. "Get lost and don't bother my son again."

Tears welled in my eyes. "But I love him."

I hadn't said those words out loud in front of anyone but Akio himself. And yet, I couldn't stop those words from leaving my mouth because I so badly wanted to fight for love and for us— even though I knew Akio probably didn't want me like that anymore.

I was willing to do anything to keep him.

Anything.

"Love?" he spit. "My son doesn't love you. Now, leave before I call the police."

Not wanting to face Dad or any other of his buddies tonight, I turned on my heel and walked back to my car. My eyes blurred with unshed tears, my feet heavy. I yanked the door open and fumbled with my keys.

After sliding into the driver's seat, I gripped the steering wheel and stared blankly ahead. I wanted to be numb like I had been for years. I didn't want to think about what had happened or about what could happen. It was easier that way.

When I closed my eyes and took a deep breath, Hannah drifted through my mind. All this time, I'd wanted to make her proud. How could I make her proud and get out of this situation if I did nothing to leave? How could I make her proud if I lived in fear?

I picked my phone up from the passenger seat and stared down at my Contacts. My fingers hesitated over the screen, my heart pounding inside my chest when I clicked the Call button. The phone rang once, then twice, and then João answered.

"Who is this?" he growled. "I'm busy."

"João, it's Nicole," I whispered. "Please don't hang up. I have information that you want."

CHAPTER
FIFTY-SEVEN

NICOLE

WHEN I PULLED up to Landon's house in the slums, I could hear my heart pounding in my ears. Maybe this wasn't the best idea, but I didn't know who else to go to. If I wanted to prove to not only Akio, but Hannah, that I wanted out, then I needed to do this.

I blew out a breath and exited the car, pushing some tears off my cheeks.

The door's slam echoed through the slums, and I walked on the dirt driveway to the door I had entered the other day with Allie and Imani. A couple of other cars were parked on the road in front of the house, which meant that more than Poison was here tonight.

Could I tell my secrets to everyone who hated me?

After gathering the courage, I opened the door and walked down the stairs. When I reached the bottom step, the entire room —Jace, Allie, Imani, and Poison—collectively rolled their eyes. I dropped my gaze to my feet, guilt rushing through me.

They all hated me.

"Hey, guys," I whispered, trying to muster up all the confidence that I had left. I lifted my gaze and met the confused stare of some other girl with red hair that I didn't even think Poison hung out with, feeling just as confused. "Weird that you're here, but ..." *Fuck, can I do this with just random Redwood students here?* "Okay ..."

Nobody said a word, so I took off my shoes at the door and walked to the couch, where the only free spot was next to Jace. Allie pulled him closer to her so we weren't touching—which we hadn't been anyway—and clenched her jaw.

"You said you had information," she said. "Tell us or get out."

My eyes widened slightly, the nerves piling up. I hoped that they believed me.

Jace placed a hand on Allie's knee and squeezed. "We'll leave soon, baby. Settle down."

Tears watered in my eyes, and I straightened myself out. "About my father ..." My throat began closing, but I forced myself to continue. "This can't ... nobody can know that this information came from me. Please, if you can make it look like you got it some other way, please do it. I don't want my father to be angry with me. I want him put away."

If I thought the room had been silent before, nobody even sucked in a breath now.

"He's using the cheer team to do his dirty work," I started because I couldn't lead with ...

He rapes me.

Landon rolled his eyes. "God, why is it always the cheer team in the drama?"

I pressed my lips together, feeling a flood of tears about to burst through. Nobody would believe me. They just thought it was all some drama that I'd caused because what the hell else would Nicole do, huh?

"I'm being serious," I said, voice cracking. "He found out that Principal Vaughn had been taping people in the locker rooms. It started with the cheer squad. He let it slide as long as he was able to take some of the film of the girls. He's been using it against us and blackmailing us into getting information about people in Redwood for him, threatening to leak the tapes and ruin our lives if we don't."

Jace shifted next to me, an unreadable expression on his face.

He and I'd had a fling—nothing too deep—at the beginning of the school year, and he had walked in on me with his arch-nemesis.

"That's why I slept with Carter," I said. "I never loved you. I just … my father wanted me to get information out of you. I knew it was wrong. I fucking knew it."

"What?" Jace asked. "He's doing that?"

I wiped tears from my cheeks with a shaky hand. "That's not all. He's roped some of the girls into a sex ring, and he was helping pimp them out at one point. He's doing it all for the money. He's so … so greedy. He doesn't care."

A sob escaped my mouth, and I held myself tighter.

"I-I-I'm one of those girls," I said, a complete and utter mess of tears and snot. "He used me, forced me to have sex with men sixty years older than me. Just to get a quick few bucks. I'm sorry for everything I've done. I'm so sorry."

I collapsed onto someone's lap, but my eyes were so blurry that I could barely see straight anymore. All I could feel was pain and relief. They wouldn't believe me—hell, they didn't even know the extent of it—but I was so relieved that I wasn't living this alone.

So relieved that others knew about it.

"Prove it," Landon said, waving me off and lighting up a cigarette. "Why should we believe you? All you have done is lie for and protect your father for the past few years. Why tell us now?"

After sitting up, I wiped my eyes. "Because … because I know that you can do something about it now. I know that you can put him away for years, if you … if you want to. And I'm begging you to do something. If you don't, I'll be stuck here for the rest of my life."

A few silent moments passed, and the dread returned.

I stood. "You don't believe me, do you?"

Instead of responding to me, João looked at Kai, who shrugged. "I didn't find any of that footage when we went through the principal's computer, but he could've stashed it elsewhere. I don't know. She could be lying, or she could be telling us the truth about her father. We know he's a prick."

João shared a look with Landon, then looked at me and nodded to the door. "Get out."

My chest tightened, and my feet stayed glued to the spot.

I want to die.

That was the first and only thought that crossed my mind at that moment.

People knew, but nobody believed me. Nobody cared. Not even Akio.

Allie's eyes widened. "You're going to make her leave? After what she told you?"

"She can't prove this. We have nothing to go off of and nothing to hurt her father with," João said, glancing back at me. "You bring me all the shit you can find to prove to me that you're not lying, and we'll help you out. If you can't, then you're stuck."

I shook my head. "But I-I—what am I supposed to get? How am I supposed to give it to you? What kind of evidence do you need? He doesn't let me into his office, and he somehow always knows if I try to sneak in there or not. I can't get you anything." I rubbed the back of my neck and stared at the ground through wide eyes. "Please, you have to believe me."

João sighed heavily through his mouth and stood, grabbing me by the arm and dragging me to the door. "I told you that I want you out," he said through clenched teeth. "Come back when you have something that we can use."

As he dragged me to the stairs, I looked back at Jace and Allie.

"You have to believe me. Please, Allie, please. You're the only one who does. I can see it. Don't let them—"

Before I could finish, João shoved me out and slammed the door in my face.

I was all alone. Truly alone.

CHAPTER
FIFTY-EIGHT

AKIO

SOMEONE SLAMMED their foot into my ribs. "Get up."

My body twisted into a ball, and I blinked my eyes open. Two guards stood at the door, never once taking their eyes off me. I whined softly to myself, the concrete ground hard and cold. I didn't know how many days it had been, but I had definitely missed school.

Another guard—the one who must've kicked me in the ribs—grabbed me by the biceps and pulled me to a standing position. He yanked out a chair and sat me down on it, hooking my bound hands to the back of the seat and my ankles to the chair legs.

The salty air hung heavily around the room as a faint flash of the light bulb flickered above. In front of me, the door opened, and Mom sauntered into the room, wiping blood off her fingers, her eyes set in a menacing glare.

"You're awake," she said flatly.

"Why are you doing this?" I growled. "Let me out."

Her features seemed even sharper under the shadow of the light. She hadn't returned to see me in days, and I felt like this was my only chance to convince her to let me go. I didn't have any other option.

"Dear Akio ..." she started. "We wouldn't be here if you had been a good son."

"I've done everything you've ever wanted."

"Not without pushback," she growled. "*Never* without pushback."

"That's not true."

"Oh, I'm sorry," Mom said, stopping right in front of me. "You only don't push back if the job I give you will benefit *you* or Nicole."

When Nicole's name left her mouth, my body jerked forward, and the binds seemed to tighten around my wrists and ankles. Why was she throwing Nicole's name around like it was nothing? Why had she stopped me from killing Nicole's father when I had the chance?!

"There it is ..." A smile twisted her lips. "You love her, don't you?"

I gritted my teeth and glared at her. "Let me out."

"My sweet boy," she taunted. "If you had only found out about Nicole and her father sooner ..."

My stomach dropped. "You knew about what he was doing to her?"

"Knew about it?" Mom chuckled dryly. "Our family runs this whole town."

Seconds suddenly felt like hours as the reality of her words set in. She'd had a hand in the sex trafficking ring happening with Principal Vaughn. And worst of all ... Mom had known that Nicole's father had been raping her this entire time.

Mind whirling, I sank my nails into my palms. "I'm going to kill you. I'm going to fucking—"

"Come on, Akio," Mom said with a smirk. "I thought you were smart."

"How fucking long have you known?!" I shouted, jerking the chair back and forth in an attempt to break free. "How long have you known he rapes her?! What have you done this all for? For power? Control?! Let me fucking out so I can kill you!"

She stepped closer to me, her moves deliberate and calculated. "He's touched her since she was five years old, maybe younger. Her sister, Hannah, too—that is, until he killed her. The feeble are trampled in this town, and Nicole's father has a weak spot for her, which leaves us as the strong—"

My body moved on its own. Shaking. Trembling. Pushing. Shoving. I hobbled in the chair, trying to get closer to her, trying to break free, trying to get my hands around her throat and kill her. She didn't deserve an easy death.

I would make her fucking pay!

Mom reached out her hand toward my face, and I bit her pinkie clean off her body. She shrieked and pulled her hand back, slapping me straight across the face with her unwounded hand. Then, she kicked me in the balls.

"Akio, I'm giving you one last choice. Join me and save her."

"Save her?!" I scoffed, spitting out her finger. My heart pounded so loudly that I could hear it in my ears. I tasted her blood on my tongue, and I rejoiced in it. "As if you would save her after what you've done!"

"Join me, Akio," Mom said again, the darkness within her words sending shivers down my spine. "It's the only way you'll survive tonight. The only way Nicole here might have a chance."

Here? What the hell did she mean … here?!

"Let me out!" I roared.

If she had Nicole here … then I had no doubt in my mind that she'd kill her tonight.

"Oh, my dear boy, don't you see? There's no going back now. You either stand by my side"—her smirk widened, and she let out a menacing cackle—"or I have the most joyous of surprises for you. I think you'll love it!"

My throat closed up, and I balled my hands into tight fists because I couldn't do anything. I … I tried and I tried and I tried, and I couldn't fucking do anything. Tears burned my eyes. I needed to get the fuck out of here.

"Please," I tried to reason, "you don't have to do anything to anyone."

"Yes, I do." Mom straightened her shoulders. "There's no other way to win in Redwood."

The door creaked open, and cries echoed through the room from the hallway. My entire body stiffened, bile rising in my throat. Someone dragged a girl down the hallway toward our room. And it wasn't just any girl.

It was *my* girl.

NICOLE

"DAD, PLEASE," I cried, trying to shuffle to my feet.

He gripped my hair tighter and continued to drag me across a hard and cold concrete floor. I kicked my legs to stay upright so his grip on my hair wouldn't fucking rip out every last strand that I had. But with my hands tied behind my back and my eyes blindfolded, I had trouble doing much else.

"I'm going to fucking kill you!" a man shouted inside the room. "Don't touch her!"

When Dad dropped me, I landed with a thud on my side. I moved back and forth in an attempt to roll onto my stomach and push myself up to my knees, but a weight was suddenly pressed against the backs of my thighs, forcing me still.

Since the night Akio had found out about what Dad did to me, the abuse had only become harsher. And I just took it because I couldn't find it in me to fight against him any longer. Akio hadn't come to save me, like I'd hoped he would.

But I had a bad feeling that something was wrong because … he hadn't been in school.

Hands traveled up my sides to my bra. Dad yanked it down

and made my breasts spill out of them. Usually, Dad stayed home and let his buddies have a go at me, but tonight was different, and I tried my hardest not to fear why he had blindfolded me.

"She's pretty, isn't she?" Dad said. "I spent a lot of money to make her look this way."

My lips trembled, but I kept them closed.

"Let her out!" the man roared again. "Don't you fucking touch her!"

The voice sounded so familiar, almost like Akio, but since that night, everyone sounded like him to me. It was my imagination playing tricks on me, taunting and tormenting me for falling in love with him when my life was doomed to end in one way.

Death.

"Nicole!" the man said again, this time softer. "Nicole, I'm here. I'm sorry. I'm sorry."

"You're a fool, Akio," a woman said.

My chest tightened, and I lifted my head a few inches off the ground as Dad slipped his hand into my panties. I couldn't see through the blindfold, but … but he … was this really him? Was he here?

I inhaled sharply, smelling the salty air, and moved my head from side to side, trying to find him through the faintest of black outlines. A tear slipped down my cheek, and I dropped my head again, not wanting him to see me like this.

He probably hates me.

"Nicole," Akio shouted, "it's me."

"Akio," I whispered.

Dad punched me straight in the jaw. "Shut the fuck up. You're hearing things."

Lips trembling, I tasted blood and lifted my head in the direction of Akio's voice again. I didn't know what or who to believe. If Akio was really here, why would he sound so soft, so heartbroken? Why wouldn't he be mad at me?

"I'm going to fucking kill you," Akio sneered. "Don't touch her!"

Dad wrapped one arm around the front of my throat and lifted my body off the ground, enough for him to finger my cunt for whoever the hell was in the room for us. Inhuman sounds—those I had only heard a hero make in anime—echoed throughout the room.

"Akio," I whispered, desperate for it to be him, "I'm sorry."

"There's nothing for you to apologize for," Akio said.

A sob escaped my mouth. "I'm sorry. I'm sorry. I'm so sorry." Sorry that I hadn't told him sooner. Sorry that he had seen what he saw. Sorry that I'd ever gotten involved with him. He deserved so much more than me. "I'm sor—"

Dad hit me harder this time.

Stars danced in my dark vision, and I blinked my eyes a few times, my blindfold loosening around my head. My arms slackened as the pain shot through me and more blood pooled in my mouth.

"Shut the fuck up, Nicole," Dad spit. "You're delusional."

"If you're going to kill me, just kill me!" I screamed, finally letting it all out. I had pleaded for him to spare my life, and yet all this time, I had wanted it to end. "Please! I can't take this anymore! Kill me. Kill me. Kill me! Please!"

Snot and spit and tears covered my face and ran down my neck. Dad slammed into me repeatedly as more screams and shouts echoed throughout the room. I didn't know what to believe anymore, and I just wanted it all to end.

I wanted peace.

I wanted Hannah.

"Please," I sobbed. "I want to see Hannah again. Please, let me see her." My lips trembled, and I cried harder than I ever had. "I miss her more than anyone. Nobody believes me. Nobody loves me. Please, just fucking do it, Dad. Please …"

"No!" Akio shrieked. "Don't touch her!"

"Join me, Akio," a woman said. "And I can stop this."

Dad grabbed me by the back of my head and ripped back my hair again, the blindfold slipping off my eyes and falling around my neck. Blinding light pierced through the darkness and stung my eyes. Blinking quickly, I struggled to adjust my eyes. And when I did, the scene before me sharpened into focus.

Akio sat across from me, bound to a chair, both eyes swollen and bruises covering his body. He jerked his body against the chair and the binds, desperately trying to escape, his gaze only on me.

My eyes softened, and I wanted to take it all back.

"Get off her!" Akio screeched. "I'll do whatever you want!"

Dad slammed my head against the concrete once, and pain shot through my nose. I stared up at Akio, refusing to take my eyes off him because I feared that if I did, then I would … I would lose him forever. He slammed my face into the ground again, and sound faded around me. When my face collided with the ground a third time, Akio disappeared from my vision.

If I made it out of here alive by some miracle, all I knew was that I needed to do everything in my power to help Akio escape too. I didn't care what it took. They had been holding Akio here against his will, just like Dad had held me.

And while I didn't have the strength to escape Dad's wrath, I could try to help Akio.

CHAPTER
SIXTY

AFTER TAKING a deep breath of Redwood Academy halls, I tightened my grip on my purse and walked into the cafeteria. Students shouted and yelled, the sounds making my ears hurt because they reminded me of Akio's screams.

My face hurt badly, and a huge bump from last weekend was still prominent on my head from when Dad had continued to bash my face into the ground. It all felt like a dream—like a nightmare. I barely remembered where I had been or what had happened.

But I remembered the salty air. We must have been down by the beach.

I glanced over at the table where the cheerleaders sat—my go-to table—then spotted Allie, Imani, and Poison sitting at their usual table. Since Principal Vaughn had died, the cheerleaders had been giving me the cold shoulder, way more than usual.

Allie offered a soft smile and waved me over, patting the seat beside her.

The past week had both dragged on and blown by in a flash. Allie had actually invited me to hang out after listening to my story, but I barely remember what we had done. All I could think about was saving Akio.

But because nobody believed me, I had to pretend like everything was fine … when all I wanted to do was sob.

Nerves zipped up and down my arms, but I pushed forward and headed toward their table. I wanted—needed—them to believe me. This was my last chance, my only hope. If they didn't believe the video evidence that I had of Dad and Pick raping me … I'd lose.

I'd lose fucking everything, even Akio, because I didn't have the money to pay Kai to help me rescue Akio. I would have to try to do that all myself, but Dad had barely let me out of his sight lately.

"Hey," I said softly, sitting down on the bench.

"What are you doing here?" Jamal, a football player who was Jace's best friend, said.

Again, Allie gave me a smile, and I faintly remembered going to Imani's house this past weekend to get my makeup done. It was all too blurry to determine if that was actually what we had done. Why else would she be so nice to me?

"I'm sitting with my"—I didn't have any friends, but I desperately needed them—"friends." The word came out as a whisper, and I didn't know if Allie would ever consider me a friend. I swung my backpack onto my lap and fished around inside it. "I have something that might help prove myself to you."

Allie leaned closer to me. "You don't have to. They believe you."

But it didn't seem like they did. Had spending time with her … changed their minds?

"I spent all night trying to find it on my father's computer. I'm not going to let all my hard work go to waste. I just … I need a place to crash for a couple of nights. As soon as my dad gets home from work tonight, he's going to know that I went in there."

Everyone stayed quiet, and I pleaded with Hannah—if she was watching down on me—to convince *someone* to offer up a place to stay. Allie and Jace's place was off-limits because he had a crazy father, too, but … I just needed to get away from Dad.

And hide.

"You can stay at my place, but what's on the flash drive? Why do you need it?" Jamal asked.

"It's"—my stomach twisted into knots—"a video of my father and me." I handed the flash drive to Kai. "If you can't find anything incriminating on my father, use this. I want this to be over as quickly as possible. I don't want any of you guys getting hurt anymore."

After pulling out his computer, he stuffed the flash drive into the USB port. The screen reflected off his glasses as his eyes widened, and he almost immediately snapped the computer closed and looked around the cafeteria. "You're not fucking with us."

Tears welled up in my eyes, but I stayed strong for Akio. It was our only chance.

"Please, use that. I don't want any of the other girls to have a video of them leaked or … something worse. If you can incriminate him with this, then do what you need to."

Kai leaned closer. "Nicole, this is a video of your father mol—"

"I know it is," I snapped. "It fucking happened to me. I don't need to relive it. Do what you have to do with it and fucking destroy that fucking bastard, so he doesn't hurt anyone else like he has me."

Everyone at the table stayed silent, and suddenly, Allie rubbed my shoulder. Tears slipped down my cheeks, but I quickly pushed them away. I couldn't cry right now. I had cried for so many nights, so many weeks.

I was tired of being weak. Akio needed me.

Allie rested her head on my shoulder. "Thank you, Nicole. You don't know how much we needed this right now. Jace and I are in your debt."

I didn't know why, nor could I find it in me to ask.

"No, you're not," I said. "I did this so nobody else will get hurt or used by the Redwood Police or disgusting old teachers who have nothing else to do than jerk off to underage students."

Another few moments passed by, and more students—friends of Allie and Imani—dropped by the table. I shifted uncomfortably and leaned toward Kai, who stared down at his closed laptop, concerned.

"Can I talk to you privately?" I whispered.

João and Landon peered at each other, but Kai stood without giving them a second glance. His jaw was clenched, and he slipped off the bench. I set down my backpack and followed him out of the cafeteria and down a hallway.

"Where's Akio?" he asked before I could say a word. "He never misses school."

"Please, help me," I whispered, my voice cracking and lips trembling. "They have him."

"Who?"

"His mother has Akio down by the beach," I said, my shoulders bucking forward. I wrapped my arms around myself. "I ... I don't know what they're doing to him, but my dad took me down there, and they forced Akio to watch him rape me."

Kai sucked in a breath. "Fuck."

"I don't have any money to give you, but I have no one else to ask." Tears burst from my eyes, and a sob left my mouth. "I don't want to beg, but I will. I can't do it myself. There are too many of them, and I ... my father has hurt me really badly. I ... I can't ... I ..."

"We'll help."

"Please, I ..." My eyes widened. "What?"

"We'll help," Kai said. "I don't like Akio, but we owe him."

"How do you owe him?" I asked. "What did he—"

"Don't worry about it, Nicole," Kai said. "All I need is information, and I'll bring him home to you. Deal?"

My chest tightened. "Deal."

CHAPTER
SIXTY-ONE

SEAGULLS CAWING WOKE me from the heavy sleep that Mom's guard had put me in last night. After hours of me trying to break free, he had straight-up socked me in the jaw, and I had passed out cold.

I slowly opened my eyes, ready for another day of trying to claw out of these ropes. The room reeked of my shit and piss from the small bathroom to our right. It had one toilet that didn't flush, just like the rest of the toilets at the public beach. The smell just stewed there.

Blood soaked through my shirt and clung to my body. I winced and bit down on my lower lip so I wouldn't let them know that I was up. Pain shot through my body from my raw wrists. My vision blurred for a moment, but I was freshly awake.

Mom had *never* held me hostage for this long, even after I had told her that I would work with her, that I would be her fucking servant as long as she didn't hurt Nicole again. I would do anything that she fucking asked.

The ropes chafed my wrists, the skin red and scabbed. I struggled against the ropes for what seemed to be the fifth day or more.

My body was weak, but I would get out of here alive to see Nicole. Soon.

A clang rattled through the building, alerting the guards. I lifted my head slightly to the door, hearing the sound again. It almost sounded like … gunshots echoing through the building. My heart pounded heavily inside my chest.

Gunshots drew closer and closer. One of the guards in the room slipped through the door, gun drawn, and shut it behind him. I clawed at the rope harder in an attempt to break free while they were distracted, my wrists burning.

Suddenly, the doors burst open, revealing a figure dressed in all black and a ski mask to hide his face. My gaze dropped to his cargo pants and combat boots—staples of Kai Koh's wardrobe.

Without hesitation, Kai moved like a snake, his movements swift and deadly. He closed the distance between himself and the guard stationed at the door, wrapped his hands around the man's head, and snapped his neck.

In seconds.

The guard dropped to the ground with a thud. My eyes widened, and I watched in disbelief that Kai, out of all people, was here to save me. He hated my fucking guts and had no reason to help me.

Why is he here?

Another guard ran into the room, gun raised. Kai knocked the weapon from his hand with a swift kick and hurled his fist into the man's throat, sending him to the ground. After reaching behind himself and drawing his gun, Kai shot three bullets into his skull.

"Say a fucking word, and I'll kill you too," Kai said to me.

Once he tucked his gun away, he drew a knife from his belt and crouched behind me. He began slicing through the thick rope, the threads snapping. I stayed still because the pain from my raw wrists was becoming overwhelming.

The restraints fell away, and then he cut the ropes around my ankles. Relief flooded through me, and I slumped my shoulders forward, so exhausted from the past five days—or more. This room didn't have any windows, so I couldn't tell night from day or day from night.

I gently rubbed my wrists and winced. I needed medication from the pharmacy for them.

Kai remained focused, scanning the room and then the hallway for any sign of danger. And when he didn't find any, he nodded for me to follow him. I stood on shaky legs, clutching my stomach wounds, and stepped over the guards.

"Let's go," Kai ordered in a hushed tone.

Wincing, I followed him and stumbled into the wall to catch myself before I face-planted in the middle of the hallway. Kai pulled off his ski mask, his hair wild underneath it, and bit it into his mouth. He wrapped his arm underneath mine and lifted me.

"Damn, you're skinny as fuck, Akio," Kai said, his words muffled. "Lighter than I expected."

After biting down on my cheek so I wouldn't grunt in pain in front of him, I stumbled down the hallway with his help and walked through the doors to get the fuck out of this place for good. We moved in silence to a car that definitely *wasn't* Kai's bike.

Though I was far from safe with Kai, at least … I was out of here.

Now, I needed to find Nicole.

CHAPTER
SIXTY-TWO

AKIO

FORTY MINUTES LATER, I sat in a surveillance room with at least twenty screens, monitoring Redwood. Kai stabbed a needle into my abdomen to stitch up my wound, and I bit back a grunt of pain because I had been through worse stuff this past week.

While Kai's place was located in the center of the slums and his windows were smashed in on the first and second floors, the basement floor was built up with more technology than I had ever seen.

Multiple complicated locks. A computer room. I'd even seen a gun range when I was walking into the room. Based on the location and the look of the house, I didn't think anyone would suspect such secrets would lie underneath this place.

"Why are you doing this?" I hissed through gritted teeth as my wound stung.

"Shut the fuck up, Akio, and don't ask questions."

After letting out a low breath, I relaxed against the chair and closed my eyes. Nicole fluttered through my mind, and I really fucking hoped that she wasn't back with her father. I hoped that she had gotten out.

But that night, her dad had made her feel like she was crazy, like she was seeing things, like her reality wasn't real. Talk about being a fucking gaslighting asshole. I gritted my teeth as Kai took my arm.

He placed down the needle and picked up some cream, squirting a bunch on my scabs. When he snapped the container closed, I rubbed it against my raw wrists and forced myself to breathe or else I'd pass out from the pain.

"Is everyone safe?" I asked, mainly worried about Nicole.

"Yes."

"Even—"

"Yes, Nicole is safe."

After cleaning up the table, Kai stood and motioned for me to follow. I stood on shaky legs and hobbled after him, down a short hallway and to a spare room in the very back of the finished basement.

It was small and only had a bed, but it would do. There was no way in fucking hell that I would go back to Mom's place now. Not for a while. I didn't know if Kai would let me crash at his place for long, but I wasn't going to ask.

"You need anything, you get it yourself," Kai said. "I'm busy with shit."

"Sounds good. Where is the kitchen and bathroom?"

"Find it yourself, but don't get into my sh—"

Someone knocked on the basement door, and Kai stiffened. With his gun drawn, he stormed out into the hallway and to the door. It was a maze, just trying to find the door. It had to be Poison, right?

I sat down on the bed and lay back, closing my eyes as I listened to the door open.

"Where is he?" a familiar voice asked frantically.

Then, I heard a pair of heels clanking down the hallway toward my room. I lifted my head off the pillow and stared at the door. A moment later, Nicole appeared, her hair thrown up in a messy bun, an oversize sweatshirt hanging off her shoulders, and two different heels on her feet. She dropped her purse and sprinted to the bed.

"Thank God!" she cried, falling to her knees by the bedside. She grabbed my hand and dropped her head, unable to look at me. "Akio, I'm so sorry. I'm sorry. I ... I never wanted you to see what you did. I'm sorry. I didn't ... I wasn't sure ..."

Biting back the pain, I tugged on her wrists and tried to pull her up onto the bed with me. She lifted her head, tears running down her cheeks, and sobbed even harder, taking in all my wounds.

"You ... I ..." She opened and closed her mouth a handful of times, never speaking another word.

"Come up here," I whispered.

Her chin quivered, yet she crawled up into the bed with me. I gently cupped her face and swiped my thumbs across her cheeks to wipe away the tears.

"Nicole, it's not your fault. Stop apologizing."

"But my father—"

"He rapes you, Nicole," I said. "You should never apologize for that. You didn't—"

"If I wasn't as pre—"

"Stop," I growled, biting back a hiss of pain. "Don't apologize again for this."

Tears wavered in her eyes. "B-but—"

"Promise me," I said, pulling her face closer. "Promise you won't apologize for him. Promise me that you'll start loving yourself. And most of all, promise me that you'll never say that you want to die again."

Her entire body tensed, and she burst out into another fit of tears and sobs.

"I don't want to die," she cried. "I want to be with you. I want to be normal."

I pulled her down onto my chest and held her tightly. "Then, be normal with me, Nicole ..."

I lied and promised her a life that we would never have, a life we *could* never have because of who our parents were. But I would do anything to give her the world, to fulfill her wishes, to love her the way she needed to be loved.

SIXTY-THREE

AKIO

AFTER MY FIRST day back at Redwood, I clasped my hands around my backpack straps and headed to my car. Nicole was staying with Jamal Simmons for a short period of time to hide from her father, which pissed me off because I wanted to protect her.

But it had been obvious that I couldn't do that. I balled my hands into fists. And I hated it.

As I walked to the car, Imani whizzed by me. I lifted my head a couple of inches to look over my shoulder and spotted Kai watching her drive off. He glanced my way, and I cursed under my breath.

He might've helped me escape the other day, but he still had it out for me. Nicole had convinced him to help me, only because I had saved Imani a few weeks ago while down by the beach. That had to be the reason.

Kai walked my way. "Did you find any information on your parents?"

"No," I said, stuffing my hands into my pockets. "Nothing yet."

While he had wanted as much information on them so Poison could finally pluck them from their Redwood throne, I'd honestly wanted to be as far away from them as possible these past few days. Nicole wasn't the only one hiding out. I had been cooped up in Kai's basement for as long as I could.

"Your father showed up while we were out shopping yesterday," Kai said.

"He did?"

Kai grabbed me by the collar and slammed me against my car. "Don't fuck with me."

"I'm not," I said, holding up my hands. "I swear, I didn't know. I don't know anything about what they do. I've been trying to find something without them being suspicious. I've never wanted to be part of the family."

He knew that.

"After Nicole left the other night, we made a deal," he hissed. "You promised me that you'd get information for a place to stay."

"I will," I said, pushing on his hands. "I promise, I will."

Because now, I owed Kai. Not just for saving me, but for protecting Nicole.

"What do you know about Nicole?" Kai asked.

"What do you mean?" I asked, furrowing my brow and attempting to look confused.

Nicole hadn't wanted me to know about what her father or the rest of those disgusting men did to her. She really wouldn't tell anyone else about it.

"Nicole—the girl you have a crush on, head of the cheerleading squad. That Nicole," Kai said. "Your parents work closely with the police, don't they? Nicole told Poison a few days ago that they're using her."

"What?" I whispered. "What do you mean, they're using her? For what? Information?"

Nicole wouldn't have told them, right? She wanted it to be a secret.

"Information and," Kai said, watching me carefully, "sex."

I mouthed the word *sex*, repeating it to myself and coming to the conclusion that Nicole hadn't just asked Poison to help me escape. She must have told them everything in order for them to actually do something about it.

While Poison might've been one of the most feared gangs in Redwood, they weren't heartless. They just wanted to clean up this town and get out of this shithole. If they were given proof that sex trafficking was happening, then … they'd stop it.

"She told us that her father is forcing her to sleep with everyone in town so he can get info on them to use for blackmail," Kai said. "Doesn't that sound like something your parents would be a part of?"

I clenched my hands tightly by my sides, wanting to fucking kill them even more now.

"You didn't know?" Kai asked, slowly releasing me.

Rage rattled through me, and I gritted my teeth.

Oh, I knew. I fucking watched it!

Part of me wanted to rest, to formulate a plan of action before wildly rushing back home to get my shit kicked in. But I couldn't see straight. All those memories of the other night flashed through me. Nicole had been sobbing, apologizing for being raped to me.

To fucking me!

"I have to go," I said, yanking open my car door and collapsing into the driver's seat.

After slamming the door and starting the car, I hit the accelerator and sped out of the parking lot. I didn't know what I was going to do, but I couldn't sit back anymore.

I was done resting.

Nicole deserved to have justice. And if I had to kill all of them, then I would.

CHAPTER
SIXTY-FOUR

AKIO

MY FOOT COLLIDED with an officer's chest, and I slammed him to the ground. I stood in the middle of a one-story home in the slums, its windows smashed in, heart pounding inside my chest.

After my *talk* with Kai the other night, I had been able to keep my cool enough to stop myself from blindly starting a war in Redwood with my family and the police force. I couldn't win that alone, but I could kill them all off, one by one.

The ones who'd hurt Nicole first.

Then, the others would come slowly but surely after that.

I slammed my heel into an officer's face, knocking out two of his teeth. Blood was splattered all over his shirt and covered his neck. But I wasn't finished. Nicole's helpless screams rattled through my head, and I kneed him in the side.

Every night, I had nightmares about Nicole being raped and me not being able to do anything about it. I drowned myself in her terror-filled screams, burning them into my memory to motivate myself.

Another punch, and I flipped him onto his back and straddled his waist. I grabbed him by the neck and slammed his head repeatedly on the tiled floor, his sanguine blood pooling underneath him, only motivating me to hit him harder.

"Die, you fucker," I growled. "You deserve all of this."

My gun was tucked away in my waistband, and there was a knife in my pocket.

But I'd much rather use my hands, like he had with Nicole.

After I slammed my fist into his chin, he stopped moving completely. I stood to my feet and stared down at him with my chest rising and falling quickly, cheeks flushed. I widened my eyes slightly, realizing that this fucker was finally dead, and then I stumbled backward and shook my head, pissed that I would now have to clean up my mess.

"Good job," someone said from behind me.

Jumping into the air, I reached for my gun in my back pocket and turned around quickly. Kai and João stood behind me. João grabbed the barrel of the gun and pointed the muzzle toward the ground so it wasn't aimed directly at them.

I blew out a breath and dropped the gun completely, then began pacing the room.

"I just killed a man," I said, realizing that they had watched. Still trying to keep up the good-boy persona that I had lived in for the past four years. Nobody knew about this side of me. Nobody except Nicole. "I couldn't stop myself."

"Why'd you kill him?" João asked, crouching beside the officer. "We could've used him."

"He did it to protect his girl," Kai said, looking at me. "That's why you did it, isn't it?"

With my back turned toward him, I gripped the doorframe and clenched my jaw. "I didn't have proof, but I found out what he did with Nicole, and I lost my shit."

João pulled up a chair from a table—which was the only other piece of furniture in the room—grabbed me by the shoulders, and shoved me down into it roughly. Then, he gripped a fistful of my dark hair, pulled it back, and shoved the muzzle of his gun underneath my chin.

"I don't give a fuck what you did. What do you know about my mother?"

What the fuck is he talking about?!

I shook my head. "I-I don't know what you're talking about."

"She committed suicide. I had two guys I trusted take her out of my house and place her somewhere safe. Today, my mother's finger was delivered to Imani, and I found those men dead. What the fuck do you know?!"

"All I know is, my parents came home with blood on them yesterday morning," I said, holding my hands up into the air. I hadn't talked to them, but I had been watching them from the security cameras. Like a fucking hawk. "I-I don't know anything else. Ask Kai. I haven't even had enough time to make it home. I-I left school—"

"Shut the fuck up," João said, hitting me in the temple with the side of his gun. "I don't want excuses. I need fucking answers. Where the hell are your parents? I'm done playing around with Redwood. I'm going to take care of them and every other problem here."

"If what you know about Nicole is true and your parents are part of this," Kai interjected, "you're going to want them dead. And besides, they've threatened to kill Imani and her family. They'll kill you, too, once they find out what you've done to one of their trustworthy men. And you fucking know that too. They don't give a fuck about what happens to you."

"Okay," I said, nodding, just to keep João happy. I didn't have time for this shit. I needed to find my next victim. "The next time I see them, I will—"

"I want them now!" João growled.

"I don't know where they are now!" I said. "Apparently, they went out to dinner with Imani's family hours ago, and they're going into hiding. They don't give me any information about anything."

"Where'd they go out to dinner?" Kai asked.

"Ocean View."

João stormed out of the room, and I rolled my eyes. Whenever I ran into him, he'd always wonder if I knew shit about random goddamn things and without giving me any context about *anything*. And it pissed me off.

"Thanks," Kai said. "You good?"

I wiped my hands on my pants and nodded. "If you find any more of these assholes, text me."

CHAPTER
SIXTY-FIVE

NICOLE

THE WARM SUN cast an orange glow on the fallen leaves on the pathway just outside the ice cream parlor that Akio had brought me to after school. I had skipped cheer practice because I didn't want to go anymore and decided that … this was normal.

Skipping practice for a boy. Going on a date. Being happy.

I dipped my spoon into the sundae smothered in chocolate syrup and took a bite of it. While the past few weeks had been absolute hell for both of us, it was a sweet relief to share a moment like this with him.

The scent of waffle cones and sugar wafted through the air. I kicked my legs back and forth underneath the booth, peered up at Akio, and smiled softly, my chest warm. His fingers fidgeted on the table, his hair a disheveled mess. I furrowed my brow.

"Is everything okay?" I asked.

Akio glanced up at me and offered me a smile, his dark brown eyes meeting mine. "Yeah, everything's fine. Just a bit busy with work." He peered down at his phone that he'd left screen up on the table. "Nothing to worry about."

But Akio hadn't really gone back to work in a while.

I nodded, decided to drop it, and continued diving into the ice cream.

Early afternoon sun bathed him in warm light, illuminating his paler features. His bruises were still healing, and his lip was scabbed over from the torture that he'd told me his parents forced him through.

Still, he'd decided that he was well enough to come out with me.

The ice cream parlor's door jingled, and my gaze shifted toward the entrance. A couple of football players from Redwood Academy entered, laughing and hollering about the party this past weekend.

Akio tensed and leaned closer, his voice hushed. "Is it okay if we're seen together?"

Oh, what a freaking cutie.

I reached across the table and squeezed his hand. "Why wouldn't it be? We're dating."

Akio's lips curled into a small smile that awoke butterflies in my tummy. Heart pounding, I leaned in to kiss him. Our lips met in a lingering kiss, and I didn't pull away, even when I knew those kids were looking over at us.

Honestly, we had been through so much shit that some people spreading rumors about us in the Redwood halls didn't really matter at all to me. A few months ago, it totally would have, but now …

I'd kiss this man in front of anyone.

Just as I pulled back, Akio's phone buzzed on the table. He immediately glanced down at it and clenched his jaw, barely even savoring the moment between us. "Nicole, I'm sorry, but I have to go."

My heart dropped, and I followed his gaze to an unknown number with an address on his screen. Bad, bad thoughts crossed my mind, but I pushed them away because Akio wouldn't hurt me. Not after what we had been through together.

"What is it?" I asked before assuming.

He averted eye contact with me. "It's nothing …"

"You've been so tense all day. Please tell me," I said, grabbing his hands. "Please."

He hesitated, then blew out a low breath. "I have information on someone who hurt you."

"And?"

"It's an address. He was taken there and is waiting for me."

"Huh?" I asked, furrowing my brow. "What do you mean, waiting for you?"

His lips twitched into a small, evil smirk. "I'm going to make him pay. Just like the others." There was something so menacing, so vile in his gaze right now that both terrified and excited me. "You should get somewhere safe."

"No," I said, grabbing my purse. "I want to come."

There was a moment of silent hesitation, and then Akio nodded. "All right."

He stood up and held out his hand for me to take. I placed my hand in his and smiled softly. We were in this together, no matter what kind of shit lay in our path. And while I wanted to see Hannah again, I wanted vengeance more.

SIXTY-SIX

NICOLE

HEART POUNDING IN MY EARS, I stood in a dimly lit room and stared at the blood dripping off Akio's fist. Tension hung heavily in the air, and the poisoned scent of piss and fear clung to every wall of this huge room.

In the center of the warehouse, a man who I was sure had touched me at some point—there had been so many men that I could barely keep it straight anymore—was tied to a chair, his face swollen from the punches Akio had already thrown.

Blood dripped onto the floor from Akio's fist, and I listened to it splatter on the concrete. Akio, the scrawny kid who was just supposed to be my science project partner, stood over the man with ferocious eyes.

Never before had I seen him like this, and, God … I thought I loved it.

Consumed by anger, Akio hurled another punch to the man's jaw. The thud echoed throughout the room, and a pained cry left the man's mouth. My lips twitched into a small smile as adrenaline rushed through me.

My breaths came in shallow gasps, but it wasn't from fear. No. Not at all this time.

I physically couldn't peel my gaze away. Every punch, every scream—it was music to my ears because the last time he had seen me, I had been the one screaming in pain and in agony, begging for him to stop.

"I'll give you anything you want!" he cried. "Just stop!"

"Anything I want, huh?" Akio taunted, slamming another fist into his mouth.

The man in the chair groaned in pain, and a giggle left my lips, one that I couldn't stop. One that I didn't want to stop. Akio glanced over at me, his eyes filled with excitement and his lips curled into a wider smirk.

"Nicole," Akio said, his voice gruff, "do you want to try?"

The room fell silent, and the man shook his head at me in horror, breathing raggedly. Akio stood over our captive, chest heaving and knuckles beyond bloodied. I was waiting for him to take it back, to snap out of this trance.

Because this wasn't him.

But he stepped back from the man and pulled a knife out of his back pocket, extending his arm for me to take the weapon. My eyes grew wider, and my heart pumped so loudly that I could hear it all around me.

"Yes," I whispered, "I do want a try."

"Here," Akio whispered, placing the knife in my hand and wrapping my fingers around it. "Hurt him."

I gripped the knife tightly and walked closer to the man who had hurt me, relishing in the fear evident in his eyes. He shook wildly and screamed at the top of his lungs for me to stop. But like my screams had driven those men to rape me, his screams only made me want to hurt him more.

With a deep breath, I smirked softly at the man, and then in one swoop, I slashed the blade across his face, happiness washing over me.

NICOLE

HALFWAY THROUGH LUNCH, I walked into the Redwood Academy cafeteria and stared at all the students chatting busily with each other. Nobody peered my way, and I wasn't sure *where* I was accepted anymore.

Not with the cheerleaders. They hated me.

There weren't any seats left with the jocks. Plus, all they wanted was to fuck anyway.

My gaze traveled to an empty table in the front of the cafeteria, near the deans and teachers who oversaw lunchtime. I blew out a breath and really wished that Akio had come to school today, but his wounds were really acting up.

I tightened my grasp on my backpack and headed to the empty table. Well, I guess—

"Nicole!" someone shouted from my left.

Standing at a lunch table, Allie waved both her hands in the air. Imani looked over her shoulder at me and smiled softly, nodding me over too. Warmth spread through me, and I … I couldn't explain the feeling inside my chest.

They sat with Vera, Maddie, and Sakura Sato, who I think had a thing for one of the teachers here. I slowly walked over to them, unsure if they actually wanted me to be here with them, but none of them gave me any sour expression.

Instead, they all looked actually inviting.

After another hesitant pause, I placed my bookbag on the lunch table and sat in the only empty seat next to Allie. She beamed at me, and the girls continued grilling Sakura about her relationship with Mr. Avery, to which she blushed uncontrollably.

I listened to the gossip and pulled out a sandwich. Allie leaned closer to me and gently knocked her shoulder against mine.

"So, where's Akio?" Allie asked. "I heard from Kai that you two are a thing."

"Is it true?" Imani asked, leaning forward.

The attention was suddenly all on me.

Sakura looked over, her gaze telling me that she was desperate to have the attention taken off her. I bit back a small smile and kicked my legs back and forth underneath the table, wondering if *this* was how it felt to have friends.

Did they gossip like this all the time with each other? Should I tell them? *Trust* them?

"Yes," I whispered. "We're dating."

"Dating?!" Allie squealed. "I would've never imagined you dating him."

"What's that supposed to mean?" Maddie asked.

"Well, Nicole is totally way out of Akio's league," she said. "I mean, no offense to him."

"He's really sweet to me," I whispered. "And way too good for me, but we work."

And we worked well together too.

"Do you want to come over and hang out with us tonight?" Allie asked. "We're going out for ice cream to see if we can get any more info out of Sakura about her bab—I mean, her relationship with our professor."

"Or are you too busy with your new man?" Vera asked.

While it was nice that people were finally being good to me

and while I really wanted to have friends who actually cared about me for the first time in my life, Akio and I already had plans tonight and for the rest of the week.

"Rain check?" I offered. "I'm a bit busy tonight."

Allie nodded. "Sure. What are you up to? Cheer?"

"No," I said, my lips curling into a smile. "Something that will actually make me happy."

CHAPTER
SIXTY-EIGHT

NICOLE

"COME WITH ME," I purred, grasping Officer Clawson's hand and leading him into a sleazy motel room down by the beach.

He kicked the door closed behind us and followed me deeper into the small room toward the bed.

With every stride forward, the gun on his hip thudded against his thigh, and his badge shone underneath the flickering room lights. Before he could notice Akio in the dark corner, I twirled us around and shoved him back on the bed.

"Is this what you want?" I asked.

Clawson's cock was rock hard inside his pants. I unbuckled his belt and pulled it off his waist. Then, I grabbed all the weapons that he could use off his waistband—first the baton, then the gun—and I set them on the side table, promising that he'd be more comfortable this way.

He lay back, his hands behind his head, and stared at me. "You've grown up."

I gazed up at him with sultry eyes, wanting to hurl. "Not a little girl anymore."

"I kinda liked you that wa—"

Before Officer Clawson could finish his sentence, Akio snuck over from behind him and wrapped a rope around his neck. Clawson tried to get ahold of the rope, but Akio tightened it so quickly that he wasn't able to grip it before it started chafing into his neck.

"Do what you want with him," Akio said, staring up at me. "Anything you want."

My lips curled into a smirk as the officer continued to fight for his life on the mattress, but Akio easily restrained him. I hurled my fist into his nose as hard as I could and relished in the crack that echoed through the room. I kneed him in the balls, slammed his baton into his head repeatedly, and clawed his eyes out with my freshly manicured fingers. I did it again and again, over and over, until my arms fell by my sides, and I stepped back.

The man had stopped moving minutes ago, but I hadn't been able to stop myself.

Akio had given me the opportunity to do whatever I wanted, and I had taken it.

I was tired of feeling weak around men who had abused me for years. I was sick of not putting up a fight, of letting them use me for their pleasure, of being raped, of people I loved dying because some men got off on hurting women.

Fuck that.

No more weak Nicole. No more pushover Nicole.

Rage-filled Nicole was here to stay. Revenge-seeking Nicole wanted payback.

I didn't care what it took. I would ruin their lives one by one, just like they had ruined mine, just like they had taken Hannah's away from her. Everyone who had hurt me in the past would be done for. And if I couldn't do it, Akio would.

Finally, Akio released Officer Clawson and stood. After grabbing Clawson's gun from the side table, Akio aimed it at the officer's head and wasted no time shooting three rounds into his skull. Blood splattered everywhere, but Officer Clawson was nothing but a corpse now.

He couldn't hurt any more children. Nor could he hurt me.

NICOLE

ONCE THE BLOOD began pooling out of Clawson's head and soaked the mattress that his corpse lay upon, my lips curled into a smirk, and a wave of pleasure rushed through me.

All these years, the police had stolen my power from me.

And I would take it back. One fucker at a time.

Akio dropped the gun on the bed next to us and wiped off some blood that had splattered onto his lip. I gazed over at him, heart pounding inside my chest as a wave of feral lust rushed through me from what he had done and continued to do for me.

"God, you're so sexy when you're angry," Akio said, grabbing a fistful of my hair and tugging back on it. He moved closer to me, his lips brushing against mine. "And you're mine." He trailed his lips up my jaw. "All mine."

Warmth fluttered through my chest and raced down to my pussy. I pressed my legs together and stared at him through siren eyes, aching for him. Now that I didn't have to hide in my guilt, now that he knew, now that he had *helped* me get revenge, I felt more powerful than ever.

I snapped my hand around his throat, squeezed gently, and

stepped closer to him so I could feel his hard dick against my stomach. He pressed his mouth to the soft spot on my neck and sucked on it, not yet releasing my hair.

"Mine," he growled, his lips all over my throat. "All mine."

After collapsing onto the pillows, I arched my back and closed my eyes, moaning softly to myself. Clawson's corpse lay on the blood-soaked bed beside me, his eyes and mouth wide open, just like it had been when we killed him.

Akio climbed between my legs and ground himself against my pussy, teasing and taunting me with his huge cock. I spread my legs wider and reopened my eyes, lips curled into a small smirk.

"Fuck me, Akio," I whispered and hooked my arms underneath my knees to pull my legs further apart and give him the view of his life. I stared up into his dark brown eyes and furrowed my brow to feign innocence. "Please, I need it."

Akio unzipped his jeans, took his dick in his hand, and laid it against my clit. I whined and tried to position myself so it pressed against my entrance. After letting a wad of spit drip from his lips onto my clit, he used the head of his dick to rub it in.

I whimpered.

Desperate for it.

"Look at my pretty girl," he murmured, his dark eyes in a haze. "My fucking princess."

My pussy pulsed wildly, and I lifted my hips off the bed, needing him inside me now. Up until this point, he had never really given me a cute pet name, especially during sex. All I had ever been called was slut or whore, even by some of my classmates.

But *princess*?!

"Please, fuck me," I begged. My breaths came out in pants, and I spread my legs even wider with my arms, my thighs beginning to tremble in anticipation. "Please, Akio. I need it. I need it. I need it."

Akio drew the head of his cock from my clit to my entrance and gently pushed it in. I threw my head back and moaned, the pressure making me feel oh-so good. He placed his arms on the pillow near either side of my head and pushed another inch inside me.

"Nerds have the best dick!" I cried, eyes rolling back. "*God!*"

Teasing me, Akio gave me another inch, but didn't move forward. I curled my toes and stared up into his hazy eyes, then seized his chin and pulled him down into a kiss. As soon as his lips met mine, he slammed all the way into me.

When I cried out into his mouth, he slipped his tongue past my lips and began pumping into me wildly. I kept my legs spread for him like a good girl—an obedient *princess*—and tightened around him with every thrust.

"More," I pleaded. "More. More. More. More. More—"

He dropped down to his elbows and wrapped his arms underneath my shoulders, using my body to plow deeper and deeper inside me. The headboard banged against the wall, and Clawson's corpse rolled off the bed and hit the ground with a thud.

Clawson had fucked me so many times that I had lost count. One last fuck on the bed with him was …

Rightfully deserved.

Akio grunted, slamming into me and stilling, coming inside me.

The longer that I waited for Akio to continue, the tighter my pussy clenched around his cock, and the higher I built myself up. He pulled out and pushed into me one last time, and I screamed out louder than I ever had.

Pleasure soared through my body, traveling down my legs and arms and to every last fingertip. My body jerked up against his, my mouth colliding with his once more as he pushed his cum deeper inside me.

"One of these days," Akio mumbled against my lips and continued to push deeper, "I'm going to make sure that you're"—thrust—"always"—thrust—"mine."

CHAPTER
SEVENTY

NICOLE

FOR THE FIRST time in a long time, I sat in front of Hannah's grave, content with myself and my life. Usually, I came here and cried my eyes out because she wasn't here with me anymore. But after Akio and I had started to get payback, I thought ... she would be proud of me.

Violence was never the answer ... until it was.

The coolness of the gravestone pressed gently against my cheek. A gust of bitter late fall and early winter air seared my face. I closed my eyes, finally at ease. We still had a shit ton to do, but we were making progress.

I was making progress.

My gaze drifted up to Akio, who stood a few feet away with his hands stuffed into his pockets. He stayed quiet, but offered me a small smile that had saved me more than he would ever even know.

A few weeks ago, I'd thought that the only way out was to either be killed or kill myself. But now, I realized that I had been so wrong. The only way out, the only way to truly ever stop this from happening to me *and* to someone else … was to become the predator and kill our prey.

Suddenly, the tranquil graveyard was shattered by my phone buzzing. I fumbled to retrieve it from my bag, to shut the damn thing off so I could finish catching up with Hannah, but when I saw the name on my phone, I froze.

My father.

Dad: WHERE THE FUCK ARE YOU?

Dad: GET HOME NOW.

Dad: WHERE DID YOU PUT MY RECORDING?

Dad: NICOLE, ANSWER ME.

Dad: I WILL COME FIND YOU AND PUNISH YOU IF YOU STOLE THEM.

Dad: I'LL FUCKING KILL YOU LIKE I KILLED HANNAH.

Dad: ANSWER ME.

My hands trembled as I tried to formulate a thought. But the memories of the past few weeks raced through my mind. He had found out that I'd stolen the video to show Kai and Poison, then erased it from his computer. He knew that … that it was me.

And now, he would really be out to get me.

"Nicole, what's wrong?" Akio said, walking closer with his brows drawn together.

I swallowed hard, my voice quivering as I explained, "It's my father, and he's mad."

Instead of texting Dad back—because there was no fucking way that I would do that, not after all he had done to me—I created a group chat with Poison to warn them that my father knew. They were the ones who had that recording. Not me anymore.

Me: My dad knows that the recording is gone.

I wasn't risking João or Kai not seeing my message. I needed them all to know.

Kai texted back almost immediately.

Kai: Get somewhere safe with Akio.

Kai: We'll release it now.

Kai: Shit is about to go down.

Fear gripped me right down to the very bone.

I stood to my feet and grabbed Akio's hand. "Poison says we need to get somewhere safe and stay there tonight. Something big is happening."

I'd omitted the fact that they were releasing the video. I hadn't told Akio about that yet. If he knew, then he would want to help Poison do whatever the hell they were going to do.

Right now, I needed Akio to be safe and with me because I feared that Dad would hunt me down, and when he found me, he would kill me.

AKIO

DRAGON BALL Z played on the TV screen in Jamal Simmons's small home in the slums. The room was bathed in the flickering glow of the vibrant anime characters battling on their planet. I sat on the couch next to Nicole while Jamal and his siblings lounged on the floor.

Everyone was quiet, even the world outside, and that made me … uneasy. The way Nicole had reacted earlier made it seem like she knew more than she was telling me.

Darkness flooded in through the cheap and thin drawn curtains. Jamal's brother inched closer to Nicole's leg, glancing up at her every so often and wiggling his brows.

Yet Nicole didn't notice as she stared blankly at the screen, her skin a ghostly color.

Nicole's phone buzzed, and she recoiled as if it'd hurt her. Her fingers shook as she retrieved her phone and stared at the screen. Then, suddenly, Jamal's phone buzzed, then mine.

Message after message poured in, accompanied by a video. Marquis, Jamal's little brother, grabbed the phone from Jamal and tapped on the video.

Nicole's screams and pleas echoed through the room from Jamal's phone, and Jamal quickly snapped it back from him.

"What was that?" Marquis asked.

"Nothing," Jamal quickly said, grabbing his brother's hand and yanking on it. He looked back at Nicole and pulled his siblings out of the room. "It's time for bed."

The anime faded into the background, drowned out by Nicole's horrified silence. It was clear that someone had leaked this to the entire town of Redwood, maybe even that fucker that she called a father.

Tears welled up in Nicole's eyes, and I quickly wrapped my arms around her trembling shoulders, pulling her close, telling her that I would do anything to protect her.

But deep inside me, fury raged.

Whoever had done this to Nicole would pay.

"I'll kill him," I growled into her ear.

"My father didn't release the video," she said. "Poison did."

"How … how did they get it?" I asked quietly, confused.

Nicole took a shaky breath, her tear-filled eyes locking on to mine. "I gave it to them," she admitted, her voice barely above a whisper. "I thought if they believed I was being abused, they'd help me rescue you from what happened."

A wave of guilt washed over me. I couldn't bear the thought of Nicole feeling responsible for this nightmare, and I certainly didn't want anyone watching her endure this torment.

"I'm sorry," I said. "I never wanted you to go through this, Nicole. I never wanted anyone to see you like that."

Nicole gently brushed her fingers across my cheek, looking into my eyes. "Akio, I needed this entire town to know the truth. I needed them to see what'd been happening in Redwood for so long. It's not your fault, and it's not mine. I know that now."

I stared at her with both adornment and amazement at how much she had grown these past few weeks.

"We'll expose everyone for what they've done to you."

"We'll get justice," she said. "Not just for us, but for everyone who's suffered."

CHAPTER
SEVENTY-TWO

NICOLE

WAILING sirens jolted me from my sleep. I shot up in the unfamiliar bed with panic surging through my veins. Akio lay beside me, also stirring from his sleep and opening his eyes as the sirens intensified around us.

"What's happening?" I whispered.

Akio rubbed his eyes and glanced at me, equally confused. "I don't know."

"It doesn't sound good," I said, swinging my legs over the side of the bed and tiptoeing to the bedroom door.

Jamal had slept with Marquis last night, graciously giving us his bed. I had never been good friends with him, but he seemed like a thoughtful guy.

The sirens grew louder, and I noticed that they were a mix of ambulances and firetrucks, but mostly just police cars. After peeking out the door to make sure that there weren't any officers here, I stepped into the hallway and then descended the stairs.

At the bottom of the staircase, Ms. Simmons sat at the kitchen table with tears streaming down her cheeks as she stared at her phone. With trembling hands, she gripped it tightly and shook her head, mumbling about how terrible this was.

My stomach turned. "What's going on?" I whispered, my voice quivering.

She looked up at me, her eyes filled with sorrow and guilt. "Nicole," she whispered, her voice quivering. She stood, reached out for me, and pulled me into a tight embrace—the first time a motherly figure had done that in years. "I'm so sorry. I didn't know this was happening to you."

"You saw the video," I said, mouth dry, "didn't you?"

"If I had known somethin' like this was happenin', I would've done somethin'."

Gently, I hugged her back and stared out the front window at the police driving by with their lights blazing. My heart raced as I watched them pass, and I really hoped that they wouldn't find me here. I wanted to ask Ms. Simmons why there were sirens, but the words caught in my throat. I knew why the police were going crazy.

They were trying to find me.

Tears blurred my vision. I clung to Ms. Simmons harder, the knowledge that the police were closing in on us sinking in so deeply. My dream life had been so close, just in reach. If they found me now, then they'd kill me.

But what would happen if we stayed here? Would they hurt Jamal and his family too?

"How's Redwood reacting?" I asked her when she pulled away.

After wiping her tears, she shook her head. "Everyone's angry." She glanced out the front window, then drew the curtains so nobody could see into the house. "I hope the rest of you kids are staying safe."

My phone buzzed in my hand, startling me, as Akio walked down the stairs.

Allie: It's insane out here.

Allie: Everyone is rioting over the video.

Allie: The police department is on fire. We just drove past.

Allie: We saw your father. He's acting crazy. He was aggressive toward Jace.

Allie: And Jace shot him.

The words on the screen sent shock waves through my body. The messages were coming in so quickly. I dropped the phone. Everything inside me was so empty. I didn't know how to feel. Was he dead? People actually cared about *me*? The station was on fire?

Akio picked up the phone from the ground and read the texts. His eyes widened in shock, but his body didn't falter like mine had. He was stronger than I was, especially when I needed him the most.

He grabbed my hand. "If your father is hurt, *if he's weak*, then we need to find him."

My heart pounded in my chest as he pulled me toward the door.

"This is our chance," Akio said. "To end this all for good."

"You can't go out there now!" Jamal's mother called.

"We'll be back," I said over my shoulder. "I promise that we'll come back."

"Alive," she said. "You'd better come back alive!"

"We will!"

I didn't know where all my confidence had come from, but Akio was right. If Jace had shot my dad, he was lying in a puddle of his blood somewhere in Redwood and bleeding out, probably at the hospital or back at home.

And I would bet that he had gone home.

Nobody in the hospital would treat him if everyone was reacting as Allie and Jamal's mother had made it seem like they were.

Sirens still blared around us, but Akio tightened his grip on my hand, and we headed toward João's house on foot, which was where we had parked Akio's car last night. We were going to find a way to escape this town and start a new life.

My father's reign of terror was over. Today, I'd make sure of it.

SEVENTY-THREE

NICOLE

I STARED across the spacious warehouse at my father. Blood seeped out of his bullet wound and created a small puddle on the ground underneath him. He screamed and tried to escape the rope that Kai had just finished putting on him, but he wasn't getting out.

No, not this time.

He was here as my prisoner. Not as my father.

I would do to him as he had done to me since I had been just a child. I would do to him as he had done to Hannah since *she* had been just a child. And I would do to him as he had probably done to Mom countless times before she killed herself.

Once Kai tightened one more rope, he walked toward the exit. "Let me know when you're done."

The warehouse door closed behind him, the sound echoing throughout the spacious room. I stood across from my father, relishing in the anger in his eyes. He screamed through his gag, his muffled words enough to make me smile.

How the tables have fucking turned.

This had been me not so long ago, except I had been blindfolded, gagged, beaten, and bruised, begging for him to stop this madness and to kill me already. Sometime tonight, *he* would get the same punishment too.

My father couldn't move, so when I knew we were alone, I walked over to him with my heels clicking against the ground. I kicked him right in the bullet wound. More blood spurted out of him, and he shrieked.

"Louder," I growled, kicking him in the same spot again.

His scream echoed through the warehouse.

"Louder!"

Another kick. Another shriek.

Akio walked behind my father and grabbed him by his hair, forcing him to look up at me as I kicked him in his wound over and over and over again. Tears streamed down his face from his angry eyes, but I didn't stop.

I had no sympathy for the man.

"My foot hurts," I said to Akio. "Your turn."

Nothing hurt, but I wanted Akio to get a chance at him. I knew that he had been waiting to kick his ass since he had found out what was actually happening to me, since he had witnessed my father raping me.

Akio released his grip on my father's hair and punched him square in the mouth.

I took a seat on a chair that Kai had placed out in front of my father before he left, and I watched in anticipation, in joy, in vengeance as Akio beat the shit out of my father for almost an hour. I didn't have it in me to hit him anymore.

No, I wanted more than him to be hit a few times.

I wanted payback.

"Stop," I said, grabbing Akio's wrist before his fist collided with my father's face. "I don't want you to kill him yet. There's something I need to do." I reached for my phone in my pocket. "Someone I need to call."

While Akio's eyes blazed with vengeance, they softened a smidgen when he looked at me. He released his fist, peering at my father once more, and then nodded, as if to say that he would wait.

I placed a kiss on his lips. "I'll be right back."

After releasing him, I scrolled through my Contacts and walked into a separate room off the main warehouse. I hadn't had his number saved because I hated the kid, but I knew that he would do whatever I wanted.

When I found our text chain, I messaged him.

Me: I have something for you.

A few moments later, the screen lit up with a response from the Redwood Academy quarterback, Carter, the asshole everyone hated.

Carter: Anything for you, babe.

CHAPTER
SEVENTY-FOUR

NICOLE

"WHY'D you want to meet up here?" Carter asked, glancing around the warehouse.

I grabbed his hand and pulled him inside, so the chilly air wouldn't come in. After tugging him a few feet inside, he spotted Akio and my father in the center of the room, then froze.

"What's going on?"

I continued to tug him forward. "You're here to fuck my dad."

"Nicole, what the fuck?" Carter said, yanking himself out of my grasp. "I don't—"

"Stop playing," I said, done with all the bullshit that had come along with having to flirt with him nonstop, all because my father had forced me to. I knew what Carter really enjoyed, no matter how much he boasted about pussy on the football field. "You prefer men, and there's nothing wrong with that, so here's your chance."

Once we made it a few feet to my father, who was screaming through his gag to let him out of here, Carter stared down at me in horror—the first time I had ever seen that emotion on his face.

Then, he shook his head. "Nicole, I …"

"It's okay," I said to Carter, releasing his hand and walking over to Akio. "We aren't going to tell anyone about this." My gaze shifted to my father, and fury rushed through me. "I just want to see him hurt the way that he hurt me."

"Nicole, I'm not going to—"

Before Carter could finish his sentence, Akio pulled the gun out of his waistband and pointed it at his head. "Do what she says, or we'll kill you too," Akio growled, the possessiveness dripping off his voice.

I had never seen him so jealous, but Akio knew that I had slept with Carter before. Carter had never forced me to do shit with him, which was surprising, but I still had been in his bed. And Akio seemed to hate that fact.

Warmth gathered between my thighs, and I pressed them together gently.

Every day, Akio surprises me.

When I had first met him, I thought he was just some nerdy, scrawny geek who had a fat crush on me. But it turned out that it was all a facade, all a perfectly woven lie. Akio had grown up around guns and drugs and violence.

And as much as he didn't want that life, he knew how to protect himself and me. Something the girls liked to call a *bad boy*. I guessed there were many bad boys of Redwood Academy that I knew. But it was safe to say that none of them could live up to Akio.

Carter stared at him for a few moments, then burst out into laughter.

Instead of giving Carter a second warning, Akio shot a bullet at his shin. It grazed the edge, but it did take off some of his pant leg and a chunk of his flesh.

Carter hissed out in pain and clutched his shin. "What the fuck?!"

"Do as Nicole says," Akio snarled. "If you make her tell you again—"

"Fine!" Carter said, wincing in pain and standing straight. "Fucking shit, dude, that hurt."

I crossed my arms. "It wouldn't have happened if you had just listened to me."

"Here I thought that you two were just working on a science project together," Carter mumbled to himself while undoing his belt and jeans zipper. He dropped his pants to his ankles, standing in his underwear. "Not taking over Redwood."

My father continued to yell, scream, and shriek, trying to escape his restraints. But Kai had tied them so tightly that he wasn't going anywhere. And I couldn't fucking wait to watch this masterpiece. I hoped Hannah was watching too.

She deserved this as much as I did. Even more actually.

"Older men with power loved being rough with me," I said, gently swiping my hand around my father's cheek and cupping his chin, loving the terror in his eyes. "So, don't be afraid to do the same with him. Okay, Carter? He deserves it."

"You're just … you're just going to stand here and watch?" Carter said.

"Yes."

"Crazy bitch," he murmured, but that didn't stop him from lining himself up at my father's rear entrance.

As soon as Carter pushed himself into my father, pleasure washed over his face like I had never seen before. His eyes rolled back into his head, his mouth dropped open, and he shivered in ecstasy.

"Fuuuck," Carter moaned. "You feel so good."

"Is this your first time with another man?" I asked Carter.

With a grunt, Carter seemed to get his footing easily as he gripped my father's hips and slammed himself deeper and deeper inside him. He stared down at his ass and smacked it, watching himself pull out his bloody cock. "Looks like it's his first time too."

I yanked off my father's gag to hear him scream.

"Nicole, you bitch!" he screamed. "I'm going to kill you! Stop this!"

"Doesn't it feel good, Dad?" I whispered, the pleasure of being the one in control consuming me. My lips curled into a smirk, and a small giggle left my mouth. "Don't you feel so fucking good?"

"No!" he shrieked as Carter went faster. "Stop! It hurts!"

"It's supposed to," Akio said.

"Harder," I said to Carter. "And faster."

As if consumed by pleasure himself, Carter began slamming himself into my father as quickly and as harshly as he could. My smirk widened, and I watched in amazement. This was what my father had felt whenever he raped me.

I didn't condone it, and I would never do this to anyone.

Except he deserved it, and I was soaking in every single last scream.

"Stop!" he screamed at the top of his lungs.

"Scream louder," I pleaded. "It only makes this better for me."

"Nicole!" my father howled. "If you don't stop this now, I'm going to—"

He couldn't finish his sentence because he was cut off my Carter going fucking primal behind him. I took one last look at my father, burning his terror into my memory for good, and then I turned around and walked to Akio.

"This is all I have ever wanted," I whispered, placing a kiss on his cheek. "Thank you."

CHAPTER
SEVENTY-FIVE

AKIO

"GET OUT OF HERE," I hissed at Carter once he finished with Nicole's father.

Nicole had left about thirty minutes ago after telling me that she wanted to be finished with this for good and never wanted to see her father again, but I had let Carter continue because *I* wanted to see him pay.

Carter refastened his pants, his wound still open and bleeding, but he didn't seem to even notice. His eyes were hazy with pleasure, and he had a different kind of smirk on his face than I had seen when he came out of the restroom with some girls.

"Didn't think you were this crazy, kid," Carter called, shrugging on his clothes and sauntering to the exit of the warehouse, where Kai stood with his arms crossed. Carter said a few words to him, then left.

I growled underneath my breath, hating that Nicole still talked to Carter. But at the same time, I didn't mind because he wasn't into her and he preferred men like her father instead. It'd made tonight so much better for Nicole.

"He's still alive," Kai noted.

"I know."

"You gonna kill him?"

"No," I said.

Kai paused beside me. "You're not going to kill him after that?"

"No," I repeated, unfastening his binds. "That's enough torture for tonight."

"Where the fuck are you taking him?" Kai said, placing a hand on my chest. "I thought—"

"I'm going to bury him alive."

After staring at me in shock for a few moments, Kai pulled his arm away from me and then turned back to the exit of the warehouse. "I'll bring Poison's van around back. It's easier to clean than trying to get blood out of car cushions."

My lips curled into a smirk, and I dragged Nicole's father's body across the warehouse to the exit, creating a trail of deep sanguine blood after him. Her father had lost a lot of blood tonight, but he was still alive. And I wanted his last moments to be *wonderful.*

Just like the life he had given Nicole.

A moment later, Kai pulled up and hopped out of the driver's seat. I hadn't known that they had another car, but I guessed they used it to take care of business like this. Maybe they'd used this van to dispose of Principal Vaughn's body too.

After opening the back, we stuffed in Nicole's father and slammed the door. I slipped into the passenger seat and clicked on my seat belt—*can't break any more laws tonight*—and then we took off through Redwood.

"I know a place," Kai said, turning onto the highway.

I stared emptily through the windshield, listening to the rain pattering against it and the sweet sounds of Nicole's father's grunts in the back. The melody was a nice one that I would burn into my memory forever.

About fifty minutes later, Kai pulled into a wooded area way outside Redwood. We exited the car. While I opened the back and pulled Nicole's father's body out of it, Kai retrieved two shovels from somewhere deep in the woods.

We found a spot that hadn't had the dirt pulled up yet, and I dropped Nicole's father on the ground to start digging. After forty-five minutes of us digging a hole deep enough for his body, I rolled him deep down into it and listened to the thud as he dropped.

A grunt left his mouth, and he fluttered his eyes open, his body still tied.

"What's going on?" he asked, his voice groggy. "What happened? I feel like—"

I dropped some dirt onto his wound, and he winced. Then, he stared up at me as if all the memories were flooding back through his head. My lips curled into a smirk as he screamed and shouted for someone to help.

But I continued filling the hole with dirt until everything but his face was covered.

"Let me out! Someone, please—"

I scooped up some more dirt and dropped it into his mouth, filling it completely. And even when he stopped screaming, when he stopped moving underneath the dirt, we finished until there was no more dirt left.

Until I knew he was dead.

CHAPTER
SEVENTY-SIX

AKIO

A BLANKET of darkness lay over the Redwood slums when I pulled up to Jamal's house. It had been several hours since we had left this morning, but Nicole had come back here after I asked her to stay safe.

Now that I had taken care of her father, I couldn't wait to see the relief on her face.

She deserved this vengeance more than anyone.

When I parked, Jamal opened the front door and glanced out at my car, giving me a stare that I would bet he gave the opposing football team on Friday nights. I exited the car to show him that I wasn't any trouble, and his expression softened.

Nicole glanced over his shoulder at me and smiled. He stepped back, said a few words to her, and allowed her to walk out with a heaping plate of food that Jamal's mom must've told her to take with her.

As she made it halfway to me, I spotted Jamal's mom behind him. "If you need anything, sweetheart, you're always welcome!" she shouted. "My home is your home. I'll cook for y'all anytime y'all want it."

"Thank you," Nicole called, waving her off.

I opened the car door for Nicole, but before she slipped into the passenger seat with her plate, she leaned over and planted a sweet, lingering kiss on my cheek. My face warmed, and butterflies fluttered through my stomach.

After waving to Jamal, as a sorta thank-you for protecting Nicole, I climbed into the driver's seat and locked the doors. Even though her father was gone, we still weren't completely safe. My mother was still alive and well.

"So, how'd it go?" she asked, chewing on her inner cheek.

"You don't have to worry about him anymore."

Her blue eyes widened, and she smiled. "Is he … dead?"

"Yes."

With the plate of food still in her lap, she reached for my hand and laced her fingers with mine. I started the car and pulled onto the road, heading toward her house. We couldn't stay for long—the danger was far from over, and she'd been living in it for too long—but I wanted Nicole to grab what she could.

Fifteen minutes later, I guided the car to a stop in her driveway.

"Are you sure it's safe to be here? There are people still out to get us."

I cupped her chin. "We're not staying, but you should grab everything that you want to keep from your house. I don't know when we will return, and I want you to keep all the memories that you can of Hannah."

Nicole had opened up to me about Hannah many times since that night, but I had never really brought her up because I didn't want to trouble Nicole. With her father gone, I felt like Nicole would be okay with it.

Eyes softening, she curled her lips into a small smile and gave me a determined nod. "Okay, but if I'm going inside to grab her things, then I want to do it alone. Can you wait here for me?"

"Yes," I said. "I'll only come in if something goes wrong out here."

After shooting me another small smile, she stepped out of the car. I couldn't help but feel a pang of protectiveness wash through me when she disappeared into the house, but I trusted her to come right back out if anything looked wrong.

Minutes felt like hours, but my gaze never left the front door.

Finally, Nicole reappeared with her school backpack, a suitcase, and a purse that I had never once seen her carry before. Instead of locking up, she walked back to the car and shoved the suitcase and the backpack in the backseat.

When she slipped into the passenger seat and clicked on her seat belt, I started the car.

"Wait," Nicole whispered, gazing at her home with a mixture of longing and anticipation.

So, I turned off the car once more and gave her the time she needed to depart with all the memories, anxiety, and heartache that she must've felt in her home. While she had been tortured in it for years, I hoped that she had some good memories in it.

Suddenly, a spark flickered through the window of the living room.

I furrowed my brow in confusion, but Nicole grabbed my hand and squeezed as if this was what she had been waiting for. The spark turned into a flame, and my heart raced as I realized what was happening.

In a matter of seconds, the entire house erupted into a blazing fire.

The red and orange flames licked at the sealed windows. Smoke filled the top floor of the house, some escaping through the upstairs windows. Nicole's face, which had been filled with uncertainty, transformed into a calm smile.

"It's over," she whispered, her voice steady and strong. "I'm ready to move on now."

CHAPTER
SEVENTY-SEVEN

NICOLE

I SAT on the bed in Kai's spare bedroom with Hannah's belongings spread across the purple comforter. Dim lights flooded into the room from the small Christmas tree that I had put up three days ago with purple and white ornaments.

While we weren't staying here permanently, somehow, Akio had convinced Kai to let me make small changes to the bedroom to make it cozier. And it really was the first time I'd ever had the chance to decorate the way I wanted.

These past few weeks had been shit, but—let's be honest—so had my entire life.

Except being with Akio made it all hurt a little less.

The pain was still there, and I thought it would follow me, no matter the years or decades that passed. But now, I could finally live a life. Not just a happy life. *A life*. One that I chose. One that I wanted. And maybe one that Hannah might've wanted too.

Akio's voice drifted from the other room as he spoke with Kai, his words hushed, but I could still hear bits and pieces of their conversation about my father. I turned my attention to the purse that I had brought with me, the one I had filled with my sister's belongings.

Hannah had suffered in silence, all to protect me, and I had never understood the depths of her pain until it was too late. Except now that my father was dead, now that I had nobody left to hurt me, I thought … maybe she would've been happy.

My fingers danced along all her little knickknacks I could find in her old room that Dad had turned into his office. A small anime figurine. A crumpled sticker that she had gotten out of a sticker machine at our local grocery store. A couple of buttons that had been ripped off her favorite dress by Dad—that was, before he'd burned the dress when she died.

And my favorite item of hers of all—her necklace.

I grasped it in my hand and pulled it close to my heart, a tear sliding down my cheek.

"We did it, Hannah," I whispered, closing my eyes. "We did it for you."

Once I locked the necklace around my neck, I grabbed her purse and opened it up one last time. It was ripped in several places from how much she'd used it over the years and refused to use any of the more stylish ones that our father had bought her. But I wanted to use it too. It fit the style that I thought I had.

Inside, there was a zipper. I pulled it open and reached inside to find small pictures that I had never seen before. Pictures of us together—sitting on a swing at her old elementary school with me in her lap, her holding me with the biggest smile on her face at the Overlook, me hugging her thigh as tightly as I could before she left on what Dad had called a *vacation*.

Only then … I hadn't known it was a permanent vacation.

A sob escaped my mouth because I had thought I didn't have any pictures of her. I'd feared for so long that the memory of her face, of her smile, was fading. And now, I had these, which I would forever savor.

The door opened, and Akio peered into the room. "Is everything—"

"I miss Hannah," I cried, pulling my knees to my chest and holding myself in a ball.

Akio slipped into the room, sat down beside me, and pulled me to him. "I'm sorry."

What we had done was necessary and what Hannah would've wanted because for so long she had been my father's prisoner, just like I had, but I wished that she could be here, enjoying this with me.

"It's not fair," I cried because I had never had much of a chance to, "that she had to die."

"She didn't die," Akio said. "Your father killed her."

While it didn't make anything better, it was a clear distinction that needed to be made.

"She should be here, but you did what you could for her now," Akio said, gently rubbing my shoulder. "And I'm sure that she's with you and she will continue to be with you every step of the way in whatever kind of life you choose to live."

Though I wasn't sure what kind of afterlife there was, I really hoped that Hannah was watching, that she approved of what I had done, and that she would be proud of me for the life that I would live for her. For us.

CHAPTER
SEVENTY-EIGHT

NICOLE

FLUORESCENT LIGHTS HUMMED ABOVE US, casting a sterile glow over our science class the following Monday. Akio and I sat side by side at the lab table, about to work on our science project. It was the first time I'd returned to school since my father's death.

And for the first time in a long time, I felt refreshed.

Curious eyes looked back at us every now and then, and I almost couldn't believe that this was where it had all started. This was where I had met Akio. This was where he had … saved me all those weeks ago.

I glanced over at Akio, his glasses perched on the bridge of his nose and his deep brown eyes fixed on our teacher. The chatter and giggles of our classmates buzzed around, and I shot everyone who decided to laugh at us a dirty look, making them look away immediately.

My father might've pushed me around for so long, but I wasn't going to let anyone bully Akio. He was mine to protect and mine to fight for. If anyone so much as hurt him with their words, I'd throat-punch them.

"You know," I murmured, leaning closer to him and placing my hand on his thigh, "this is where we met."

"This is where *you* met *me*," Akio said, glancing at me. "I'd had a crush on you for years."

Warmth rushed through me at the thought of *anyone* truly liking me and not just wanting to get in my pants. I gently bit my lip, watching Akio's gaze drop to it, and I glided my hand further up his pant leg.

"Nicole …" Akio froze, leaning closer to me. "We're in public."

"Remember the last time we did this?" I asked with a smirk.

He swallowed, his eyes turning a shade darker.

I slipped my hand into his pants, gripped his already-hard dick, and stroked it discreetly underneath the table in the back of the classroom, so if anyone did want to look back and laugh, then they'd see my boyfriend—the geeky anime nerd—getting his dick stroked by me.

They could get jealous all they wanted, but we all knew that they weren't as lucky.

"Well, you're going to come for me like that again," I said, tightening my grip on him and moving closer so my tits rubbed against his upper arm. I jerked his cock faster until he let out a soft grunt. "And it's going to feel *sooo* good."

While Akio stared at our teacher, I pulled the head of his cock out of his jeans and leaned over to let a wad of spit drip from my lips onto his dick. When I swiped my thumb across it, he shivered.

"Fuck, Nicole," he murmured quietly so nobody else could hear. "You're going to make—"

"You come?" A small giggle escaped my throat, and I shook my head. "Not yet."

Before he could stop me, I slipped off my seat, and when Mr. Woodward turned to the board, I dropped to my knees and crawled underneath our table. I pulled more of his cock out of his pants and crawled between his legs.

Akio stared down at me through huge eyes from behind his dorky glasses, dick twitching. I wrapped my hand around the base to keep it still and swirled my tongue over the pre-cum on his head.

Stiffening, he gripped the bottom of his seat and watched as I took inch after inch of his dick inside my mouth. I sucked every bit of him, down to his balls, into my throat and stared up at him through teary eyes.

While I thought he expected me to pull back, to use his dick to throat-fuck myself, I stayed completely still and swallowed around him. His hips jerked up harsher against my lips, and suddenly, I felt hot cum roll down the back of my throat.

The power I felt, watching him squirm without making a sound, was so fucking unholy.

Once he finished, I finally pulled back and licked my lips. He had earned that.

CHAPTER
SEVENTY-NINE

REDWOOD ACADEMY'S cafeteria buzzed with toxic energy, students gossiping and bullies laughing, pointing at other students. I walked into the cafeteria by myself and scanned the tables. I hated this part, not knowing who to sit with, who accepted me, who *wanted* me.

Allie stood up from her table and waved her arms. "Nicole! Over here!"

I eyed their table, spotting the same group of girls as last time they had called me over—Allie, Imani, Vera, Maddie, and Sakura. The boys were nowhere to be found. Swallowing my nerves, I walked over to them with my lunch.

Despite having grown closer to them over the past few weeks, I still felt like the odd one out. I had bullied them, against my will, for the past four years. And I wished that I could take it all back.

When I sat down and started my lunch, Imani broke her sandwich in half. "So, how's it going with Akio?"

"Good," I said softly, trying to make up for all the years that I had unintentionally tortured them.

My father was gone, but what he had made me do to everyone

still haunted me. Remnants of him still lingered around Redwood Academy, within the students and staff and even faculty that he had made me fuck.

"Have you met his parents?" Imani asked.

"Only in passing."

At least for the most part. These past few months had gone by in such a blur, and lately, I'd begun to realize that I'd been repressing memories. I was sure I'd had a conversation with Akio's mom, but I couldn't remember where or when or even what we had talked about.

But, boy, did I know about her.

She was a witch, evil, and deserved to die. Just like my father.

Imani leaned in, her brown eyes wide. "Good."

My eyes widened slightly, mirroring hers. I had been reading a bit lately and learned that mirroring someone's expression might make them like me a bit more. But I didn't know if I was that redeemable.

The other girls shared a quiet look.

"She's," Allie started, looking over at Imani, "a bit of ..."

"A bitch," Imani said, crossing her arms and glaring down at her food. "I think she literally has it out for me. My parents were stupid and asked for her protection a long time ago, and now, she owns them."

"She owns this entire town," Vera whispered, curling her arms around herself, too, and unable to keep eye contact, her entire expression turned down.

And I recognized that she must've had personal experience with her.

I sat up taller and furrowed my brow. "What'd she do to you?"

Vera opened and closed her mouth a handful of times, then glanced at Maddie.

Maddie pursed her lips. "Kidnapped her and tried to sell her into their sex ring."

My entire body froze up, and I scrunched my sandwich between my fingers. My father had used me for so, so long. *This* was unacceptable. I didn't want any girl to go through that, and I could only imagine how someone as sweet as Vera must've felt.

"She does own everyone," Sakura whispered. "Mr. Avery too."

I looked around at the faces of my new friends, and they stayed quiet.

"Well then, we need to do something," I said, a protective urge surging through me. If Akio didn't want to do anything, it would be fine. But I didn't know how many lives she had truly affected. "We can't let her get away with all this."

"We can get Poison on it," Imani suggested.

"Do we need Poison?" I asked. "Why can't we do it ourselves?"

For me, revenge felt best when *I* was getting it myself. Not when I watched Akio do it. We were capable of making Akio's mother's life a living hell by ourselves. She couldn't outrun or outfight all of us.

While the other girls seemed hesitant, Imani smirked. "That's not a bad idea."

"Imani, we can't—" Allie started.

"Yes, we can," she said, glancing around the table as the lunch bell rang. "And if you girls want in, meet me in the back of the student lot tomorrow morning before school. We'll come up with a plan to destroy this town for good. Together."

Students bustled by us to dump their trays in the garbage and head to their next class, but we stayed seated, all looking at each other and slowly agreeing that we would do this ourselves, that we didn't need anyone else.

"Let's go, girls!" the dean shouted from the doors. "Lunch is over. Get to class!"

AKIO

I STOOD at the door to my parents' mansion. I hadn't been back in weeks, but after Nicole had told me that she planned to take on my parents with her new friends, I knew that I had to do something. Her intentions were golden, but she didn't know what my parents were capable of. They had done things far worse than what I had done for Nicole.

If Nicole got in their way, they'd kill her without a second thought.

After I typed my code into the lock, the door clicked open. Being back here made me sick to my stomach, but I had no other choice. I stepped into the house and decided that I wouldn't take my shoes off. I wasn't staying long anyway.

As if she had been waiting for me, Mom sat in our cushioned armchair and watched me walk into the room. Her men kept their eyes and their guns trained on me, and I knew that I had to make this as convincing as possible.

"Back already, Akio?" she murmured, the edges of her words like ice. She stood up and stalked toward me, her heels clicking against the ground. "Has the real world been too cruel to you?

Decide you needed to crawl back to me and beg for forgiveness?"

I held her gaze just long enough to hold my facade of the son she had always known, but then dropped it in defeat and slowly slumped my shoulders together. "I hate you," I ground out. "But I need your help, and *we* need your protection."

"*We?*" she repeated. "Who? You and that whore?"

"She's not a whore," I said through gritted teeth. "I love her."

"She's slept with the entire town."

Because her father—and you—forced her!

I wanted to scream that back at her so fucking badly, but I bit my tongue. It wasn't Nicole's fault that she had been through hell and back every single day, but I needed to get Mom alone so I could kill her.

If I made a wrong move now, she'd kill me. She'd made that clear.

"I know," I whispered. "But I don't care."

"I do," Mom said, stopping a few feet from me and staring me right in the eyes with the most heartless expression. "She'll make us more money as a whore than my future daughter-in-law."

My hands instinctively balled into fists, and I held myself back from hurling one into her face. I wouldn't make it halfway before they filled my chest with holes, and I couldn't leave Nicole without protection like this.

"I know that it's a lot to ask, but I wouldn't have come back here if it wasn't necessary."

She stayed quiet for a long time, a smirk twitching her lips. "Very well, Akio. I'll consider it. But you know the rules, don't you? To gain my trust, you'll have to prove yourself. And this time, it'll be harder than all the other times because you've betrayed me."

The rage bubbling inside me slowly subsided as I realized for the first time that she truly didn't want to kill me. She had no other children to continue her legacy, so she was willing to give me chance after chance after chance.

Even when I'd fucked up. Even when I'd betrayed her or told her off.

But she wouldn't be so giving to Nicole.

Which meant that I really had one chance to get her alone, to get close to her. It was a treacherous path that I was willing to take, all to protect Nicole and eventually dismantle the empire my mom had built.

"Okay," I said quietly. "I'm prepared to do whatever it takes."

"Good, because we start tonight."

"What do you want me to do?"

Her lips curled into a deeper smirk. "We're going to pay Imani and her family a visit."

My throat dried. "Why Imani?"

Sure, Dad had wanted me to get together with Imani for as long as I could remember, but Mom never really liked Imani. Imani always got too much in her business, always back-talked my mother despite *her* family's wishes.

She stepped closer, her gaze unyielding. "Imani is your friend, isn't she? If you're truly serious about gaining my trust and protecting those you care about, this is the first step. It's a test of your loyalty and willingness to do what it takes."

What was she planning? Should I warn Imani? Did I have time?

Reluctantly, I nodded. "Okay, I'll come with you to visit Imani's parents."

"Good." She nodded, satisfaction evident. "We'll leave soon. And remember, Akio, this is just the beginning. Prove yourself, and you might earn your place within the family. One wrong move, and you'll lose everything that you care about. Even Nicole."

CHAPTER
EIGHTY-ONE

AKIO

HANDS COVERED IN BLOOD, I stood in front of Imani's mother and father, who Mom's guards had bound and gagged an hour ago. Blood seeped out of their wounds, their eyes were swollen, and bruises had already formed on their bodies.

I hoped—to a god that I didn't believe in—that Imani wouldn't get home anytime soon.

But as luck would have it, headlights shone through the living room windows. Mom chuckled darkly and sashayed in front of Imani's parents, shaking her head and clicking her tongue, as if to taunt them.

After tightening my grasp on my gun, I stared down at her parents with as little remorse as I could muster. Imani's mother sobbed uncontrollably and stared at the door, shaking her head. Mom smacked the side of her gun against her temple, silencing her.

My gaze flickered up to Mom, then to all the guards around the room, who hadn't taken their eyes off me since I had walked into my own living room two hours ago. I gazed back at Imani's parents, trying to come up with something quick.

I was doing this for Nicole, but could I kill my friend's parents in front of her? Was that what Mom would make me do? Would Imani hate me after that? Would she understand? Why was she here right now? She should be with Poison.

Suddenly, the front door knob jingled.

"Mom!" Imani shouted.

Mom looked at Imani's mother and gestured for her to respond.

Imani's mom squeezed her eyes closed and shook her head. "In here, sweetheart!"

One moment, Imani walked into the room while texting on her phone. The next, she looked up and let out a piercing scream that shook me to my very core. I tightened my grip on my gun and realized that this was much bigger than me.

That tonight someone was going to die, and it might be someone that I cared about.

"Wh-what's happening?" Imani asked, looking at me.

I averted my gaze, unable to hold eye contact with her. I was doing this for Nicole.

To keep her safe and to keep her alive.

"Cooperate with us, Imani," Mom said. "And I'll only kill your parents."

"Kill them?" Imani whispered.

"Kill them."

Hot, rage-filled tears welled up in Imani's eyes. "What do you want?"

A long, heavy silence filled the air, then Mom stepped forward. "Join me."

My gaze shot up to Mom, and I furrowed my brow. What the fuck was she …

"I'm not giving you—" Imani asked, then mirrored my confused expression. "What?"

"Join me," Mom said, lowering her gun and stepping toward Imani. "I want you to work with me, Imani. Your mother and father have betrayed me these past few years. They're backstab-bing assholes who can't follow orders. But you …"

She stalked around Imani like Imani was some sort of prey and pushed some hair back behind her shoulder with the barrel of her gun. I tensed and swallowed hard. Was this one of Mom's sick games?

"You interrupted Poison's agenda. You've pushed them to do more than they thought capable. They are nothing but loyal to you, as you are loyal to them. You're stronger than you think. And"—Mom walked all the way around Imani and stopped right behind her, her lips dangerously close to Imani's ear—"you've done some work on my son too."

My eyes widened, and I finally looked at Imani.

"What do you mean?" she asked.

"I mean that my son would've never held a gun and shot at someone before you," Mom said, which wasn't true. And she knew it too. "I've tried hard so many times. I've relentlessly tried to inspire him to join us. And tonight, he told me that he would."

While glancing from me to my mother to her parents and back a handful of times, Imani teetered from foot to foot. Mom placed her gun into Imani's hand and wrapped her fingers around the grip. I swallowed hard and gripped mine tighter.

What should I do?

The guards were here *for me*. If I stepped out of line, they'd shoot *me*. Maybe not fatally. But they would.

"Kill your mother," Mom said to Imani.

To my surprise, Imani grabbed the gun from her and aimed it at her own mother. From her knees, Imani's mother stared up at her daughter and let her tears fall down her bloodstained cheeks. Imani's hands shook, and while she looked confident in herself, I knew she couldn't do this.

She had no fucking idea what to do either.

But this was better than Nicole, Imani, Allie, and the rest of the girls getting themselves killed. If they had thought for a second that they could capture and kill my mother by themselves, then they had been wrong. I would gladly sacrifice my life for theirs.

"I can't," Imani whispered, lowering the gun. "I won't."

Mom grabbed the barrel in her fist and aimed it right at Imani's mother's forehead. "Do it."

"No," Imani growled.

All this time, Dad had stayed quiet behind Mom, holding his gun by his side.

"Do it"—Mom took the gun from my father—"or I'll kill you."

"Imani," Imani's mother whispered, tears streaming down her cheeks. "Just do it, please. I don't want you to die at her hands. Kill me and your father. I've been nothing but a pain for you all these years. Get your revenge."

Tears streamed down Imani's cheeks. "I can't."

"She's done nothing but trap you in this house and hold you back, Imani," Mom said firmly. "You've thrived with those boys and become something admirable to our family. We've been watching you every step of your journey. We've watched you become a killer."

"A killer?" Imani's mom whispered. "Imani, have you killed someone?"

"No," Imani whispered, shaking her head.

The sick games Mom played unraveled in front of me. The lies

...

Mom smirked. "Kill your mother and prove yourself to me."

Something in Imani snapped, and she gritted her teeth, her eyes turning sour.

"Let go of the gun," Imani said to Mom, her frown turning into a scowl. "And let me do it myself."

Mom curled her lips into a devilish smirk and released the gun, turning her body to face Imani's mother. She shot me a smirk, as if she knew exactly what she was doing. My gaze shot to Imani, who looked at me for the briefest moment before she turned the gun on *my* mother.

And I realized that this might be the only chance that I would get to end this for good.

CHAPTER
EIGHTY-TWO

AKIO

EVERYTHING HAPPENED IN A MOMENT. Imani shifted the gun from her mother to mine. All the guards had turned their attention to her. And I lifted my weapon to meet my mother's head. Imani had the chance to shoot, but I wanted to kill my own mother first.

So, I pulled the trigger.

And then Imani did, seven times in quick succession.

I took out the guards that I could before they could kill Imani, watching Dad scurry out of the room toward the back door. He had never been cut out for this life and valued his life more than the ones his wife brutally had killed.

Bullets whizzed in every direction, and I ran after my father. Before he could slip out the back door, my fist collided with the side of his face, over and over until he finally toppled onto the ground. I crawled on top of him and slammed my fist into his face.

All this time, he could've saved me if he didn't want this life.

All this time, he'd let Mom run things. He'd let Mom hurt me and the ones I cared about.

Dad's head bounced off the hardwood floor, splitting open and staining it in blood. When I knew he was dead, I shuffled to my feet and scanned the room for Imani, who sat in a corner, covering her head.

"Get out of here, Imani," I shouted, shooting a bullet through the ceiling. "I'll take care of this."

To my surprise, all the guards looked at me. I had never commanded such attention from them before, but their leaders were gone. They were chickens with their heads cut off, idiots who didn't know who else to kill or who to obey.

"Now, Imani," I growled when she hadn't moved.

Imani picked up a gun, held it tightly to her chest, then dragged her mother's beaten body across the hardwood floor and toward the front door. Her father crawled out behind her, a bullet hole through his shoulder and blood everywhere.

"Things are going to fucking change around here," I growled to the guards when the door slammed shut. "*I'm* your new boss. And if you have a problem with that, then you can suffer the same fate as my mother and my father, who lie in blood at your feet."

"You're not going to do shit," Kingston, one of the guards, shouted. "Get the fuck out of—"

When I lifted my gun and shot him in the head, all hell broke out in the house. I ducked behind a couch as they unloaded bullets into it in an attempt to kill me. One shot right through the cushions and caught the side of my arm.

I winced and picked up an extra gun off Mom's corpse. After checking to make sure it was loaded, I peered into a mirror that had fallen and broken on the floor, spotting three to my right behind the couch and two to my left.

As they reloaded, I shot two of them in the foot. And when they fell to clutch their wounds, I shot them in the heads. Then I killed two more of them, leaving only Randall left—the seven-foot-tall monster of a gangster.

He barreled at me without a gun in sight, wrapped his hand around my throat, and hurled me across the room. I landed with a thud against the wall as a five-by-nine-foot piece of art fell onto my head.

Stars danced in my vision, but I had to finish this to protect Nicole.

Before I could stop him, Randall picked me up and pinned me against a wall with his forearm pressed against my throat, cutting off my airway. I lifted the gun in a shaky hand, pressed it against his gut, and pulled the trigger. Except no bullets came out.

I was out of ammo.

After cursing to myself, I dropped the gun and grasped on to Randall's forearm, desperately trying to peel it away. But he was too strong. I scanned the room for anything I could reach and spotted Imani standing feet away.

My eyes widened, and I shook my head.

What the fuck is she doing here?!

Imani lifted her gun and shot Randall in his head. Blood splattered everywhere. Flesh flew in every which direction. Randall stumbled back, and then his body smacked against the ground, a puddle of blood forming underneath him.

I doubled over, spitting and choking on air.

A few moments later, the front door burst open. Imani quickly grabbed a loaded gun from one of the corpses and aimed it at the doorway, waiting for someone to walk into the room from the foyer. Poison hurried through the doorway and stopped when they saw us.

"Akio!" someone shouted from behind them.

My heavy gaze lifted to Nicole, whose brow was furrowed. She ran over to me and dropped to her knees by my side, grasping my head and pulling it to her chest. She sobbed and hugged me tightly.

"I've been trying to call you all night," she cried. "Are you hurt?"

"A little," I said, glancing at my mother's corpse and pushing some hair out of Nicole's face. "But it was all worth it. You're safe

now. Nobody will ever hurt us again. I will make sure of it ..."
Even if it killed me.

EIGHTY-THREE

NICOLE

I LOOKED over the edge of the Overlook, my hands gripping the armpits of a corpse. The moonlight cast an eerie glow on the crashing waves below, and the salty sea breeze tugged at my hair that I had thrown into a messy bun hours ago.

While holding the corpse's legs, Akio scanned the dark street around us, then nodded at me to continue down the rocks so we could toss another body into the Atlantic Ocean. Redwood had long been plagued by the corrupt police force and Akio's crime family, and we wanted to clean up the mess.

We wouldn't be able to find everyone—at least not before the school year ended. We had both seen so many people involved with the family and police that it would nearly be impossible. But I wanted to protect my friends as much as I could.

Nobody would get away with what they had done.

My grip slipped on the heavy corpse, and his head collided with a rock and split open. Blood splattered all over my shoes as the water sloshed over them. Akio hopped down onto the next rock, tossed the body over his shoulder, and looked out into the water.

"This should be good enough," he said, launching the body into the water and watching as the waves dragged him down. "Besides, it's not like the police will care when he washes up onshore. They're too busy trying to save their own asses."

The corpse had been a man responsible for countless lives ruined, including mine. We had tracked him down, and this would send a clear message to the others who thought they could get away with their crimes.

After wiping his bloody hand on his jeans, he gripped mine and squeezed. The moonlight illuminated the determined look on his face. We were making the hard choices, but we were making our town safer, ridding it of those who had preyed on the innocent.

A dark shadow moved in the distance, and I spotted Kai's motorcycle behind our car.

"What's he want?" I asked.

"I don't know," Akio said, but led me back up the path to our cars.

When we reached our car, Kai stalked over to us, shaking his head and clicking his tongue. "Looks like the king and queen of the Redwood Mafia have been enjoying themselves."

The chilling waves crashed below, the constant push and pull of the ocean like a symphony to my ears. The Redwood Mafia had transformed into something entirely different under our leadership—no longer a force of crime, but a force of justice.

Once my father and Akio's parents had gotten out of the picture, the positions had fallen into our hands. Except our reign was one of protection, not terror. And most of the assholes who had been working with Akio's parents didn't know what that meant.

So, we had shown them. Ironically, by killing them. But life was better without them.

"We didn't choose this, Kai," I said.

"Sure you did," Kai said. "When your father died, you had a choice. And you chose the same path that Poison had. Cleaning up this town for good. Getting rid of the corrupt who think they run it."

"What are you doing here, Kai?" Akio said.

"I'm here to propose a partnership."

"A partnership with Poison?" I asked.

"You're now the leaders of the Redwood Mafia," he said. "And we're on the same path."

I glanced over at Akio, who shrugged his shoulders, then my gaze found Kai's again.

"Does João know that you're proposing this to us?" I asked.

"Nah," Kai said with a slight laugh that I had never heard. "Not yet."

"And if we say yes," Akio said, "how will he react?"

"Let me handle that when the time comes," Kai said, extending his hand. "So?"

We might now be known as the king and queen of the Redwood Mafia, which we had earned through blood, sweat, and a relentless pursuit of justice. But we had many targets on our backs, and we couldn't do this alone.

After peering back at Akio, I grabbed his hand and shook it. "We'll join you."

CHAPTER
EIGHTY-FOUR

AKIO

THE SOFT GLOW of the screen illuminated the room, casting a warm and inviting ambiance that enveloped us, along with the moonlight flooding in from the sheer curtains that Nicole had put up last week.

Nicole and I were nestled on the couch, her head resting on my shoulder, her fingers gently tracing circles on my bare chest. We were in the heart of our own little world, content and at peace, watching *Jujutsu Kaisen* together after school.

I gently rubbed her thigh and pulled her closer to me, closing my eyes at the hum of Nicole's gasp of surprise. She popped a piece of cheese, a slice of soupy, and a cracker between my lips.

After I bit into it, crumbles fell from my mouth onto my chest. Nicole giggled softly and swiped them away onto the floor for the time being. Our housekeeper would be here tomorrow morning anyway.

The faint scent of the wine we had opened earlier wafted in the air. We weren't old enough to drink, but it sure as hell felt like we had lived two goddamn long lives after what we had been through. So, I was calling this an exception.

Suddenly, Nicole sat up. "Did we ever finish that project?"

"Which one?"

"Our science project."

Once I finished chewing, I grabbed my glass and took a sip. "Yeah."

"When?"

"I finished it last week."

Nicole snapped her head toward me. "Without me?!"

I offered her a sheepish grin. "I didn't want to stress you out, love."

While I knew she had just been about to go off on me for doing it all myself, she stopped herself as my words drifted through her pretty little ears. Then, her cheeks rounded, and she gave me a soft smile. "You can't just call me a pet name whenever I'm mad at you."

"Why not?"

She grabbed a pillow and hit me with it. "Because, you nerd, that's not fair."

"Sure it is."

When she playfully hit me with a pillow again, I grabbed her wrist and pulled her toward me until her lips pressed against mine. With her, the weight of the world seemed to disappear, and all that mattered was the here and now.

Jujutsu Kaisen continued to play in the background. I had pulled her in to kiss her because I loved her, but also because I didn't want her to fall in love with that white-haired, blue-eyed Satoru Gojo on the screen, who I had caught her ogling earlier.

My lips curled into a smile, and I tugged her closer.

Who would've thought that Nicole, the head cheerleader and my only crush for years, would love anime as much as I did, have the biggest heart, and want the best for her newfound friends?

But best of all ...

She was mine.

. . .

Continue reading Nicole and Akio's story in the epilogue.

ALSO BY EMILIA ROSE

Stepbrother

Poison

The Bad Boy

Detention

My Brother's Best Friend

Excite Me

Mafia Boss

Mafia Toy

Mafia Betrayal

Sex Education

Bound By My Father's Best Friend

Pornstar

Submitting to the Alpha

Come Here, Kitten

My Werewolf Professor

The Twins

Four Masked Wolves

Monster Lover

My Bad Boy Alpha

Alpha Maddox

Summoning Sex Demons

The Breeding Cave

Next Door Incubus

ABOUT THE AUTHOR

Emilia Rose is a USA Today bestselling author of steamy romance. She loves writing about dirty-talking bad boys who are obsessed with innocent, and sometimes insecure, virgin heroines. She currently lives in a small town in Connecticut USA with her husband and three playful cats.

Join Emilia's newsletter for exclusive giveaways, early chapter releases, and more!